# Mortal Magic
## Thea Atkinson

Thea Atkinson, Author

**Have you got your free ebook yet?**

Be sure to visit http://theaatkinson.com to get your freebie.

# Chapter 1

I was in love with a monster. That was what Layne told me moments after we'd buried the ashes that were supposed to be mine.

We had just laid 'myself' to rest with my father's remains, and his comment took me off-guard. I let it go at the time. But then he said it again, hours after we'd left the graveyard.

We were alone together, finally, in the library of his father's manse. The sun had set behind the taller buildings in the borough and I could see the silhouettes of bare branches through the window. The library was not in the pack wing, but in the family wing. That alone should have raised alarms for me because as Parrish's lover, Layne shouldn't have brought me here. The optics were too dangerous for us both.

I sat on the edge of the sofa, the same perch I'd taken upon our return to the manse. I was disguising my true identity from the pack, because the alpha was in league with the black coven trying to kill me. The black wig was getting itchy, so. I peeled away the silk scarf I'd wrapped around the braids to keep an errant breeze from lifting the wig from my head at the cemetery.

A bottle of wine sat on the coffee table in front of us. Two glasses, filled with some Italian blend, flanked each side of the bottle, but neither of us had touched a drop. I wasn't even sure why Layne had poured it.

That's when he'd said the words again: "You're in love with a monster."

I stared at my glass, wishing right then that I could pluck mine from its spot and down it without looking like his words had gutted me so badly. As it was, I knew the act would appear as desperate as I felt, so I left it on the table and felt my body rocking subtly back and forth as he kept talking, repeating the same thing as though multiple passes over the same damn lie would help me hear better.

I heard him just fine. He was done with me. After all we'd gone through. It was finally over.

I tapped my bare leg that peeked out from beneath the skirt I'd worn to my internment. I didn't know what to say, so I stayed silent. I brooded and stewed like some helpless mute and hated myself for saying nothing.

He sat across the coffee table from me in the love seat with his legs crossed. So carefully distanced. Layne was always careful. It was the detective in him, I guessed, or maybe the werewolf, the predator. Whichever it was, his caution was as stoic a thing as he was at times.

Dressed in one of those fancy suits he preferred that showed off his wealth even though he didn't wear a stick of jewelry to augment it, he looked all wound up. Like gears about to let go.

"You understand, don't you?" he asked, pressing me again. "I'm a monster."

My gaze trailed from the scarf I'd dropped in my hands to his trouser leg. The muscled thighs tensed beneath the expensive fabric and let go as he sat tensely enough that I thought he wanted to bolt to his feet but was controlling the urge.

I blinked away the sting in my eyes. "I understand you're done with me," I said.

I dropped the scarf beside me on the sofa. The crimson spots looked more like spatters of blood on the black fabric than I'd thought when I first put it on. I decided to shove it beneath my backside so I wouldn't have to look at it. I'd seen enough blood for a lifetime already.

"Brie?" he said. "You heard me, right?"

The sound of my name on his lips pulled my gaze to his and saw within its depths a chasm of pain and trauma. Grief, too. I knew the look of grief that deep. I'd seen it in my mother's face when my father had died, and now it was in his eyes as he looked at me.

I was dead to him. The realization put a hitch in my breath as he waited patiently for me to acknowledge his comment.

Looking at him was a physical hurt. Even if he hadn't been so damned handsome, there was something about the angle of his jaw, the look of power in his face, his eyes, that drew me. I'd given myself to him. I thought he'd done the same. Didn't matter what either of us were. We belonged to each other.

I watched his jaw tighten as he braced for my response, and I tracked that tension all the way down to his collarbone, then to his biceps and finally to his hands. Such amazing hands, too. The way they smoothed out my skin made me possessed in ways so delicious, I never wanted to belong to anything or anyone else so badly.

But he hadn't touched me since the moments in the graveyard when we'd tossed the soil over the urn meant to hold my ashes.

I'd thought at first, his reluctance came from the need to be careful. He was protecting me, the same as he'd done before. One false move and Owen or anyone else in the pack might realize I was still alive when we needed them to think the woman who rested in her father's grave was really me. Really Brie.

We needed them to believe Desiree, Parrish's lover, was the woman held at the manse until the pack could trust me to keep their existence secret. Something that might never happen and that everyone but the supposed Desiree—me—understood.

If Desiree and Parrish broke up. Desiree would be deader than Brie.

A human with the knowledge of the werewolf world was a liability to the pack, and so they tolerated me, and I fully expected that Desiree would die in a tragic accident the moment Parrish finished with me. Thus, the surveillance we'd both been subjected to. All done on the alpha's orders.

So for Layne to avoid touching me the entire ride home in Parrish's car, for him to walk with Zach instead of me to the manse, for him to avoid meeting my gaze all made sense to me. I accepted it with a sort of nervous qualm.

Because it couldn't last. Because it would all be over soon. Because I knew that deep down, he still loved me. At least, that was what I told myself. That's what I thought.

Now, with the manse empty of everyone except Layne and I as the pack took Parrish out to a celebratory dinner for pulling Layne out of his feral state, I knew the truth. Layne was finished with me. That's what his words meant. He'd brought me to the library because it was a neutral space to break it off.

The entire travail had been too much, and he'd realized I wasn't worth it. Hell. Who would be? He'd gone feral, for fuck's sake. I'd drove him to it. The cult, the curse, the killings. All because of me.

I did my best to keep my lip from trembling as I faced him. I'd be brave, though. I'd lived without him before. I could live without him again.

I pushed aside the scarf so it wouldn't fall on the floor when I got up.

"I understand perfectly," I said to him, and took a deep breath. "You're telling me it's over."

He ran his hand through his hair. A shag of locks fell over one eye.

"I'm telling you, I can't be trusted. Do you really want to be with someone who wanted to tear the throats out of innocent people?" He looked away, letting his gaze land on the spines of books. "I wanted vengeance, Brie. I wanted to sink into the blackness of revenge and stay there. It was something to feel that was stronger than the grief of losing you."

"You didn't lose me," I said, standing in relieved surprise because he hadn't said it was over. Not yet. I rounded the table and sat next to him, hopeful but afraid. I ran one finger over the back of his hand. "I'm right here." When he didn't pull away, I felt emboldened enough to lay my entire palm down.

I was sure I felt the rippling effect of my touch as he closed his hand into a fist beneath mine and I curled my fingers over the backs of his.

"Don't shut me out. Not now." I sank onto my knees in front of him, pulling his hand to my chest as I nestled between his knees. "You're not a monster, Layne. You didn't hurt anyone."

He dragged his gaze to mine. His lips curled back in a sort of self-loathing smile. "But I wanted to. I would have. Given enough time, I would have killed someone. I'd have mangled their bodies just so I could feel something other than that soul-crushing grief."

He swallowed, and I watched the lump in his throat plunge. "I can't live without you, Brie. I don't even want to."

A ball of emotions knotted itself into my stomach at his confession. So he didn't hate me. He just hated what he'd become. I remembered the way he'd looked at Parrish when she'd tried and failed to call the man out from behind the wolf in my shop. It had been terrifying.

I wondered if he remembered much of it, if that was why he was so adamant that he wasn't human anymore, despite the man sitting right there in front of me.

"You're not a monster," I said again, this time firmer, with more conviction. I believed it and I needed him to believe it, too. "You smothered the monster. You came back. That monster is gone."

He snorted. "That's not all of it," he said in a voice thick with subdued rage. "A black fucking coven nearly killed you," he said. "And the monster inside wanted vengeance. It's waiting for the moment it gets to face even one of the bastards who hurt you. It's biding its time and sharpening its teeth on dreams of revenge. And the man is plotting to make that happen. He wants it to happen. I want it. I want them to fucking pay for every second of your pain. You need to know this. You need to know that I will fucking ravage each witch who laid an evil hand on you. The wolf inside will sing at the taste of their blood and the man beside him will savor it right along with him. That's what I am now. That's what you need to know. That my beast is capable of that. That the man is."

He tugged me toward him so fiercely a jolt of pain snaked its way to my wrist as I tried too late to adjust my position to accommodate the sudden movement. "Can you live with that, knowing you love a man who fully intends to fucking tear the beating hearts out of their chests and devour them as they watch. Can you still love a man like that?"

I swallowed hard at the clump of confusing emotion that rose and clutched at my voice box. "I think," I said, carefully because I knew the tension in his body indicated he meant each word and I didn't want to condone murder, not for him. Not for the man who upheld the law. "I think there is a very real part of my lizard brain that feels safer knowing you would do that for me."

"But," he said.

"But the rational mind knows that you don't want that. I know you want justice. You chose law and order as your vocation instead of taking care of your father's business. You want to do what's right."

"What's right and what I want are not the same thing right now, Brie." He placed my hands against my waist as he stood. "I can't make any promises except that I will do my best to make them pay. One way or the other. Does that make you afraid?"

I brushed my skirt down over my thighs as I stood with him. "I'm done being afraid," I said. "What you don't understand is that I feel the same. You think I'm going to be docile and timid like a mouse under a hawk's gaze, and that's not me either. Not anymore. The coven nearly killed me. It did everything it could to use me and it failed. I told you at the cemetery, I'm done playing victim. What did fear get me except more fear?"

I crossed the room to run my fingers over the spines because the rage was so strong I could barely contain it as it tried to climb up my throat. I pulled out a book and held it by the spine.

"They'll pay," I said. "And it won't be you or Parrish who slays the dragon, but me."

I spun on my heel to face him, and the anger swelled with each breath.

"They've taken things from me. Things I didn't even know I had, and they used them for their own evil intents. They took my father. They took my mother. They took my damn childhood and tried to take my life. But they woke the bitch in me and as God is my witness, I'll send them back to the Devil they dance with and I'll laugh as they suffer in his embrace."

He prowled toward me, the bright amber of his eyes filled with something that looked more primal than delight or pride. Lust. That's what it was. The recognition of one monster for another, the primitive lizard brain lusting for its equal.

"Is it so horribly wrong to think that's fucking sexy?" he purred. "Am I crazy to want you so bad right now that I'm ready to tear your clothes off and take you right here on the floor?"

I held his gaze boldly, my throat thick with the same desire, and I knew he saw it. He took one more step, just enough to bring him close enough to smell his aftershave and hear the rustle of that suit.

His voice went soft. "There's more, though," he said. "And you should know that too."

I swallowed and backed up against the bookcase, suddenly anxious as I remembered his words. He was a monster.

"You know what you did to me, don't you?" he asked with a growl in his tone. "You lied to me. In a pack, we have to trust each other. We have to believe every movement, every word, every expression that crosses our faces. It's what keeps us safe."

I felt behind me for the shelf and clutched at it out of instinct. A book's edge caught my thumb, and I grabbed it. A weapon. Dear God, was I really searching for a projectile?

"I had no choice. You know that."

He prowled closer, the wolf high in his eyes. The set of his shoulders made the muscles roll. "Even so, you lied. Liars need to be punished."

# CHAPTER 2

THE MONSTER STOOD DIRECTLY in front of me, and while the tentative fluttering of fear tickled the base of my spine, so too did excitement.

I lifted my chin as the book slipped from my grasp. When it struck the floor, I barely heard it. "I'm sorry," I said. "I did it to protect you. To save you."

Layne made a sound deep in his throat that indicated he might believe me, but he didn't approve. I thought of my lie to him, the one greater than the untruth that I'd died. To protect him, I'd told him I'd slept with his father. It was unforgiveable, and I'd known it. I'd used it.

"I know you're sorry," he said. "And now you're going to show me just how sorry you are. I suffered," he said with a tightness in his voice that was half memory and half desire. "I ached inside when you betrayed me. I ached so much I thought my soul was burrowing out my chest."

He was a breath away and I could smell his cologne and beneath it that true scent of him. "All I could think about was you with my father. And I hated you. I hated him. Do you know what that feels like, Brie?" he asked so softly I thought for a second he was going to embrace me with a soft hug. "Do you know how much that hurts? You think you'll never come back from it, and then you think if it's true it's not worth coming back from and still that want is there. It bubbles beneath the betrayal and you feel angrier still because you can't stop it."

He backed me up against the bookcase, and I jerked as my spine crushed against several volumes and the edges of two shelves. One of the books fell to the floor, pages splayed open like a hooker showing her wares.

His calloused thumb roamed my chin. "I'm going to replace that image right now. And when this is over, I'm going to make him pay for what he did to you."

"You can't."

Molten gold stared back at me, his eyes heavily lidded. "No? You think I don't know you want me? You think I can't smell how excited you are?"

I swallowed hard because he was right. I did want him. I would want him till I died, I knew. But that wasn't what I was rejecting.

"No," I said. "That's not what I meant. I meant you can't do that to your father."

He grappled for my hand and planted it on the shelf beside me, pinning it there beneath his. He caged me there, both hands holding mine, his chest, the whole lean, hard length of him trapping me against the shelving.

"The books, Layne," I said in a pleading voice I barely recognized as my own. "They're hurting me."

"Not as much as I'm going to hurt you," he said.

There was a moment when he inhaled sharply. His nostrils flared and his eyes dipped down to my face.

"And you want that, I can tell," he said. "You want to be punished."

I couldn't speak for the lust and mingled fear that clogged my throat, but it didn't seem he needed an answer. The way my body strained against him was all the response he needed. It told me what I hadn't the courage to admit to myself. That I deserved to be hated and hurt. That the things I'd done to him were unforgivable.

"Let me fuck the guilt out of you, Brie," he said. "If that's what it takes for you to forgive yourself, let me do it. I promise I won't be gentle. I'll be as hard and as thorough as you need me to be."

His gaze was hooded, filled with liquid heat.

My gaze flicked to over his shoulder, revealing the walls of books and diaries, the leather-bound spines with gilded lettering beyond him, the tomes that filled the four walls of the chamber as though the room had been wall-papered with them.

What he wanted was too kind. I didn't deserve absolution. Not like this.

"It's not enough," I said. "It's too good for me."

"The way I'm going to fuck you, Brie, isn't going to be a picnic."

He ground against me, the wolf high in his eyes, all primal and wild. "And if you think it's going to be a leisurely, swelling pleasure that I bring you to, think again. I'm going to take you to the crest and leave you hanging there. I'm going to wait until the tide goes back out and then take you again. And when that wave recedes, I'll drive you to it again and again until you beg me to finish it."

"The sofa," I said in a breathless voice. "There. Take me there."

One of his hands planted itself on my chest, the thumb stroking the collarbone while the fingers reached for my pulse. I felt it hammering against the pads of his fingers. "Oh, hell no," he said. "The sofa is far too damn comfortable for you."

He strained against me, pressing my back into the shelving. "Right here," he said in a gruff voice. "Right here is where you'll take your punishment."

"The books--"

"Fuck the books," he said and while he held me with one hand, the other tore the books from those shelves, scraping them to the floor with a loud clatter until there was just enough lip, just enough space to nestle inside to hold me there, trapped with the wood at my back and the hard length of him at my front.

He scooped beneath my ass with both hands and yanked me against him. Of their own volition, my legs wrapped around him, my ankles harboring him, anchoring me to his hips.

He drove me into the bookshelf and I winced as pain sliced up my back.

"I'm going to take you here," he said." And I'm going to be as rough as you need so that you remember to never do that to me again."

He lifted my skirt with his free hand, keeping his eyes on mine as he did so. I heard fabric tearing and the fluttering of my panties slipping free. I couldn't speak, couldn't tear my gaze from his. I wanted him so badly and I wanted him to drive the pain away, the guilt, the image of him looking at me like he wanted to eat me.

I could feel him working at the button of his trousers as he claimed my mouth with his. We were close, so close. All I had to do was hoist my hips a mere inch up and open myself to him.

A sound behind him made me freeze. Layne's back muscles went rigid beneath my hands and he lifted his lips from mine. An almost languid inhale moved through him.

"Charles," he said, the note of certainty indicating he knew the scent of the man without turning around.

Charles. Although I would have given anything not to open my eyes, I peeled them open and peeked over Layne's shoulder. A big ball of shame and embarrassment lodged itself in my throat as I caught Charles's eye. His smirk all but scalded my face.

I started to unravel from Layne's embrace, but he held me all the tighter, preventing me from escaping. My legs had no space to drop down beside him. Awkward and humiliated, I let them hang over his hips. My feet dangled stupidly.

"What do you want, Charles? Can't you see I'm busy?"

"All I see is Parrish getting screwed by her supposed lover, and I couldn't be more delighted by it." Charles's eyes roamed my face and darted to my bare legs, clenched around Layne's waist.

I had to hook my ankles together again as the exhaustion in my thighs took hold, and when Layne growled deep in his throat and sounded so much like the feral wolf in the basement, I didn't dare move another inch.

"You hate Parrish so much that you enjoy seeing me fuck her lover?" Layne asked him without taking his eyes from mine.

"Parrish doesn't know her place," Charles said. "I think you tapping her lover's ass just might teach her where she belongs in the pack."

It occurred to me that Charles didn't realize how close Layne was to turning on him. And it made me realize how close to his wolf he was in the moment. He'd really meant it when he said he was going to punish me. He was nothing but a wild and primal beast right then and a nervous hitch caught my breath at how close I'd come to letting him take me that way.

I felt a shudder move through Layne and with a long, bracing breath, he tugged my skirt back down over my legs and lifted me off the shelf. My feet had barely touched down when he pivoted on his heels and lazily zippered back up, facing the other shifter and blocking me from view.

I ducked down to grab at the pieces of fabric that puddled around my feet, then I stood, doing my best not to catch Charles's eye. Layne's silence hurt my ears. I had the feeling the look he was giving Charles was enough to slice through the man's nerves like a razor through shaving cream. I clenched the tatters in my closed fist.

"Listen," Charles said nervously when Layne didn't speak. "Your secret is safe with me." He angled his head so that he was aiming his glance over Layne's shoulder at me. "Can't say I blame you. An ass like that needs a good tapping, and I don't think Parrish has the equipment to give it what it really needs."

I sucked in a breath and blinked at the wolf, shocked he'd say something like that in front of me, in front of Layne. I wasn't sure what I expected, but it wasn't the tense balling of Layne's shoulders, the coiled electricity in his posture.

"Have you ever gone feral, Charles?" he asked in a voice so sweet it might be a matronly check on whether the man had eaten all his peas.

"If I had, do you think I'd be standing here watching you fuck some lesbian's lover?" He had the foolhardy nerve to snort. "Owen would have taken me out in a heartbeat."

I heard the comment his words didn't say: but for being the alpha's son, Layne would be dead.

Layne ignored the unspoken sentiment. "The sensation doesn't all leave you," he said, punching himself in the chest. "The beast is right there, right at the surface like water just about to boil."

He reached back for me, sensing I had myself straightened away, and when his hand touched mine, I felt the heat in his fingers burning my skin. "I'm sorry, Desiree," he said, angling his chin over his shoulder. "I lost control."

He said this all without looking at me or taking his eyes from Charles, and I edged sideways, enough to make it seem as though I wanted to bolt from the room. Which wasn't entirely an act. The image of the relative safety of my pack room flashed through my mind and I'd have given anything in that moment to be there.

"It's... It's fine," I said in a shaky voice.

"No. It isn't fine. I lost myself," he said, still keeping his eyes on Charles, but this time he'd begun to prowl forward, not quite abandoning me, since his body blocked me from Charles's view as he moved.

All I knew was that whatever Charles saw in Layne's face made him take an abrupt step backward.

"I'm still not quite myself," Layne said, and in one horrifyingly fast movement, he had Charles pinned against the door. His hand was on the other's throat and... dear God, Charles's feet were an inch off the floor.

The violence unfolding in front of me freed my feet. I sped across the room, sliding on one of the open books we'd knocked to the floor. I slipped to my knees.

I went down hard, my hands catching on yet another damn book and wrenching my shoulder. A yelp of surprised pain escaped me, and my clumsiness seemed to accomplish what I'd intended when I'd charged for Layne.

He dropped Charles back onto the floor and reached his hand out to me. I looked from his face to Charles. The controlled rage in Layne's was a stark contrast to Charles's relief.

I let him help me to my feet while Charles lifted his chin, angling his head back and forth as though his neck ached and needed to be stretched out. By the time he spoke, I was standing and Layne's expression had softened. He tugged the fabric of my panties free from my fist and tucked it into his trouser pocket.

Charles's eye trailed the movement. "Look," he said. "It doesn't matter to me who you fuck. I told you that. No need to get all huffy. Hell, screw her in Parrish's own bed for all I care. Let Parrish catch you at the deed. I got no reason to tell Parrish what you're doing. I got no reason to say anything to anyone."

Layne's back muscles tensed. "What did you come in here for, Charles?"

Charles cleared his throat twice, obviously having a hard time getting his voice box freed of the compression that made his voice raspy. "The pack is back," he said.

"That's obvious since you're standing in front of me," Layne said and I swung my gaze to his at the bald, cold tone. "What else is there?"

"Your father wants to see Desiree," Charles said. "They've come to a decision about her."

# CHAPTER 3

THE WHOLE WAY TO the big room, Layne was silent. I couldn't let go of the feeling that while he had beaten back the feral side of his wolf, he still wasn't quite Layne. He was harder, somehow. As though he'd gone through a kiln and been cured. I watched him and the way he strode beside me. There was a difference in his movements.

He moved more like the predator and less like the man.

Charles seemed to sense it and kept his distance. I saw his gaze dart to me and then to Layne several times as we trekked to the meeting room. I kept trying to tell myself the knot in my stomach was because I was worried about what Owen and the pack had decided about my future, but if I was honest with myself, I knew the unease was more than that.

Charles hadn't expected Layne to react the way he did. And it was clear by the way he stole looks at the both of us that he was measuring something else, something that worried him.

I did my best to keep a respectable distance, trying to maintain the illusion that I was Desiree, a woman the beast inside Layne had tried to seduce and not the lover he'd gone feral for. Because that was the only thing that might hold this whole charade together long enough to bring down Owen and his merry band of black witches.

By the time we arrived at the broad double doors with European style handles, I'd shrugged off the unease that Layne would kill Charles before we reached the conference room, but the other dread, the one that made me think the pack had decided to rid themselves of the threat of a human like me revealing their existence, that one rode my nerves like a hooker trying to finish out her day.

So when Charles swept the doors open, I squared my shoulders, ready to face whatever waited inside.

Charles stepped aside so Layne could enter. I thought for a second he'd let me go through after, but he held out his hand, palm facing me, blocking my path.

"Mortals last," he said, but not with any hint of rancor in his voice. His gaze drifted to my throat and my hands fluttered to my skin as though they could see what had caught his eye. "You might want to hide that," he drawled into my ear, soft enough that I barely header the words. Then he did the most surprising thing. He tugged my collar tighter around my neck.

"Not because I care about the bitch-wolf's feelings, but because we just survived one feral," he said. "Don't think we're ready for Parrish to go off, too."

I lifted my chin defensively as I realized he was covering up a hickey. "Thanks."

He flashed me a quick smile, one that made him look boyish. "Maybe you'll remember my kindness later," he said. "And pay me back with a taste of what you gave Layne."

I immediately regretted any thought that the man had a naïve side at all. "Layne is an alpha," I said with acid in my tone. "I doubt a paltry omega wolf could raise enough lust in a lesbian to keep her from kneeing him in the crotch."

I brushed past him to stride into the room.

Inside, I got a much better look at the chamber. Large black velvet drapes took up one entire wall, and since they were closed, I couldn't tell if they hid a window or were there to create a stark display of the oak dais positioned in front of them.

The entire room had to be three hundred square feet, and while paintings hung on the walls, there were no chairs. A dozen men lined the front of the curtain, and in the middle stood Owen.

It looked so much like a coven. I had to bite down on the nausea that stole through me.

"What in the Hell?" I whispered to Layne as I drew up beside him. "Thirteen? Really?"

He leaned sideways, talking beneath his breath. "It's not the way it looks. The Council of Elder Wolves has fourteen members. But they excluded me today. I guess they didn't want to risk a tie."

I wanted to ask what he'd been excluded from and what in the blue blazes the council did, but Owen had already stepped out of the line of shifters and looked like he was about to speak. He nodded at Charles, who nodded and pivoted on his heel.

I cringed, expecting by the way Owen caught my eye that he wanted Charles to grapple me forward, but the lesser shifter brushed past both Layne and me to open a door built into the paneling.

The room grew deathly silent as Charles stood to the side of the open door, gesturing for whoever was within to come out of hiding and into the chamber.

I held my breath as I felt Layne go rigid beside me, and I kept holding it as Parrish staggered into the room and nearly fell to her knees. Charles did nothing to catch her from falling, but she righted herself before she tipped ass over kettle.

The sole female shifter of the pack was not the sort of woman to be awkward on her feet. She had a litheness to her movements that was absent in the moment she lurched into the room.

My heart leapt into my throat as I scoured her for signs of abuse or wounds.

"They hurt her," I rasped. Every muscle in my body went on high alert as I imagined what they must have done to her to steal that usual smooth grace of hers. Without thinking, I bolted forward, not sure what I could do to help her in a room full of shifters who were far more powerful and way more swift than I, but knowing I had to do something, even if it was just to offer her my shoulder.

Layne hooked my elbow, pulling me back. "Look again," he said.

I blinked and narrowed my gaze. I couldn't see any sign of bruising or blood except for a scurf on the tip of her nose that looked more like a scrape you might get on your knee when you skid along asphalt.

Closer scrutiny proved useful. The way she held herself, the way she looked far too loose and uncoordinated, told me exactly what was wrong with her. It had nothing to do with anyone hurting her at all.

"She's drunk," I said and gawked at the way she staggered toward Owen. She caught sight of the two of us and snapped off a salute that nearly made her reel backward. It took several seconds, and three long blinks, before she displayed some equilibrium again.

When she broke out into a broad grin, Layne mumbled beneath his breath that she was one stupidly lucky wolf.

She tore her gaze from us and approached Owen, standing with her back to us as she then weaved in front of the alpha. I thought I heard her hiccuping. Charles took his place a few feet away from her, facing the opposite wall, with his shoulders back and head held high.

In profile, without the hard lines of Charles's face and hateful gleam in his eyes, he was a handsome man. He stood at least an inch taller than Parrish, and if she wasn't slouched so deeply into her own posture, she might have looked regal beside him.

As it was, there were twigs in her hair and what looked like a tangle of cobwebs.

I couldn't hold back an exclamation. "Dear God."

"God is a useless benediction to call upon when it comes to Parrish," Layne drawled. "Trust me, I've tried."

Owen side-stepped her and caught my eye. I felt my face blanch at the way his gaze roamed over me, and when he waved me forward, a sharp hitch of breath caught in my throat.

"Go to him," Layne said through gritted teeth. "If he raises a hand to you, it will be torn from its wrist before it reaches your skin."

Trying not to look at Layne with anything other than gratitude in order not to give us away, I minced my way toward the lineup of council members. Owen indicated I should stand next to Parrish, so I took the spot on her right. The strong smell of booze and puke clawed its way through my nostrils.

"Parrish Fiennes," the alpha intoned with a generous amount of command to his voice, "you have been granted one boon from the council in gratitude for bringing one of our own back to the fold."

"Enough with the fucking formality already," she said and leaned sideways, obviously trying to nudge me playfully but ending up stumbling against me. I braced myself, but it was only Charles's quick action that caught us both before we fell. She tipped an imaginary hat to him. "Much obliged, pardner," she said and tittered.

"Good gravy. How much did you drink?" I rasped against her cheek.

She waved me away, but the long, slow blinks told me she was about ready to collapse. She looked like she needed about twenty-four hours of coma just to process half the alcohol in her blood.

"Don't worry, sweet cheeks," she said, loud enough for Owen to grimace. "I'm not too drunk to clean your clock later." She licked her lips with what she must have intended to be a sultry look, but that just ended up looking like she was a dog lapping at air bubbles.

"Enough already," Owen barked.

Her eyes shot to him. "Oh, come on, Owen," she said. "We both know there's never enough pussy."

His eyes narrowed, and Layne grabbed her by the elbow from behind and gave her a shake. How he'd crept up to us without me noticing, I'd not figure out.

"Get it together, Parrish," he said beneath his breath.

She blinked again, slow and unfazed by the warning tone in Layne's voice. She raised one auburn eyebrow as though she thought everyone else was being a bit too prim. Then she lifted her chin and snapped her heels together along with a little salute toward Owen. For an instant, she gathered herself together and managed to look sober.

"The fine feral fellow to my rear has spoken. I shall endeavor to be on my best behavior as you all clench those sticks further up into your tight asses." She snickered and mumbled something beneath her breath and collapsed again, hanging over her knees and slapping her thighs at the wittiness of her remark.

Owen rolled his eyes and sighed. "It's my fault, really," he said, directing his attention to Layne. "I encouraged the pack to buy her drinks as a thank you. I had no idea she could hold so much liquor."

"Lick her," Parrish tittered. "I'll do my best, sir."

"Let's just get this over with," Layne ground out. "Best for all of us."

He shifted protectively between Parrish and I as he put his arm around her back and draped her arm over his shoulders. "She's about to go into a coma."

Owen gave a short nod that indicated he wanted nothing more keenly than to get this over with, then turned his eye to me. Immediately, every hair on the back of my neck rose to attention. I shivered beneath the sweater I'd worn for the graveside service. I felt a chill under my skirt.

"Parrish has requested one thing of the pack as her boon and that request involves you, Desiree. Are you ready to hear what it is?"

I wanted so badly to slip my hand into Layne's confident grip, that I nearly spoke the need out loud, but I was alone standing there facing the alpha of the pack who had sold his soul to a black coven that wanted to kill me.

It took everything I had in me to hold his gaze and nod. To wait demurely until he spoke, and when he did, my heart near dropped to my feet.

"Desiree, Shifter Fiennes has asked the pack to make you a mortal ally."

The tension in the room prickled over my skin. A few gasps escaped to echo through the chamber.

"What... what does that mean?" I asked.

Owen tugged on the cuffs of his suit jacket. "It means the pack has decided to trust you with our lives. In return, you may trust us with yours."

In other words, as long as I kept their secret, I could live. I inclined my head, not trusting my voice. I knew that everything was weighted in what came next, from the way I moved to the way I reacted.

That one word from a throat that sounded like Brie's and not the Desiree they expected to hear would seal my death warrant.

# CHAPTER 4

The room went deathly quiet. Several of the shifters in the council shifted back and forth on their feet and I was aware they were all watching me.

Owen canted his head as he held my gaze. "You know what will happen if you break that trust?"

I tried not to feel those eyes on me. "I won't break it."

"She won't break it, oh alpha of alphas," Parrish said, alert now for the moment.  She bumped me with her hip. "And there's more too. Don't forget the more. Tell her the more, Owen."

Owen's nostrils flared at the familiar use of his given name, but he didn't correct her. Instead, his gaze skated over me. "Parrish says her friend Brie's lawyer contacted her about Ms Duncan's will. Apparently, the witch left our Parrish everything."

I nearly choked on the term 'our Parrish' but managed to remain stoic. Parrish gestured at him to continue, an impatient movement of her hands that would accompany a rolling of the eyes if I could see her, which Owen must have because he shot her a glare.

She ignored it and continued waving at him until he sighed heavily and folded one hand over his other wrist in front of the zipper of his expensive trousers.

"God knows Parish is busy enough in her job," he said, addressing me. "And God knows her apartment is no place for anyone except a wolf like Parrish, so she's letting you caretaker both Brie's apartment and manage her shop." He offered me a subtle bow. "That is, if you accept."

My heart stuttered. I didn't dare look at Parrish, because I knew if I caught her eye, I'd break down. It was cunning and clever and so wholly unexpected that I hung my head as I swung from my waist to face her. My hands trembled and my stomach felt tied into silken knots.

I barreled into her, then, wrapping my arms around her waist and nearly toppling both her and Layne. It wasn't just a show for the pack. My throat ached with the excitement and pleasured surprise. She hugged me back, then lifted my chin with her finger and...

Kissed me.

The shock of it left my lips open to hers, and I remained still as a stick as she wound her arms around my neck and pulled me roughly against her. I knew she was doing it for show, but it was so thorough and so passionate, I nearly gave myself away with a flinch.

I gathered myself as quickly as I could, hoping I'd done so fast enough to make the reaction look merely surprised. This kiss was far too close for anyone watching to mistake a simple press of lips to lips for real passion as we'd done in the car when pack eyes were watching.

So with Layne beside me, and with an awkwardness creeping into my body that I feared everyone else could see, I did my best to shove all those thoughts aside and forced myself to lean into her, to open myself to her kiss.

She bent me back ever so slightly, my spine arching as the clumsiness disappeared into an effort to stand beneath her crushing weight. Gods, but she was heavy, but when she slipped her hands on the small of my back and supported me, I felt like I could float there, and let my weight go.

I thought I heard Layne growl beneath his breath, but before I could gage it, Parrish released me with a sheepish grin.

"It's all I could give you, baby," she purred. "I hope you love it." She looked askance at Layne. One single arched eyebrow seemed to dare him to react.

I took her hands in mine, mindful of the eyes on us, of Layne's drilling into my back. "I do love it. You're amazing, Parrish." I almost tacked on an I love you, but I thought that might be a bridge too far. I could already feel Layne's icy stare digging into my neck.

Parrish let go my hand and draped my shoulders with her arm. "Let's get you moved in and out of my apartment. Not that I don't love you, but a gal needs space, and you spread a bit too much for my comfort."

Charles guffawed. "Sweet Jesus, someone catch that innuendo, please."

She swung her gaze to his. "Just so you know, she spreads like butter. Or were you aiming for some other ridiculous insinuation no one cares to hear?"

He squared his shoulders, a knot of tension bunching up his neck. "Maybe something about that trash can you live in?"

"How would you know my apartment is trashy," she said, "unless you've been in there? And I don't recall inviting you in." One perfectly arched eyebrow lifted an inch over her eye. The inference was clear, and Charles backed up a step, obviously eager to indicate he'd not once broken into her apartment.

It took several long, uncomfortable seconds, but she finally angled herself toward Layne, pulling me along with her and effectively dismissing Charles altogether.

"Do you think you could help us get Desiree settled?" She squeezed my shoulders, and I almost toppled her with my sudden weight shift until Layne laid the flat of his palm on her chest, bracing her until she got solid footing again. "I don't think I'll be much use tonight."

Charles snorted again as he slid a lecherous look my way. "I'd be happy to help," he said.

Layne's glare could have cut a diamond, and Charles snapped his mouth closed. He made a big show of digging something out of his pocket as though he was looking for something and Layne didn't take his eyes off him for one second while he did so.

It was only when Owen cleared his throat and gestured toward the pack of elders that Layne shifted his gaze away. I could feel the change in Charles when it happened. The tension went out of his shoulders. He was afraid of Layne. That was clear. But he'd also felt emboldened enough in the room to push things past what he should have.

Maybe he expected the rest of them to back him up, and when they didn't, he wasn't sure what to do. Whatever the case, the council hadn't just convened to deliver Parrish's boon and allow me my freedom. Something else was going to happen once I left, and I got the feeling there was more that went on than a few shifters getting together for a rousing game of charades.

These wolf shifters all looked stoic and hardened, like Spartans before battle. I wondered what battle they were going to fight once we'd left the chamber.

One by one, they came forward to shake Parrish's hand and offer me a long, meaningful look before touching me lightly on the shoulder. I held each gaze as bravely as I could, searching for one friendly face in the lot. No one gave away an inch of emotion as they held my gaze, then stepped back until Owen took his place again in the center.

"We are all agreed, then," he said. "Desiree, lover and partner of Parrish, you are free to roam without escort or surveillance for the rest of your days, or until you betray our secret. See that you abide by our trust."

I nodded, hearing the threat in the words as well as the promise. I almost took Layne's arm out of habit until Parrish pulled me close to her and away from Layne's side.

"Free, free, thank Gods we're free," she said. "Let's go home and celebrate, baby."

I caught Charles's lifted eyebrow. I read the thought of what he'd seen of Layne and me in the library race across his face as clearly as if he'd spoken. Thankfully, he kept his word to Layne and said nothing.

We were trooping out when Owen called Layne back, and I yearned to look over my shoulder to see what was going to happen.

"Keep walking," Parrish said beneath her breath. "For the love of all that's holy, keep fucking walking."

My head shot in her direction, surprised. She no longer sounded the least bit inebriated. I wasn't sure what amazed me more, that she was such a great actor, or that I expected her to be drunk in the first place. She ignored the look and kept eddying me toward the exit, as silent and as steady as the tide.

When we got to the door, she all but shoved me through and closed it behind us. Safely on the other side, she sank against the wood and laid her head against it as she released me.

"I fucking near died in there," she said, sliding her gaze to mine. Her expression was unclouded by intoxication, and something in her eyes flashed yellow. "Honest to God, I fucking near died."

"What's going on?"

She grappled for my elbow. "Later," she said. "Once we've got you safely home and out of bionic hearing."

We didn't so much leave as flee the manse. Her car was parked expertly between two larger vehicles in the back lot and, with a sigh, she tossed the key fob at me. "I shouldn't drive. Think you can handle her?"

I lifted an eyebrow. Parrish's vehicle wasn't such a sporty model as all that, but it was clear it took some sort of mania to brave its temperament. It took several tries before I got the car backed out of the space and aimed in the right direction. I didn't mention her feigned intoxication, giving her the time to explain it to me when she felt it was right, but I was dying to know what was going on.

She blew a long breath out when we hit the street. Her head burrowed deep into the headrest. "Fuck, that was intense."

"Mind telling me what that was all about?"

"Pull over," she said as we got to the intersection. "Find the next good spot and haul the car to the side."

I looked over at her. "I thought you couldn't drive."

"I said 'I shouldn't drive'," she said. "Not that I couldn't drive."

"That sounds pretty much the same thing."

"Not remotely. Saying a thing and being a thing are not the same. I am so far from drunk I'm going to need a drink when I get home."

"I'm not letting you drive."

"I am a bad ass werewolf, Brie. I can make you let me drive."

"You've been drinking. Quite a lot," I said, even though I had the feeling she'd not been shocked sober but had feigned the whole damn thing and wanted her to come clean. Like now. "The stink of booze is all over you."

She chuckled. "Oh that. That's the beer I upended over myself in the bathroom of the pool room they brought me to. I know better than to let my guard down with that lot. I just acted drunk so they would stop trying to feed me booze. Besides, you'd be surprised what people say around you when they think you're blasted."

Now it was making sense. The subtle note of secrecy veiled behind her tone was a good indicator that she knew something juicy. "So, what did you discover?"

She didn't even look at me when she answered. "That Owen is going soft."

I choked on my own spit at the insinuation that the pack alpha was off his game. That had to mean things were going badly for the cult. Hope flared in my chest like a firefly signaling in the darkness.

"Owen," I said. "Pack alpha, who turned two poor homeless sods into werewolves and let them die so he wouldn't be suspected of killing his son's lover. He's going soft?"

"Honest," she said and grabbed the roll bar as I turned onto one more street that would take me home. "It was him who petitioned for me to be granted a boon. To be clear, we don't have boons very often. The last time, I think, was when Zach saved a kid who got bit by one of the pack. We could have lost it all then, got murdered in our sleep by government officials. That was long before social media. Hell, it was long before we had the Internet, and I don't know how he managed to keep it hush-hush, but he did and the pack granted him one boon in gratitude."

She rapped her window with her knuckles, indicating I should pull over.

I turned sharply down a one-way street. "I am not pulling over. I have no idea if you're even legal." I tapped the gas, giving the car a bit of head as I left the intersection and found a lengthy straightaway. She huffed to herself, but didn't argue.

"So you're saying—" My thought cut off as a car jumped in front of us from a side street.

Parrish swore and clutched at the dash. "I swear, Brie, I can drive better than this drunk, which I'm not. Please pull over. You've got me all a-sweat."

"I'm a good driver," I said.

"I'd hate to see what you think is a poor driver. You ran a red light back there."

I flicked my gaze to the rear-view mirror. "Oh," I said. "You were freaking me out."

"Sure," she said as her foot jammed into the carpet so forcefully her thighs lifted her from the seat.

"So, what did he ask for?" I said, as I noticed the light ahead had changed to red and braked a little too harshly. Both of us rammed forward.

She turned to me with an eyebrow quirked up. Her lips were pursed tightly.

"I'm just not used to this traffic," I said in a needling voice I didn't enjoy hearing coming out of me. "Last time I drove, I was on rural Nova Scotian roads. Not quite the same."

"No shit," she said and went quiet as the light changed. We drove in silence for a long while before she spoke again. "A horse," she said. "A white one with a black mane and a red leather saddle. A tall, willowy blonde riding it bareback dressed in nothing but white muslin that showed every pink hue of her nipples and the dusty triangle of hair between her legs." She sighed audibly, longing thick within the sound.

"What's that?" I said. "Are you hallucinating?"

"Zach's boon." This so quiet I barely heard her. "That's what he asked for."

"Why in the hell would he want a horse and a... did you say, a willowy blonde?"

She sighed as my apartment building came into view and I wasn't sure if it was relief the ride was over or some sort of reminiscent sentiment. I pulled over to the curb and cut the engine.

When I turned to her, she was looking out the windshield with a far-away look on her face.

"So?" I asked, prodding her to swing her gaze to me, but that expression stayed on her face despite my digging for the fob and tossing it at her. "That's a pretty odd request. I'd think he could ask for anything."

She caught the key fob and tucked it into the pocket of her plaid shirt. "He could have asked for a fortune. What he did for the pack was incredible. No one would have questioned what he wanted. We'd have given him the shirts off our backs."

"So why didn't he?" I asked. "Ask for a fortune, that is?"

She swung her gaze to mine, and for a moment, I thought she might cry. Then, she slapped her thighs, done with the conversation and punctuating that end with a loud thwack of skin to jeans. "You'll have to ask him."

"Meaning you don't know."

She grappled for the door handle and pushed open the door. "Meaning there are some things a gal doesn't want to revisit no matter how much she loves a friend. If you want to know, you'll have to ask him."

The sound of the door reaching its maximum swing groaned into the car. "OK, let's get you back into that lovely, clean apartment of yours."

I knew she was joking. She'd seen the mess I'd left behind, the mess I always left behind. I wasn't dirty. Just... unorganized.

But it was my mess, and I was excited to see it again. I followed her to the curb and waited for the beep of the fob to lock the wreck of a car she drove, and then, still keenly aware I might be watched, let her lead me to the front porch of the apartment building.

She fished into her jeans and extracted the familiar-looking ring of keys and tossed it to me. With a longing bridging on excitement, I fitted the key into the lock and twisted.

The excitement lasted for all of two seconds.

# CHAPTER 5

My home had been broken into. That meant it was no longer safe. I was no longer safe.

Those two thoughts took up all the space in my mind as I peered past the foyer into the living room. All the furniture had been upended. Papers littered the floor. The book I had been reading and left on the end table splayed open with its spine pointing to the ceiling.

My favorite coffee mug, a gargantuan bucket of a cup with the words, I whiten my coffee with the ashes of my enemies, was broken in two. One half, the part with the handle, sat at my feet in the foyer and the other half lay on the first tread of the stairs to the second level as though someone tossed it after drinking the last dregs of a cup of java.

As if to prove that notion, splatters of dried coffee spotted the wall by the coat tree. The stink of burnt coffee and electronics pulsed in the undercurrents of air.

"Who would tear my place apart and take time to make coffee?" I muttered as I toed the nearest piece of my mug.

Parrish gripped my elbow. "You see," she said. "That's the thing..."

I looked sideways at her, squinting suspiciously. "You know who did this."

She had the grace to look sheepish as she shrugged. "It's not what you think. It's not the cult or some thief looking for money."

"I didn't think either of those things," I said flatly.

She pursed her lips and dropped her gaze. I knew how I sounded. Accusing. But dammit, this was my place. What had she allowed to happen here?

"Come with me," she said and tugged me toward the kitchen. "You see, one thing werewolves do not like is anything that has anything to do with domesticity. None of those bastards wants to seem as though they are doing women's work."

"Misogynists," I spit out.

She nodded. "Indeed. But that worked in our favor here."

She pulled me along with her to the kitchen sink then jerked her chin toward it. "Owen demanded that before I could hand this place over to my human lover, that the pack made sure there wasn't anything in here that could do them harm."

I pulled my arm from her clutch and ran my hand along the counter. My palm met the grit of flour and cornmeal and coffee grounds. "Meaning they wanted to make sure Brie wasn't hiding out here," I guessed. They wanted to make sure I was truly dead. "They wanted to see for themselves that there was no evidence I might be holing up here."

Parrish reached for the coffeemaker's plug and tugged it free of the socket. The coffee inside was burnt down to a film on the bottom of the pot. "My boon gave them the excuse to do this," she said. "I'm sorry, Brie." She shook her hands out as if to remove the stain of guilt on them.

I heaved a long, hard sigh. "Not your fault, I guess," I said. "I should have realized things wouldn't be this easy."

Parrish grinned so broadly that I canted my head at her. "What?" I asked.

"Check underneath the sink. Way in the back behind the dish detergent and floor cleaner."

Curious, my eyebrows scrunched together as I squatted in front of the sink and yanked open the door. Everything inside was as I had left it as far as I could remember.

I laid my forearms on my knees as I peered up at her. "So they left my cleaning stuff all neat and tidy the way I left it," I said. "What a lovely sunrise."

"Not the way you left it," she said, beaming down at me. "Keep looking."

I reached in, far past the bucket and the cleaning supplies. When my hand fell upon a stack of damp paper, my heart sped up.

"Fuck," I said and fell from my squat onto my bottom. "My mother's papers. They're here."

Parrish crossed her arms over her chest and shot me a happy smile. "I had to put them somewhere they wouldn't find them."

"You put them here?" I pulled out one folder after another, noticing that despite being a bit damp, they really were all there. "You are one cagey bitch," I said, lifting my eyebrows in salute.

She fluffed the edges of her hair where they stuck out below her kerchief. "Sometimes my brilliance amazes me too."

She stretched her arms over her head and arched her spine. "So now you have the evidence that I've been the most loyal and stodgy of executors for your worldly possessions, you should take me out for a drink as a thank you. Layne said he'd hire someone to put the place to rights tomorrow. And we have hours and hours until dawn."

"Haven't you drank enough already?"

"On the contrary," she said. "If I don't get a beer in me soon, I'm going to collapse." She canted her head at me. "Get dolled up, doll; I know just the place for two gorgeous chicks to shake their respective asses."

The place was a bar I'd never seen before, on the very outskirts of the high-class borough, edging on the retail sector, but still on the edge of the water. Yachts moored at sloops instead of container boats to wharves.

I was nervous about going until Parrish informed me while she updated my costume and forced me into a sexy black dress that only the supernatural community knew about the establishment.

I wasn't sure what that meant by community, but I was happy to resist the urge to ask. I didn't want to know any more. I was neck-deep in things I wished I could unknow already.

So when we arrived, me in a refreshed black wig and black dress that showed a bit too much cleavage for my tastes, and she in the same damn plaid shirt and jeans she'd been in for the council meeting, I felt far too overdressed.

I was tugging on the hem to pull it further over my ass when she opened the door for me. "You look great," she chided. "Stop fidgeting."

"I didn't even know I owned this dress," I said.

"You didn't."

I looked askance at her as she shoved me through the door.

"Yes," she said. "I bought it for you. But don't get any ideas about getting into my pants. It was all on Layne's dime. Now stop looking at me like you want to cut my throat and start looking like you can't wait to tear the ugly plaid shirt from my back. Show's on."

I stumbled over the threshold, the inch heels twisting subtly to the side as I gathered my footing. Inside, the place smelled of old booze, vanilla, and jasmine. Pine and woods coiled in the air as well, and while I found it a pleasant aroma, I also recognized it as something completely unusual.

When I caught a whiff of brimstone, not much, just enough to make my nose itch, I knew the source of the smell. Magic. Sulfur was the chemical of science. A witch's blessing transformed it into something different. Something magical.

Show's on. Meaning we weren't finished with the charade just yet.

I drew myself up, squaring my shoulders, thrusting my boobs out for maximum drama.

"Humans are not allowed here," she said, "except as pets or thralls or lovers." She adjusted a lock of the wig I wore, tossing it over my shoulder as she leaned in close. "This club belongs to Owen's pack. He owns it. You're safe here. We're safe here. So long as you're Desiree, no one will blink an eye."

"Safe as a thrall, a pet, or lover?" I asked, feeling the greater weight of the inference behind the first part of the statement more than the threat in the latter.

She worked her fingers through her hair, tucking the errant locks behind her ear. "As a mortal ally, of course," she said. "Did I forget to mention that?"

The look on her face told me she had not forgotten.

"Bitch," I muttered, and she chuckled beneath her breath.

"Careful, werewolves have incredible hearing. Wouldn't want anyone to overhear us having a lovers' spat."

She wrangled my elbow and spun me to face the interior. I peered around the space and took in the wall-length bar with a shelf behind it that stretched to the ceiling up two full floors. A sliding ladder, much like in a huge library, shook with the beat of the music pulsing over the room.

Somehow, that music was loud, but also managed to stay in the undercurrents, like the most cleverly planned background sounds. Magic, I realized. The music was spelled to allow the customers to speak to one another without shouting.

Probably a useful thing in a world that was still in the shadows the way the shifter and witch world was.

"This is even ritzier than I expected," I said.

Parrish eyed the area along with me. "Glad I stuffed you into that slinky dress now, aren't you?" she commented.

Opposite the wall-length bar that stretched up two storeys, and spread out like a banquet, sprawled dozens of white-clothed round tables in a cabaret style arrangement. A piano trickled out soft notes from beneath a pianist's fingers, that couldn't quite cut through the din of the bar, but I knew moved him as he swayed in time with his fingers.

Between the two spaces, several plush sofas created a conversation area reminiscent of a piano lounge. Although it was filled with small clusters of crowds in animated conversation, I couldn't hear a thing but the noise from the bar.

Youthful, attractive servers meandered through the building, carrying trays of champagne that shifted to beer steins and draft glasses when they hit the lounge, and as I followed a server with my gaze, shifted again to colored cocktail drinks.

Throughout the entire building, candles flickered with mauve flames from tall, black wax pillars set within what looked like crystal holders. Sconces lined the walls and lit the room with the same purplish flame.

One look at the unnatural hue of the tongues of fire and I knew magic was at play in the lighting as well. So Owen had access to his witch's coven, still, and was no doubt using their power in his club.

Dread prickled at the base of my spine as I wondered what other magics were at play in the space.

"Yup," Parrish said as though she had read my thoughts, but when I checked, she was looking directly at me and had no doubt just read the trajectory of my gaze. "The club is cloaked from the norms. When they pass by, they see a large painted mural. Very artsy. Once a year, they even hold an outdoor gala in front of it and toss money into a pot to hire another up-and-coming artist to whitewash it and create a new one. It's become quite a tradition these last few years. Owen's foundation holds the kitty. They 'hire' an artist, and everyone thinks they're doing a grand thing for some poor starving artist."

She sighed. "Owen uses the money to pay the warlock for another year of cloaking and no one realizes they are paying money to keep themselves from seeing what's right in front of their eyes."

I flicked my gaze past the bar to the lounge. "And the sounds? They're controlled too," I guessed, and she nodded.

"Part of the magic of the place. You'll see once we pass the bar perimeter. No noise leaks from one quadrant to another. All self-contained by the magic. You'll also notice you can't really make out any faces in each section either. Not until you break the barrier."

"Impressive."

She pursed her lips thoughtfully. "The warlock is paid well."

A snort escaped me, and she laughed. "And yes, it could be the coven, too," she said. "Maybe it's Owen's pay for being a crafty bastard." She gripped my elbow tighter. "OK, she said. "I'm going to need a drink for this." She panned my face with pensive eyes. "You too. What do you want?"

I gave it little thought. "A soda."

"Margherita it is."

She plucked a glass of pale green liquid from a passing server and passed it to me before double-fisting two shot glasses from the same tray. "Tequila," she said with a grin before tipping one back. "Best to keep it in the family." She shot the other one and blew out a bracing breath. "OK. Time to face the music. Let's go."

She guided me toward the lounge where a cluster of tall men and several willowy women were either sprawled across the sofas or preening delicately next to a man of choice.

There was a moment when my entire body tingled and my skin sang a note that my blood recognized. Like meeting like, I guessed, as the magic washed over my skin when we stepped over the barrier into the lounge.

We weren't spotted right away, and it gave me a few seconds to take in the crowds. I recognized most of the men from Owen's pack, and guessed the ones I didn't find familiar were ones I hadn't yet met.

I presumed from conversations with Layne and Parrish that a pack order kept the pack running smoothly, but I'd never truly seen it in full view. From my perspective, it grew obvious quickly who was more dominant to whom.

Here, I noted several men going out of their way to avoid touching one man with his back to me, a tall, lean woman in a tight-fitting red dress trying time and time again to lean on or hang off him, but being rebuffed over and over in such polite, subtle ways, she didn't realize she was being rebuffed.

A couple of other men seemed to hold similar sway over the others, with the lesser rank wolves avoiding direct eye contact. It didn't surprise me to discover, in those moments I broke the barrier, that two of them were Zach and Charles. Both of them with their own small bevy of admirers vying for their attention.

Both of them flanked the first, a man, who no doubt would have a view of the entire building from where he stood.

While Zach smiled politely at the woman gazing coquettishly up into his face, I could see his jaw had gone tight with the effort, even as Charles did his best to poach her from him. That was all I gathered before I blinked it all into focus as the magic that cloaked the sections from each other gave way. My breath hitched as I recognized more.

I knew who the man was standing back to, who it had to be from the set of his shoulders, the way he commanded his space. And in the same moment I recognized him, Layne pivoted on his heel and met my gaze.

He held my eye with such direct possessiveness that my knees nearly buckled. The woman, a black-haired beauty with full painted lips, tracked his gaze to mine, and hers went to half-mast as she ran it over my height.

In the same motion, she lifted her slim hand to Layne's elbow and curled her fingers around his biceps. The painted nails caught the light and sparked the gloss.

"Hold on, Desiree," Parrish, who must have caught the exchange, said. "It's going to get messy up in here."

I dragged my gaze to hers. "Mine," I said. It wasn't intentional, those words. Just what came out, and she grinned as I tried to shove past her.

"Just a second," she said, barring my path and hiding me from view. She lifted my hand and tipped my drink toward my mouth. "A soldier does not go to battle totally sober."

I flicked my eyes over her face. "Is that what we're doing here?" I asked. "Going to war?"

"By the look in your eye, I'd say yes." She stepped sideways as I did, trying to get out from around her. "Her name is Rowan. She's been after Layne for the last three years. He never gives in, not even before he met you. But she gives it her best try and he's too gentlemanly to tell her to fuck off."

"I hate her."

"Most of us do," she drawled. "Mostly because she won't give any of us a second glance, no matter how hard we try." A look of mischief flashed through her gaze. "I love trying. Gets her so pissy. I secretly think she's a vampire looking for a lycan thrall."

That shifted my attention.

"Yes," she said. "There are vampires. Witches. Werewolves. Hell, I wouldn't be surprised if there are faeries, although I've never seen one." She dropped her gaze to my glass then gave me a pointed look.

With a sigh, I took a swallow. It was bitter and sour and perfection. I downed it.

"Good girl." She took the glass from me and set it on the nearest table, then grabbed my hand. "Time for subtleties is over."

# CHAPTER 6

THROUGHOUT OUR ENTIRE PATH through the lounge toward Layne's group, he kept his eye on mine, and with each step I took, my body flushed hotter. If anyone noticed, I couldn't tell. My eyes were only for Layne.

By the time I sidled up next to Zach, with Parrish corralling me into him as though she wanted to hide me from view, my nerves were alight with the feel of Layne's eyes on me.

Parrish made some foolish comment to Zach, who took affront and swung out around me to face her.

Whatever she said after that was lost to my ears during the time my attention was on Layne, but Zach's hearing was not affected. His face blanched white. She grinned. I felt as though the war was about to begin.

But before Zach could respond to Parrish, Charles slid in next to me, shoving Zach out of the way. When I felt his hand on my ass, I wheeled on him.

"Get your fucking hands off me," I growled, catching Layne's attention.

I warned him with my gaze to stay out of it. I was Parrish's date. We needed to act like it. He tensed visibly in response so acutely, Parrish had to tear her grin from Zach, and turn it, with a lot more furious rancor, toward the man with the roaming hands.

"What in the fuck are you doing, Charles?" she demanded.

His fingers whispered along my thigh, and I shoved at him. I didn't manage to move him one inch.

He addressed Parrish. "Your lover was making eyes at me," he replied. "I thought I'd try her on."

Parrish's eyes narrowed. "She's not a pair of shoes."

He shoved his hands in his pockets and rocked back on his heels, displaying how threatened he was by Parrish. "More like a pair of dirty drawers," he said, and the sharp intake of her breath was like a piston.

I fully expected Parrish to barrel at Charles, to defend my honor, and her face was so flushed, I was sure she'd do so with much prejudice.

What I didn't expect, and I guessed no one else did, was for Layne to reach over Parrish and grab Charles by the throat.

The werewolf jerked sideways, catching everyone's attention, and each of us stared in shock as Layne hauled him close and bit down on the man's neck.

Charles went still in Layne's grasp.

A quick glance showed Layne semi transformed. Even Parrish seemed shocked to see the elongated jawline, the claws at the ends of his fingers. I held my breath. The entire section of the lounge sucked in a shuddering inhalation and held it along with me. Those who hadn't witnessed the action, seemed to sense the shift in energy, and all eyes were on Layne and the werewolf who went slack in his grip.

Zach was the one who moved first. His hands extended toward Layne in a supplicating, peace-making stance, his eyes downcast. Submissive. Entreating.

"Layne," he whispered. "You don't want to hurt him. He's your father's third. Think about this. You know Charles. You know his value."

A deep rumble came from between Charles's skin and Layne's mouth. Layne's eyes flashed bright yellow.

"She's Parrish's concern," Zach said. "She's not yours. Let Parrish handle it."

Another rolling bit of thunder from the two wolves locked together, neck to mouth. I edged closer to Parrish, not sure what exactly I should do, and sensing the smartest move would be away from that furious knot of limbs and fur.

That was when everything shifted, and so quickly, I barely saw the machinations behind it. Parrish turned to me, her eyes blazing with hurt and fury.

"You bitch," she spat out.

I swung on her, confused and hurt as she slipped her hand behind my neck to cup my cheek.

"You and Layne," she growled. "I should have seen it. Oh my God. You fucking bitch."

Her thumb stroked my skin, and I froze out of shock and fear because the touch was so gentle and the words so pained that I knew no good could come from any reaction. I had no idea what was going on, but I was a human in a club filled with werewolves. I didn't dare move a single muscle. The tension was so high I felt it whistling through my ears like wind through a tight wire.

"You broke my heart, Desiree," Parrish said, a little too loudly to be authentic. "After all I've done for you?"

Zach pulled her away, his eyes soft and pitying as they ran over her face.

"It's not her fault, Parrish," he murmured and rolled his eyes toward Layne, and only then did I realize her touch had been purposefully nonthreatening so not to poke a stick in an already angry werewolf. "You know the alpha allure. If Layne wanted her, what hope did she have to resist."

She pouted. "But she was mine," she said, looking at Layne and the words eased his grip on Charles just a bit. Enough that the other werewolf was able to reach up and tap Layne on the shoulder. Layne gave him a shake and Charles gasped.

"She's yours," the man ground out, and the grip slackened even more. "I'm sorry. I swear I'll leave her alone."

Layne let go and Charles sucked in a breath as he ran his hand over a bruised throat. It took several moments for him to adjust his collar and as he did so, I didn't dare look at Layne.

"Saw them together," Charles said to Parrish, who held her ground with her fists balled at her sides. "It's true. She and Layne. I thought maybe she was just a—"

"Don't say it," Parrish's voice was like broken glass when she regarded him. "Don't you fucking say it, you bastard."

"It's not me who stole your girl," Charles said in a needling tone. "Maybe level that fucking ire on the bastard who cuckolded you. Learn your lesson about where you belong in the pack."

What fire had been extinguished blazed again, hotter than before.

Parrish took Charles out at the legs, but not before Layne's elbow snapped back into his nose. The man fell to the floor with her straddling his chest. Her fists landed in his face with sickening cracks that sent blood spraying sideways and upward into her hair.

Something shifted in the pack in that instant. I felt the zing of blood lust and tension ripple through the air as each werewolf surrounded the three of them, cutting them off from view of the rest of the building.

I edged toward a break in the ring, instinctively searching for an escape as my stomach roiled with each nauseating crack of bone on bone.

Other than the sound of Charles's moans and Parrish's grunts as she leveraged her fists into his face, his throat, his chest, the room had gone eerily silent. All eyes, all attention was on the outcome, and even Layne stood back after his initial attack, letting her show the revolting prick exactly how well she knew her place.

Just when I thought it would never end, Layne stepped over her, looming behind her back. He didn't reach for her, but his posture was stiff and everything in his body language screamed that he wanted to put his hand on her shoulder.

Whether he was afraid or merely showing her respect, he did not touch her. His voice held all the shadow and quiet of a tomb when he spoke, but the command in the one word he uttered was unmistakable.

"Enough," he said.

"Fuck that," she growled in a voice that barely sounded like her. She punctuated the comment with a blow that Charles only managed to avoid by an inch as he found the energy to turn his head to the side.

Her fist smacked into the floor, and she yanked back, shaking off the pain with a roar.

Her knuckles were bloody and bruises already bloomed beneath the skin as she drew back again. Charles's face showed beneath her arm as a mess of meat, swollen and glistening at the skin surface as inflammation pushed the skin to its limits.

In the brief time it took her to pull her fist back and aim again, he spit a gob of lumpy blood up at her.

When it struck her in the face, she ran her tongue out to catch the edges. She laughed, her fist quivering with the lust for violence.

"That's enough, Parrish," Layne said again in a low voice as he grabbed her wrist where it hung in the air over her shoulders.

She abandoned her attention of Charles and turned on Layne, a snarl on her face.

Feral, I thought in that instant. She'd lost her desperate hold on reality and finally returned to the beast she'd always feared. The horror of what she must have once been peered out from behind her gaze as she tore herself from Charles's chest. In the next instant, she threw herself at Layne.

She caught him full in the chest with the entire force of her weight. He barely staggered, but his hands went around her in a sort of bear hug. His grapple for her took a heartbeat, and as mine stuttered anxiously, I thought he'd get her under control.

He must have believed it too, because his shoulders sagged as he caught her behind the elbows and eased her away from him so gently she might have surrendered.

Then, her knee came up so quickly I didn't see it move until Layne bucked upwards with the force. His growl ripped from him, and I knew, just knew, that feral beast had met feral beast.

In that second, something critical shifted.

She let go a roar that turned her green eyes bright yellow. I could have sworn her jaw elongated with a terrifying speed. The muzzle sprouted cinnamon-colored fur and her spine snapped as vertebrae created a lupine form from her human one.

She ripped at her clothes because shifting was taking too long to free her from their constraints.

He launched himself at her. Before she could complete her transformation any further, he dove. His face buried in her neck as she tossed her head back, her face dressed in a mania that made me reach out for a solid arm to cling to. Zach's, I realized as he slipped beside me and wrapped his arm around my back.

"Come," he said and tried to draw me away.

I shook him off. "No," I said. "They're going to kill each other."

"They won't," he said. "Only one of them will die."

I swung on him. "What in the fuck, Zach? Is that supposed to make me feel better?"

I made to barrel toward the two werewolves, already tangled together in a din of growls and hair-raising roars. I was stopped long before I got more than a step away.

"Are you really that foolish?" Zach said. "They'll kill you."

"We can't just let them do that to each other."

He used his considerable size to wrangle my arms back to my sides and pulled me against his chest. I struggled, but it was like trying to move against cold taffy.

"Calm down," he hissed in my ear.

"Someone has to do something."

"Someone *is* doing something," he said. "Layne is defending himself."

A pained yelp came from the mass of limbs, and I jerked again.

"Let them be," he said. "She went too far challenging him. He has to do this."

"You'd let him kill her?"

He hauled at me again, this time more roughly, and it made my teeth clamp down hard on my tongue. He shook me. Twice. I sagged in his grip but couldn't tear my gaze from Layne's back. His suit had been torn. I could see blood and fur beneath.

"Sweet Jesus."

"Too late for Jesus to do anything," he said. "Maybe start praying to his superior because no one short of God himself is going to stop this now."

I quailed into his side, then, squeezing my eyes shut and knew that every other set of eyes was watching the drama with deadly earnestness. He put his palm against my ear, but the sounds of battle still reached me.

I caught sight of Charles sliding along the floor until he was out of range. He obviously didn't want to get caught in the crossfire of two werewolves intent on doing deadly damage to each other.

I found watching him distracted me. I could drown out the noise, pretend my world wasn't collapsing in on itself.

Someone coiled his fingers around Charles's biceps and tugged him free of the fray. I swallowed down my nausea at the sight of his face. Cuts tracked down one whole side, and bruises had bloomed a lovely purple shade around his eyes.

When he gained his feet, with the help of the companion who had reached for him, he started to tug off his shirt and kick free of his pants.

He'd shift, I realized. Hadn't Layne told me that shifting helped them heal?

For some reason, I didn't want to see Charles come through this unscathed while Parrish and Layne fought for their lives against each other because that bastard couldn't keep his stupid mouth closed.

I pushed away from Zach, who was distracted by the battle roiling about the area. Freed, I launched myself at Charles.

"Bastard," I yelled at him as I bowled into his back. "You did this on purpose, you fucking bastard."

Charles was about as yielding as a brick wall and as my shoulder struck his spine, I wrenched it painfully.

Blind in my rage, I shook it off and threw my arm around his neck, hauling him backward with me... at least, that was the plan, to distract him so he wouldn't shift and relieve himself of the wounds he deserved while Parrish and Layne still fought behind me.

Charles turned on me, his face half-transformed and terrifying. I hiccuped at the sight and dropped my arms to my sides submissively. As a growl erupted from his throat, the sounds of fighting behind me went suddenly dead.

I knew from the look on Charles's face, the bright fear in his gaze as he flicked it over my shoulder that Parrish and Layne had halted their battle. I didn't need to see the werewolf in front of me flinch to know the ones behind me had turned their enraged attention to him.

He backed away, hands up as both Parrish and Layne shoved past me. Layne reached him first, leaving Parrish standing by my side, her breath ragged in my ear.

"Touch her again," Layne said in a deathly quiet tone, "and you will die."

"Agreed," Charles said in a tight voice, guttural from the near shift to lupine cords.

Both men stood rigid for a long moment, one with his eyes traveling the floor as it searched for a safe spot to rest.

Then, finally, mercifully, the air relaxed. Layne's shoulders sagged. All hint of beast retreated back into his skin. The snuff of magic tinkled in the air and then popped as it let go.

Funny, how I'd never noticed the sense of magic before this, but now, with so many pack right there, it must have magnified enough to reach my senses.

I swallowed down a clump of tension, finding the smoothness of relief in my throat, enough to breathe normally again. Without thinking, I reached out to Parrish, and she took my hand, squeezed, then let go.

Layne waited until Charles gave up his attempts to shift and stood before him as fully man, with every inch of wound still plain on his skin. Only then, did he speak again.

"She's mine," Layne said and panned the pack with a long, meaningful glance, forcing each of them to catch his eye. "If any of you doubt my sincerity, then by all means, try me."

"Don't bother," Parrish muttered to the group as a whole, and made a show of rolling her shoulders free of stiffness. "It's just not worth it."

I rankled a bit at Layne's term of possession, but another piece of me, a much deeper, primal part, felt the zing of pleasure at the words. There was something else too, something strange that I couldn't name about the way Parrish angled her body to show off every cut and bruise to the pack while Layne stood there with squared shoulders, his expression devoid of emotion.

They had planned it, I realized. Her cryptic comments upon arriving about things getting messy, her bracing sigh. All because she and Layne had planned this pass over of lover from her to him.

It was cunning. I had to admit. In one bloody event, I'd gone from having to pretend to be in love with Parrish to being free to show my true feelings for Layne. I had my home back, my shop. I'd have been thrilled with the craftiness if I wasn't so damned furious at them both.

And then there was Rowan. Rather than showing the face of defeat as Layne claimed me as his, she looked even more determined. Her eyes ran over him hungrily, all but vibrating with lust as she licked her lips and ran her hand absently over her collarbone.

If Layne noticed, he showed no care as he reached behind his back for my hand. I took it with all the victory of a lover and decided that whatever I had to say to him about this little show of force would be for his ears only.

Because something else had gone on here that I barely understood, but I knew it was important for him, and I knew Parrish had been part of that.

As Charles limped toward the bar and blurred out upon stepping over the barrier, Parrish held her hand up to Layne with a grin lighting her face that was most unapologetic. He returned her grin and struck her palm in a high five.

All as though she hadn't just challenged the pack's second and nearly gotten killed.

"Fuck, that was fun," she said. "Like old times." She shook out her hands at her side, bouncing on her toes like a boxer about to enter the ring. "God. I feel alive."

She turned her green gaze on me and ran the length of my body, then back to Layne. "We could share," she said. "I'm all amped up and need a good fuck right now."

In response, Layne pulled me to him so roughly, I almost staggered, but for the solid hold he draped over my shoulders. Possessive, commanding. My knees went weak for a different reason.

"No offense, Parrish," he said as his mouth dropped to my hair. "But if you touch her again, I'll have to tear your throat out."

"Fair enough." She shrugged. "What's a little pussy to the flat out fun of a cat fight like that?" She grinned so broadly no one could have taken her comment to mean anything derogatory toward me. She stuck out her hand. "No hard feelings, Desiree?"

I took her hand and shook it. Business like. As though the woman I was pretending to be and the woman I pretended to love had no more history than the passing of a business card.

"No hard feelings," I echoed.

"Great," she said, and in an instant, the smiling facade dropped. It was quick, but I saw it if no one else did. When she caught my eye, the grin was back in place again.

"Well," she said. "I'm off to find a willing victim for the night." She smoothed down the plaid shirt. "Take care of her, Layne," she said. "I'll be most pissed if this was all for nothing."

Layne's jaw went tight as he nodded. She pursed her lips and sent a casual look in my direction before spinning on her heel and following Charles into the bar.

I watched her go, not limping as Charles had done, but with a limp in her posture, one that said she had lost something even if she couldn't admit it to herself.

I had the feeling the face-off with Layne had done something irrevocable to their relationship, even if both of them pretended otherwise.

# CHAPTER 7

A CHORUS OF HATEFUL sounding whoops and laughter sounded as Parrish pushed through the barrier, and I realized in that moment how out of place she was in Owen's pack. I clenched Layne's hand hard until he swung on them all and silenced them with a single look.

It was Zach who spoke, almost as though he read the thoughts running through our minds. Maybe he was just thinking the same thing.

"Shut the fuck up, you stupid pricks," he said and pushed past several larger members toward the barrier, obviously intending to trail Parrish out of the club.

What he didn't know that he should have for a man who loved her was she didn't want him to follow. She didn't care one bit what the rest of the pack thought of her. I watched the blur of her shape square its shoulders and change direction toward a group of young and beautiful women and knew she'd find a way to feel better all on her own.

I looked up at Layne, suddenly tired. "I want to go home," I said.

His lips pursed together as he nodded. "Me too," he said and swung a nasty glare around the few pack members still lurking about after his initial glare. If his gaze landed on Rowan as she cocked her hip sideways and dipped her finger into her cleavage, he ignored her. "These bastards have no idea who they're messing with when it comes to Parrish."

He led me through the club to the door, winding between and around dancers and servers until we'd made it to the exit. He was about to push it open when someone stepped out of the shadows of the club to do it for him.

"My pleasure, sir," the young man said with a flash of yellow in his gaze that swept over me and back again to Layne. "I'm glad you put a licking on that bitch. Don't know what I'd do with a female second."

Shocked, I halted mid-stride as Layne rounded on him. Did that kid just say what I'd thought? Had the fight between them been more about rank than me? I watched Layne's expression, but it didn't change at the comment, except to flicker over the young man's frame.

"She'd wipe the floor with you, you little shit," Layne said in a voice thick with both compassion and firmness. "And then you'd either be dead or you'd show her the respect she'd deserve."

The youth dropped his head, staring at his sneakered feet. I touched him on the arm, unable to help myself. "What he means is, Parrish would die for the right friend," I told the youth. "And she would die for her pack. She would make a good alpha, let alone a second in command."

The boy lifted his eyes to mine and something strange moved within its depths, something that made my skin whisper with prescience. I felt like I knew him.

"Still," he said, "the misogyny fostered in a pack of all male members is hard to undo. Good luck with that."

He saluted us both, then evaporated into the shadows again. It was so unexpected, so mature, from a man that young that I was left speechless until we were seated in Layne's car, the engine purring as it pulled out into the streets and headed to the middle of town.

"He thought Parrish was fighting you to take your place," I said.

Layne clenched the steering wheel all the tighter. "Yes and no."

My hand trailed to his thigh, feeling for the tension I knew was in his leg, testing for it. "That's ridiculous," I said. "Parrish loves you."

He sighed and patted my hand, letting his lay atop it. The muscles smoothed out beneath my palm. "She loves me, yes, but the wolf inside—the beast—she fights it. That she-wolf was testing me, seeing once more if I was worthy of her loyalty."

"So that's what that was about."

He curled his fingers around mine. "She hasn't done that for several decades. The last time was when Zach gave her a lady Godiva for her birthday. She told one man about that fantasy, and he wanted to please her so badly."

I almost choked on my laughter. "She said she didn't want to talk about it."

"She wouldn't," he said. "She took that woman to her bed for several weeks, only coming out to complete her exams, and long enough to invite Zach in as a thanks." He chuckled beneath his breath. "I dare say two women was too much for him. He refused. All he wanted was her happiness, and she felt so damn guilty about not being able to give it to him."

"So why did she fight you, then? What did you have to do with it all?"

He glanced over at me. "Who do you think that one man was that she told that fantasy to? "

"Oh my god, you didn't."

"I did. She'd been particularly troublesome at that point and I had to either teach her a lesson or kick her out of the pack. Once she was finished with her Godiva, she came gunning for me. Although she didn't fight me quite so hard then as she did today. Her beast keeps wanting to go it alone and every time I best her, she stews for a while. I doubt I'll see her for a few days while she and her beast work out some compromise that lets them both settle back in."

"She hates it," I mused out loud. "Pack life, I mean."

He sighed. "She doesn't hate it. Her beast wants to be rogue. It wants to be ruled by no one, not even the woman that houses her. But Parrish needs a pack. Without one, there's no telling what damage she'd do. I'm not about to let that happen to her."

I thought that over. I had the feeling he didn't want to admit that pack life, however horrible it might be for her, kept her from going feral. It gave her purpose. "They're too prejudiced and sexist."

"And typical men aren't?" he asked. "Women have been fighting that battle since time began. Men are animals. Werewolves just haven't evolved quite so much as human men. At least many of us."

I squeezed his thigh. "Sometimes I like the animal."

He let go a low growl, full of possession and desire and my spine tingled. "If you mean that, I can show you just how primal I can be when we get to the hotel."

"I thought I was going home."

He shook his head. "I can't let you stay in that mess. My men aren't going in until the morning to clean it up. We'll go to a hotel. I've already booked the penthouse. We have a few hours left until dawn, and I intend to make each moment memorable."

I thought about my house, the mess inside, and the fact that I was free of the surveillance. "That was no small feat you and Parrish managed back there," I said. "Thank you."

His palm ran up my thigh to cup the tender place between my thighs. "You can thank me when we get there. But really, the idea to use her boon to free you was her idea. I was the one who decided I couldn't stand to have you kissing her in front of me. Once Charles caught us in the library, I decided to use him to instigate the fight, but then, of course, Parrish let it get out of hand."

"She loves you," I said, leaning my head back to enjoy the feel of his hand on me.

"Enough about her," he murmured. "Just think about me and my hand on you."

I was more than ready to do just that, except one question kept niggling into my mind, ruining the soaking sensation of desire threading through my body.

"Who was that young man?" I asked him. "I hesitated to say werewolf because I knew by Layne's own admission, only those with a certain bloodline are changed, and then only after they are old enough to make the decision. Besides, the boy did not look wolven to me. He looked...other.

He glanced sideways at me as he took a turn down a side street. "No idea. He must be new. Now, no more questions. Not for at least a few hours."

This said as he pulled over into a parking spot several yards away from any other cars and streetlights. The area looked all but deserted; the shops closed and the parked cars all dark within as they sat in sporadic places along the street. I knew the area, and it was mostly commercial, lined with tourist shops and parking lots.

He cut the engine and swung over the seat to gather me into his arms. His kiss took my breath away and when he slipped his hand into the waistband of my jeans, burrowing his finger deep inside me, rough and commanding, I yielded like warm butter to a slice of hot bread.

In moments, he had me so hot, I didn't care where I was or who might see. I climbed over the seat to straddle him, thankful that I'd decided to forego underwear in favor of a smooth, pantyline-free back view.

Then I thanked him good and proper. And he showed me how happy he was to be mine.

Then, smelling strongly of each other, and exhausted, I kissed the side of his cheek and begged for sleep.

"I'm not sure I can sleep," he murmured. "Not after that."

"*That* should be enough," I said, but I knew what he meant. It might never be enough.

"A tease," he said. "I want to lay you out where I can see every inch of you, not just grab release like a thief."

"I thought it was pretty hot," I said and adjusted my skirt.

His fingers slipped beneath the material and brushed my thigh. "My idea of hot isn't the same as yours, obviously," he said in a low, smoky voice. "Looking at you makes it hot. Seeing your face, watching your belly ripple from pleasure, that's what makes it hot for me." He pinched my skin lightly. "Soon," he said.

I leaned back in the seat and let my eyes travel the scenery, so content that I barely registered what blurred by.

When he pulled up to the hotel, my brain started to seize. It was *the* hotel. The place where Owen and

Honey had nearly killed me, but for the magic my mother pulled from me to push them back.

My throat went dry as I took in the twinkle lights wrapped around miniature potted cedar trees. The broad glass doors led up to the penthouse Owen had booked for me that night, knowing Honey and her coven waited for me there.

I dug myself deeper into the seat and clutched at the door handle out of an instinctual need to keep it closed.

"Why are we here?" I asked in a small voice. Didn't he know this place was a haunting for me?

"I want to know what went on," he said. "What really went on."

"I told you," I said as he leaned crossway over the seat, his opposite hand on the steering wheel to give him leverage to angle himself closer to me. "I told you everything."

Everything was a horror. I didn't want to revisit it.

He braced himself on the seat and gathered me close as his hand left the wheel. "I wish I could believe that," he said. "But you're keeping something from me. I had hoped seeing the hotel would encourage you to tell me what it is."

I swallowed nervously. "You mean you intentionally brought me here to see my reaction." I shoved his hands away.

He didn't need to reply for me to know it was true. "You purposefully fucked me in this car on the side of the road because you wanted me good and pliant when you brought me here."

"An obvious misjudgment on my part," he said. "If this is pliant, I'd hate to see what would have happened if I'd not fucked you on the side of the road."

"You can be a prick," I said.

His sigh was long-suffering. "Cops often are. We study behavior. We know when someone is lying, or when they are telling near truths."

I could barely hold his gaze in the light bathing his face from the hotel and the street, but I knew I had to.

I sighed and braced myself for the inevitable. "You're right," I said. "I am keeping something from you."

"You can tell me, Brie. You can trust me."

"You are not going to like it. You might even flip that feral switch."

"Is it that bad?" His eyebrows furrowed down.

"Yes," I murmured. "It's all bad."

# CHAPTER 8

I WAS GOING TO die. That was the long and the short of it. Bad couldn't even encompass that problem, so keeping it from Layne and Parrish seemed to be the smartest thing to do because there was nothing they or anyone could do to avoid it.

The person I'd been once, the kind of woman who conned her clients for a few coins had long evaporated into the ether of the 'magic' I'd used to pretend I had power. I knew too much now. I'd experienced the real thing, and I was left knowing that if someone didn't stop the cult, they wouldn't just hand over my mother to Lucifer in an ages-old vendetta.

They would use the power he gifted them to live forever. And who knew what kind of horrors they'd inflict on the world then.

But sitting in front of the hotel where the cult had nearly done me in with the man I loved, I found I couldn't lie to him through omission anymore. He deserved to know. After he'd done everything he could to keep me safe, even fighting the only friend I had to allow me some sort of normalcy, he needed to know.

I gripped his hand tight against my stomach and took a bracing breath.

"You know Lucifer set the cult on my mother," I began, and didn't wait for his acknowledgment. I felt his expectation and blustered on. "She fought them after my father died, vowing to bring them down and bring my father back to her."

"I know this," he murmured. "She became mortal to be with your father and Lucifer was left without a companion to guide his lover back and forth from his realm. It's an age-old myth."

I nodded although I wasn't sure he could see it in the cabin. "I'm pretty sure the cult killed my mother's mortal body, but she was a god. They couldn't really kill her or extinguish her power. She knew this, of course, although I don't think they did. Before she died, she broke herself into several fragments to keep the power safe from them. I know where all those pieces are."

"The dog," he guessed. "The amulet. The grimoire."

"That's only three," I said. "She is a goddess of numbers. Three, seven. Thirteen. We saw those numbers in the cult's sacrifices, invoking her spirit because they knew they had taken her body. They just didn't know where her powers were stored."

"You think she put her magic into more than three vessels."

"She had to. John Smith makes four, but that's not one of her sacred numerals. Thirteen is too many."

"You're thinking seven vessels to hold her power," he mused aloud, "so where are the other three?"

I leaned my head back against the headrest. "Honey took what she could, those inanimate things that could be stolen. The amulet, the grimoire. When I was in the hotel room, Abbi and John Smith came to the circle. There was a chest there as well. I believe the cult still has the chest, and that it's one of the vessels. I think the cult broke into my house to find the photo of my mother. The one John Smith gave me along with the knife that night in the cellar. That photo, or at least my mother's blood is the other vessel. Touching it triggered my magic."

"So," he said, ticking up each finger of one hand, "amulet, grimoire, photo, dog, Smith, chest. That still leaves one more."

I turned to the window and blew condensation onto the glass. Tracing a heart and arrow with our initials in the middle, I pondered how to tell him the rest. It should have been so easy. The conversation was leading me right to the truth, but I found I couldn't. Not yet.

I dotted the initials then laid my hand over the heart. "I always wondered why my mother didn't fight to keep me when I petitioned the state to keep me. I was a kid. Her kid. She should have wanted me with her, not some strangers in another country. I was mad and hurt and broken by grief even at that age, but even so, it broke my heart that she just let me go."

"I imagine it did."

I sighed. "But I know now why she did it. She taught me what she could as a child, letting me see her magic, letting me believe she didn't love me as much as she loved my father."

I swallowed to free the constriction in my throat that made my voice hoarse. "I think I understand her better now. Things changed once I went to Hell and saw her there. She ferried Persephone back and forth for centuries. She was weary. My father loved her unconditionally."

I closed my eyes, letting the memory of Hecate's broken spirited self in front of Lucifer, the way my father looked at her. It was heartbreaking.

I blew out a long and heavy sigh. The rest of it, all the things I knew now, could wait. Maybe it should wait until he was less vulnerable. "Let's go," I said. "I'm ready."

"Ready?"

"To go in." I swung my gaze back to him. "It's what you think I should do, isn't it? Face the room, feel the space, chase the ghosts away."

He shrugged with one shoulder. "I didn't think that far. Do you think you should go in?"

"Only one way to find out. I told you. I'm no victim. Not anymore."

His fingers spasmed in mine. "You've never been a victim," he growled low in his throat. "You're fierce. You just didn't realize it."

I smiled for him, letting him think I believed his lie. We both knew I was weak before, riding the currents of trauma and using them to make excuses for everything I did.

Without waiting for him to realize I'd not answered his question, I pushed out of the car and slammed the door behind me. Several steps of the path to the hotel lobby were behind me when he caught up with me and slipped his arm around my waist.

"You won't be alone," he said into my hair as he hugged me close. "I'll be with you every step. No one will hurt you. Not ever again. Not as long as I live."

I squeezed him back reassuringly. It was alright for him to think he could stop what was coming. I loved him all the more for it, and when we approached the reservation desk and the clerk smiled at us, I knew before we could ask that the penthouse would be ready for us because he'd known I'd say yes and booked it.

He laid his hand down on the desk and leaned toward the clerk, a pinch-faced young woman with long nails painted with star bursts on her thumbs. She beamed up at him as he turned on the charm that enabled him to wrestle the most frightening details out of witnesses traumatized by horrors no one should see.

"Can I help you check in?" she said, skirting over me with her black eyes and giving all her attention to the large man with the expensive suit. The girl knew her stuff. Even though I was dressed in the gorgeous black dress, I realized at the moment, that it probably looked like I was a high-class prostitute. I snickered to myself.

When he indicated he had booked the penthouse for the night, she must have sensed an opportunity to make a bit of money on the side and made a polite moue with her chocolate colored lipstick.

"I'll need to see Identification, Mr. Wayne."

Her fingers flew over the keyboard as she stared glassily at the screen. "I have the reservation under Bruce, is that right?"

She hesitated just long enough for Layne to clear his throat. Her gaze flicked over the counter where his hand lay palm up. The one-hundred-dollar bill was gone into her fist so quickly I was sure she had to be some sort of magician.

"No need for that I.D," she said once any evidence of the money was gone. "I see you've booked with us before. We're happy to have you back."

"Wonderful," he said with that dazzling smile playing over his mouth. "We'll take two keys, please."

I tried not to gape at him at the assumed name as she passed us a small folded bit of cardboard with the fobs inside.

"Certainly, Mr Wayne."

I had to work at holding my tongue and couldn't do so any longer by the time we hit the elevators. "Mr.

Wayne?" I asked with a snicker. "You fancy yourself a hero, do you?"

He shrugged as he jabbed at the buttons. "Every man is a hero in his own story, don't you think, Ms. Kitt?"

I stepped inside the shaft and waited till he muscled his way in, herding me into the corner beneath the camera and out of sight. "And you fancy me a criminal, do you?" I said breathlessly, as his hands planted themselves on either side of me.

He shook his head. "That's not why I gave you that moniker. It's because you have nine lives." He dropped his head, claiming my lips with his and kissing me so thoroughly we both barely missed the moment the doors opened to the top floor.

I gasped as he released me, it was so swift. He spun on the door like it was a man with a machine gun, barring me from view of whoever might be standing there.

As it was, it opened to a brief hallway, the way I remembered, and I shivered in reflection.

"I wonder how many of those I have left," I muttered beneath my breath, and he looked at me over his shoulder.

"What was that?"

"Nothing," I said. "Let's just do this."

He reached behind his back for my hand and I gave it to him. Together, we approached the door. I suffered a moment of déjà vu and expected that if I looked sideways out of the corner of my eye, I'd catch sight of Abbi, waiting there for me, knowing I was entering a trap.

But although my spine tingled as though someone was watching me, she didn't appear. Layne eased the door open, and we strode across the threshold. He hit a switch, and the room flooded with light.

It looked as it did the last time I'd been there, except this time there were no rings of candles and chanting witches standing in a circle to drain me of life as they sacrificed me to their god. I'd thought that god was Hecate when this all began. Now I knew it was Satan himself.

While the scene looked benign, there was a subtle difference.

"I sense the magic," I said as I scoured the room with my gaze, forcing myself to take in every detail and see the danger had passed. I was safe there, with Layne at my side. I wasn't a victim anymore. I had to repeat it over and over to bolster my courage.

"How?" he asked. "Is it the coven's magic or your mother's?"

I sighed. "I'm not sure. Maybe both. It was...it was a lot to take in that night." I felt my chest trembling and my fingers lifted to the runes instinctively. I was barely aware of the thought that I might try to use my magic, but he must have noticed.

"Don't be afraid," he said.

My fingers trailed across the neckline of my dress, nearly dipping to the skin beneath, but as I realized what I was doing, I shook my head. "I'm not. I'm just...the power in here is still strong. Don't you feel it?"

He leaned his head back, focusing. He drew in a breath through his nostrils. "I smell something. Spices or herbs. And something else. Something that makes the hair raise on the back of my neck."

"That's the magic," I said, watching the way his features changed as he looked at me, all fiercely protective and wary. I tried a smile, thinking it might defuse the charge of energy he was giving off. When he caught my eye, I noticed the gold flared behind his irises, then turned to a molten honey.

"I don't smell sulfur," he said hopefully.

"I don't either." I pivoted and spread my arms out to my sides, my eyes closed as I let the magic sweep over me. It felt familiar. "I think it's just residue," I said. "Not real magic or power. Just the film that's left when you wash a greasy window."

I took a few tentative steps further into the room. The sunken floor of the entertaining space seemed bigger somehow than I remembered. As I moved through the chamber, studying each detail and trying to lay it over the images from my memory of that night, something caught my senses, a prickle just behind my ears.

"Or maybe there is something," I said as that sensation trickled down my neck and twined around my throat to lodge beneath my ribcage, spreading out from my solar plexus to encompass my body.

I tracked the curling, ribbon-like tether that tugged at my fingers as they touched down on my skin where the dress gaped open at my decolletage.

The tether there was whisper thin, but it was as clear in that moment as a tendril of smoke from the tip of a cigarette. I didn't need to follow it to the shadowed corner near the bed to know what would be on the other end.

Abbi. She hunkered in the corner, barely visible in the shadows but for the gleam of light coming from her eyes.

"Do you see her?" I asked, my voice just audible enough to hear.

Layne immediately tensed and put his arm over my stomach protectively. "Honey?"

"No," I said. "Look again."

His strides devoured the distance between us as he squinted into the corner, following my gaze. "Fuck me," he said, as the shape there must have made itself known to him as well. "Your familiar. My God, Brie, that's your dog."

"It is," I whispered, unsure of my voice as I noticed the truth of what I was seeing. "At least, she's the dog I keep seeing. My mother's familiar, really." I held out my hand, knowing how scared she was. "The magic here. It's the only thing keeping her alive."

"She's not well?" he said, so close on my heels that I felt his breath sweep over my hair. "How do you know?"

Pausing at the spot where the sunken part of the floor met the raised dais of the bedroom, I lowered my chin, peering closer at the huge black beast lying with her paws in front of her. "I know because she's barely there," I rasped. "And I know because she is part of me. I can feel her weakness."

He crouched beside me, carefully, the way a man might if he wanted to encourage a reluctant stray to eat from his palm. "Those eyes," he said as he peered into Abbi's face. "I know the look of a soul peering out from a beast's eyes."

My head snapped in his direction. He understood. It both surprised and pleased me. Maybe explaining the rest of the truth to him wouldn't be so bad after all.

"She needs my magic," I said. "She's failing. Without it, she might disappear altogether."

He made a sound in the deepest part of his chest, one of thoughtful agreement. "And if you don't just give her your magic?" he asked.

I swallowed. "I'm afraid she just might take it."

# CHAPTER 9

I WASN'T ABOUT TO let myself be attacked by a ghost dog, but I wasn't ready for Layne to attack the familiar either. I grabbed the tail of his shirt just in time to use it to propel myself along with him. Abbi evaporated, gone like smoke. We were left in the wake of magic she left behind. It stung my nostrils.

"She needs me, Layne," I said, stepping in front of him. I wasn't sure if the dog was still lurking in the shadows unseen, so I didn't want to leave him an opening to find out.

"She might need you, but I won't let her hurt you." His jaw was white with anger. Not at me, at the thought that I might let myself be hurt to save the dog.

"She's not alive," I said. "She's energy, magic, power. She's a vessel. My mother's vessel."

"I won't let her hurt you."

"She won't hurt me."

"How do you know?"

"Because I'm going to give her what she needs."

He stared at me for a long time before he laid his hands on my shoulder. "I don't like this."

I slipped into his embrace. "She saved me," I said. "Time and time again, she saved me. I can't just let her fade, let a piece of my mother go. Every time she makes herself known, it's to warn me. But it costs her to become corporeal. Please, Layne. Don't make this hard for me."

He dropped his hands to his sides, but they clenched into fists against his thighs. I held them there, trying to reassure him with my touch that it would be alright.

"Trust me," I said. "I know what needs to be done now. Let me do it."

His jaw tensed. The words came out tight and constricted. "I trust you."

I let go a long breath. "Good." I lead him to the bed and urged him to sit down. "If it makes you feel better, you can stand guard," I said, then started a sweep of the room, looking for something sharp or pointed.

The corkscrew sitting atop the mini fridge looked about the best option.

"What are you doing, Brie?" he asked when I clutched it in my fist.

I held the corkscrew over my chest. "Calling to my power."

I'd never seen him move so fast. Before I could even drag the point of the corkscrew over the skin of my chest, gouging into the runes so that I could tap into my blood and the magic with it, his hand closed over mine. He squeezed my fingers, forcing me to release the instrument.

"No," he said. His fingers were gentle when they pried the corkscrew from me.

I swung my gaze toward him, lowering my hand to my lap where it touched his fingers.

"You don't understand. She needs me, the magic that's inside me. That last vessel? It's me. I'm number seven. Abbi isn't just a familiar meant to protect me. I'm joined to her and the others through my blood, through my mother's blood. My magic isn't my own. It's hers.

Triggered when the cult forced the grimoire and the dog and the amulet to spark into life again."

The tension in the room made my skin sing with electricity. The runes on my chest, the ones invisible to everyone but me, ached with the confession I knew I needed to speak but couldn't.

The final moment was coming, the time when Hecate's power was strong. That was the night that would be best to make my move against the cult, and yet I had nothing to go on. No place to cast my spells, no sacred space to call her magics to me and initiate her resurrection. Weeks away and yet far too close.

"I love you," I said to him. "These weeks have healed me even as they've broken me apart. You and Parrish. You're my world now."

He tossed the corkscrew onto the bed. It bounced twice. "I hear a but coming."

"But...you also know this can't continue. The cult can't keep doing what it's doing and if we don't strike, then they will. They'll come for those vessels they don't own so they can finish what they started."

"Then let her go," he said. "Let the dog fade and the magic with it. The cult can't take what it doesn't have."

I pursed my lips. "If it was that easy, I'd just destroy them all. But she's in there. My mother. She's in me. Would you kill your own mother to save yourself?"

His voice turned gravelly. "I'd kill whoever or whatever I had to in order save you."

I touched his cheek. "You won't have to. My mother will want her vengeance. There isn't enough power in any one of her vessels to fight the cult. I need them all. Hecate needs to be whole."

His eyes searched mine, and I tried to let him have what he needed to acquiesce while keeping from him the truth of what that really meant. That for Hecate to be whole, I needed to surrender the magic that filled me. I wasn't sure I was ready to face that truth for myself.

"Fair enough," he said with a heavy sigh. "I trust you. But you don't have to use your magic for Abbi. Werewolves were made with magic too. It's in our blood and marrow. Let me provide what she needs."

My brow furrowed as I took him in, and his features softened as he continued in a voice so gruff it was barely a rasp.

"I told you I would never let anyone hurt you ever again. That includes you." He guided me to the bed and urged me to sit. "Let the dog take my magic if she needs it. I won't let her needs cause you pain."

I sank onto the mattress, suddenly spent and anxious at what he was suggesting, and he knelt in front of me, slipping in between my thighs as though my legs were mere water. "It shouldn't matter what sort of magic," he said as he cupped my chin with his hand. "Magic is magic, isn't it?"

I nodded, although I didn't want to. I felt like Jesus in the garden of Gethsemane and the relief made me feel guilty. I had decided I'd do what it took to destroy the cult's hold on my life, but the doing of it... maybe I'd not really been ready for that. I wasn't even sure just how much of my magic Abbi would need to regenerate.

Relieved as I was, I knew he didn't understand fully what he was getting into.

"I'm not sure how to give her yours," I confessed. "With me it's—"

"Blood, I know," he said and shifted to pull me down onto his lap as he sat on the floor. I straddled him, our chests pressed together.

He laid his palm against my heart. "You told me the dog was bringing you things to reanimate, using her magic to kill them and then, when you didn't catch on, she ate them to reclaim her power." He waited until I nodded, then said, "And she consumed Farrel in the hospital room."

I started at the inference. "I'm not going to let her eat you."

He chuckled and smoothed my hair back. "I'm not going to let her do that either."

"Then what do you propose?"

"You also told me your mother cast spells to create the vessels, to create the dog."

I sighed. "That was my mother. She has an affinity for dogs of all breeds. It's part of her power. But I won't lie. She sacrificed small dogs to create Abbi. Used their life force to draw out the parts of herself she wanted to place inside her vessel, used them to give that familiar form and life."

I shook my head. "I'm not sure I'm ready for that even if they live on in her. It's a brutal business."

I canted my head at him. "Plus, there aren't any pet shelters open this time of night." I tried to smile at the bad joke, but my lips wouldn't form it. I ended up clamping my mouth shut.

His own expression worked silently for a few moments as he mulled over the situation, and then he stood suddenly, briskly, lifting me effortlessly to my feet as he did so. Each motion an efficiency as though he'd decided to complete some distasteful business as quickly as he could.

"There's another way, I think," he said with a flash of honey in his gaze.

He back-stepped away from me several feet, almost a skip, then spun on his heel and headed for the bathroom. "A way to give her parts of me without her devouring my flesh." He said this last with a grimace that was both full of distaste and humor. "A way that will be familiar to you and to your magic. Something sacred enough to fuel the spell."

I heard him muttering to me as he went, and I followed him to where he'd disappeared behind the bathroom door. From within, he kept up his trail of thoughts as though he was afraid he'd forget them and needed me to hear while they played about his mindscape.

"You said every time you see her, it's to warn you," he said. "What do you think she's warning you of now?"

"Who knows?" I said as I crossed into the room. "If she's prescient, I wish that she'd give me better warnings than just glowering at me."

I found him standing beside the walk-in shower, peeling off his clothes.

"Although I do like where your mind is going, I don't think it's the right time."

He smiled at me as he kicked out of his trousers and stepped into the shower. That smile stayed there, distracting me until he dragged a knife across the skin of his arm, drawing my notice. A knife I'd not seen him holding until it left a long, bloody seam on his forearm.

Alarm bells pealed behind my ears. I rushed him, thinking he needed my help. Fast.

He held his hand up to me.

"Do what you need to," he said. "I trust you. Just do it quickly. If you're fast enough, I can shift and heal before any damage is done."

He was offering himself in my stead, giving me the magic of his blood.

There wasn't time to argue, not with his arm bleeding like that. He'd known, obviously, that I wouldn't let him hurt himself anymore than he'd let me harm myself. If I wanted save him, I had to call to the magic and I had to call to it right then.

I let instinct take me, trusting the power that swelled inside me to do what needed to be done to initiate the magic. I stepped into the shower stall with him and, with trembling fingers, I touched the seam of blood that tracked itself upwards from wrist to elbow.

So much blood. It was pooling on the floor, making the stall slippery. My stomach tried to quail at the sight of it, and it took all my will to swallow down the nausea and fear and let the years of pretension and sham take over where concern tried to stop it.

All those years, I practiced with a professional distance, carefully guarding my emotions from what I was doing. I pulled that experience out as my fingers began to trace symbols in the blood. My inner eye knew them.

I'd seen them for months in the mirror as they scrawled themselves across my chest and down my arms, those invisible runes pulled from a power deep inside, raising to the surface the way an old stain creeps back into the pile of a carpet.

I worked as fast as I could and even though I did, he sagged against the back wall of the shower. Once, my gaze met his and the glassiness that he turned back to me sent shivers of terror up my spine. I almost balked, but he somehow managed to wrap his fingers around my elbow and squeeze.

"Don't stop," he rasped and slid another inch down the wall.

With throat clotted with fear so dreadful I could no longer swallow, I slid my free hand behind his back. I used what weight he had left to hold me erect as I smeared the viscous fluid into symbols that barely held their shape before drooling down onto his thighs.

"Brie," he whispered as the last of the symbols closed off its circuit on his chest. He sounded barely conscious, and I knew he was at his edge, the last bastion of his awareness when he could transform and heal the damage he'd inflicted on himself.

As if my magic knew that edge, a sharp and pungent sort of electricity struck my senses. It wasn't a smell, not in the sense of inhaling and catching a whiff of something, but it was a tickle against my sixth sense, and I knew the circuit had been closed.

Whatever needed igniting sparked in that second and a gush of air left my lungs as if I'd been holding my breath.

I collapsed into the pool of blood on the shower floor, and the magic lifted me in cradling arms. In some faraway part of my mind, I expected Abbi to poke her head into the stall and start lapping at the blood, craving the magic it held.

I did not expect for one second what happened instead.

# CHAPTER 10

AN EVIL, SLITHERING DARKNESS enveloped me. One that felt thick and sickeningly familiar. A flash of images rode my mind as I felt myself spiraling out of control, twisting like Alice as she tumbled down the rabbit hole.

Scarlet's face yawned out from the shadows. I heard a rush of her voice as it yelled at me to stop. To get away. To run.

Too late, I thought. This was the thing I'd always sensed in the darkness. The thing that had reached for me as I'd reached for the magic, the thing Scarlet was afraid of. This thing had a name as old as the earth's core. Its name was Legion, and it was swallowing me whole.

Screaming was impossible. There wasn't space in this darkness for thought let alone speech. All that existed was a pressing, claustrophobic crush of pain and grief. I plummeted with my heart in my throat until it all stopped at once.

I had landed. I was at the bottom of that well of darkness.

It took sheer will to force myself to scan my surroundings. I recognized the hallway I stood in, even though I'd only been there once before.

A leather map sprawled over a wall that seemed to have no end, and I knew the vellum to be that of human skin because I'd seen it before.

I spun on my feet to take in the veins of energy that ran the other walls, veins that pulsed with the life energy of those trapped here, playthings for a creature who gathered souls like a collector hordes stamps.

Hell. The magic had taken me to Hell. That was the warning Abbi had for me that I didn't heed. I'd thought myself safe because I'd weathered the magic before, because Layne was with me.

I was wrong about my safety but what of his? My knees went to water as I thought about him lying in that shower stall, hunched over and probably dying. I had to reach out to the wall to steady myself.

I prayed that Layne was okay where I'd left him, that Abbi had taken what she needed and he'd shifted to his wolf self, letting the transformation heal his body. I prayed for those things because I knew I couldn't let worry for him distract me now. Hell would take me if I lost focus.

If I was to survive, I had to trust he was fine, and put his survival to the back of my mind. The cards had been dealt, and it was time to strategize. To find a way out again before it was too late.

A sound from behind me drew my attention before I could reason out more than that. I froze. My skin crawled as though a thousand ants were burrowing between the first and second layers.

I turned slowly, my heart hammering in my ears.

A beautiful man stood in front of me. Glossy black hair framed a perfect face. Eyes the color of a summer sky gazed out at me from beneath a high brow. I felt as though for one second, the darkness slid away like shadows in the heat of a noon sun. I knew the man even though he looked different from the last time I'd seen him.

"Lucifer," I said.

He beamed at me. "I'm flattered you remember since I took a more pleasing form for you than I did the last time you were here."

The base of my spine crawled. "I haven't been here before," I lied.

He tilted his head at me. "You think you can fool the king of liars?" he asked with a chuckle. "Oh, you are a rare treasure."

When he approached, his strides ate up the distance between us so quickly, I barely saw his legs move. His fingers curled around my elbow softly and the feel of his touch was like the radiation from a warm and cozy fire.

"I've been waiting for your return." He winked.

He began guiding me around the large mapped wall and toward an expansive chamber lined with what appeared to be shelves of artifacts and relics. Some, the largest ones, took more than one shelf and were hung in nooks that broke the shelving into display cases here and there. Smaller relics lined taffy-colored shelves with golden lights illuminating them from the bottom up. Everything within smelled subtly of brimstone and unexpectedly of vanilla.

He paused to cast a look my way. "Last time you were here, I'm afraid you didn't see me in my best light." In a charming manner, he inclined his head just slightly to the left, making him look both playful and boyish.

I wasn't fooled.

"The last time I was here, I didn't mean to come," I said. "And I'm pretty sure what I saw was exactly what you are."

He flashed a very wide smile. "Do you?" he asked thoughtfully. "If that's all you think I am, then please tell the religious freaks. They spread such evil gossip about me." His grin was so playful it near melted my heart.

With a flourish, he invited me to sit, and immediately, a plush sofa appeared with dozens of tapestry pillows of all shapes and sizes. The fireplace sparked to life, one I'd not noticed when he'd led me to the room.

The blood-red carpet gave the room a rich, gothic feel. Strangely enough, the fire made no sound. If it gave off heat, I'd not have noticed because the sofa all but slipped into my knees and buckled them. I suffered a moment of panic, thinking bonds would fly out of the arms and backrest and pull me tightly into the cushions.

He laughed as I started. "I would never do such a thing to a guest," he said. "At least, not a guest I've been waiting so eagerly for, and not so soon after her arrival. Best to save such delights as bondage for a time when we both know we're going to indulge in it."

I found it very difficult to avoid looking at him, and when I did catch a glimpse of him, the more certain I grew that he was the most beautiful being I'd ever seen. And the more I studied his looks, the more they shifted, always seeming to respond to scrutiny, always turning into something more perfectly aligned to my own standards of beauty. I was afraid in moments he'd be so gorgeous he'd hurt my eyes.

His height made it difficult for him to hold my gaze without stooping and so he pulled up a chair (again, one I hadn't noticed until it was there in his grip and scuffing across the carpet) and slid onto the seat as though it was mere water and he moving into the wake of it as it moved around him.

He crossed one leg over the other, and pinched the crease in the trousers. I noticed he wore a suit very much like Layne wore, rich looking and perfectly tailored.

With a long sigh, he planted his hands on the armrests and let his eye travel from my face to my feet and back again. "You are beautiful," he said. "I only caught a short glimpse of you before, what with you peering around corners like a little thief."

"I wasn't—"

My words cut off at the lift of his finger to the air. "Please," he said. "Don't ruin it by lying again. We both know you were here, and we both know what you saw and what you heard."

Instead of admitting anything, I merely nodded. I was here for a reason. I had the horrible feeling I'd not get out again unless I conceded the truth.

He smiled. "As I said, I've been waiting for you ever since I caught that glimpse."

He leaned forward, his hands leaving the armrests and whispering across his knee until his elbows rested there, both hands hanging on either side of his legs. He inhaled, much the way Layne or Parrish did when they were sensing for something too fragile for a mortal to notice.

"I smell her magic on you," he said. "But in you it's like a delicate flower, not the full blast of eucalyptus that she carries. It's because you're more delicate, I think. An orchid." He shifted even further into his posture, leaning so close, so low, that I thought he might slide right off the chair. "A hothouse orchid. So delightful. So rare in this realm."

"Is that why I'm here?" I asked. "Because you are in need of a little floral arrangement for this dreary place?"

He chuckled darkly. "If you find this environment dreary, I've not read your desires correctly and you must forgive me. But as to why you're here, little mourning dove, *you* must tell me. I didn't call you. I didn't ask for you. You just came."

He gestured toward the room around us and the room shifted from a chamber filled with bookshelves and relics to an elegant, if not sleek and black boudoir. The bed that took up most of the chamber shone with jet colored satin sheets. I all but shivered looking at it.

"Were you aching to return as well as I was aching to see you?" he asked.

My throat went thick with fear so acute, I could barely swallow. "My arrival wasn't intentional."

He pursed his full lips thoughtfully, as though considering a problem that had been eluding him despite giving it solicitous attention. "Were you casting magic?"

I bit my lip at the tone in his voice. Not inquisitive in the least. He knew the answer. He just wanted me to say it out loud, as though I should know what would happen.

"I was trying to help my moth... my familiar. She's... she's not well. I thought perhaps I could help her. Give her some power."

He pursed his lips knowingly. "Ah yes. The daughter knows not the strength of her mother's power. She knows not of its source, for how could she?"

He stood and frowned down at me. Nervous, I tried to move but discovered that the sofa had indeed caught me in its clutches, just not with any bonds I could see.

"Your magic is death magic, my dove. Didn't you know? Don't you understand your mother's essence at all? She is the mother of necromancy, the goddess of death. Where else could your power come from? You draw from those poor unfortunate souls whenever you claim the power in your blood. Although, I do believe your mother used death on your side of the realm, not this side."

He sent me a wry smile. "As a god, she had her own power. You? It must be strong if it can whisk you to my side at a mere spell." He eyed me with lids at half-mast, an expression that made him look even more beautiful somehow. "Why you're even still dressed when most mortals come to me naked as the souls they house. Why do you think that is so?"

Again, a tone that sounded competently indulgent and knowing.

I thought about the possibility that I'd never considered before. That my mother's magic, and so mine, was rooted in death energy and I shuddered.

"I have my mother's blood in me. I am her vessel—"

This time when he laughed, it wasn't a pleasant chuckle. It was a riotous guffaw that threw his head back.

"Oh, I know all about her vessels," he said. "You think a seventh vessel with a seventh blood can transport you to my world so easily? No, my dove. Your power straddles both worlds, yes, and you have some of her strength, but that is not all you are, I'm afraid."

He got up so suddenly I fell back on the sofa.

"You are a born necromancer, like your father. Hecate made a mistake when she infused you with power. She was so blinded by vengeance that she didn't look beyond your small form to see what lay beneath." A smug look fashioned the boyish charm into something unattractive. It gave me the boost I needed to argue.

"It wasn't vengeance that drove her," I quipped. "It was fear. Fear for me." I'd struggled with that truth all my life, but seeing her and sensing her, I knew the accuracy of it finally. I wasn't going to let that hard-won truth go.

He waved away my words. "Perhaps that motivated her a little, but vengeance drove her in the end. She shed her godhead to be with your father and to do so she stored her power in three places. Once she came to me, I knew her truths. I knew of the things she'd done to become mortal and the things she did later to keep you from me. Three places to become mortal in the first place. Seven vessels to keep her power from my servants. The same magic shed and reclaimed and broken apart again."

He peered down at me with a knowing smile. "Her familiar, the one you so desperately want to power. Her grimoire. Her amulet. A photo of smeared with her blood. Those were easy. The others? Far more difficult, needing true magic to accomplish and what a feat. The spirit of a loyal servant. Her mortal remains." His fingers reached for my chest, tapping the space over my heart. "You."

"I know the vessels," I said, filling my voice with a patronizing tone because while I wasn't shocked at their existence because I knew them already, I was shocked that he knew of them. And that he knew them made me feel very afraid.

His palm flattened against my chest and slid down to my ribcage in a caress that made the hairs on my arm rise. Despite the revulsion and fear, some part of me responded to his touch.

"That last, that was where she made her mistake. And for more reasons than she or you think. She knew her mistake the moment she tapped into you. She felt it, the truth, and she knew. That's why she hid you. That's why she cast the wards to keep the vessels silent and out of reach. It's why she wove protection charms and invisibility around you, bound to those very vessels. Magic upon magic in layers like an onion. Only a god could perform such magic. Only the right vessel could accept it. She should have known better the moment she was able to cast it."

I thought of the way the amulet could render me invisible and my mouth went dry at the loss of the protection I might have kept if Honey had not stolen it from me. My mother had tried to protect me from more than just the cult, it seemed. Some other danger lurked behind the mortal threat of a black coven.

I had a hard time swallowing, and I scrabbled back into the cushions, my body desperate to get out of range of those truths. He seemed unaffected by my fear and knelt between my knees, pushing my thighs apart as though my muscles were butter to a hot blade. His eyes flashed with lust.

"She knows me," he purred. "She knows what excites me. She tried to keep you hidden. She cast oh so many spells to dampen your magic and keep you blissfully unaware. To hide you from my allies while she was trapped here in my menagerie."

He grinned evilly and the boyish charm evaporated. "She was drawn to your father so strongly she couldn't help herself. The death power was intense in him, so intense it was like a magnet locking them together like dogs fucking."

He paused expectantly, as though he was hoping I'd see the cleverness of his use of her sacred animal.

All I could hear was the crassness, and when I said nothing because it was disgusting, he sighed in disappointment and continued with much less zeal.

"But for all his latent power, your father was, unfortunately, mortal. They sacrificed many to gain him long-life, but alas, a mortal is a mortal and death inevitable." He flashed a grin filled with white teeth. "And for all her cleverness and preparation, I am the god of death and I take what is mine eventually. Such black magic must come home again."

His hands slid up my thighs to rest on my waist. "But the combination of her magic and his, coursing through your veins, throbbing through your very tissues. That thing is more tempting than all my treasures."

Deft fingers slid beneath my shirt in a whisper of possession and traveled to cup my breasts. "It's the most I've been tempted in a very long time. You feel it, don't you?"

He swallowed so hard I saw his throat muscles working. "You feel the pull between us. I sense you do."

Every place his hands touched down on my flesh burned with an ache of desire even as my mind rebelled. I didn't want him. This was dark, dark magic he was spinning.

"Why are you here when you didn't ask to come?" he asked me again. "That's what you want to know. But that's not what you should be asking. You should want to know how you could come here so easily? Imagine. A mortal with a god's magic traipsing across my threshold with a mere drop of blood and a whisper to nascent magic."

He shifted so that he was no longer kneeling but spread the length of my body, pulling me close as he swung me from the sofa into his arms with the same motion it took for him to stand. "You came because it's natural to be here. You came because you belong."

I tried to struggle, but something within me held back and he chuckled into my hair as he nuzzled my neck and whispered into my ear.

"You're here because you're mine."

# CHAPTER 11

I WAS LOST IN the devil's arms. Within his embrace, darkness was as smothering as a ton of earth, even if it did smell of vanilla and rosemary. A whiff of brimstone tainted the air as I found myself all but giving myself over to the way his muscles twitched, the hardness of his chest against mine. His breath in my hair felt so hot, a furnace might have back-drafted.

"Mine," he murmured. "Such magic. Such power. It belongs here."

With an adroit movement, he hefted me higher. My legs had to wrap around his waist to keep from dangling beneath me as he arched me back, one hand on the small of my back, the other cupping the back of my head.

I peered up at him, grateful to be out of the smothering embrace, out of the shadows that felt as if more was there in the darkness than muscle and flesh. I savored the air, pulling in long drafts, terrified that in a single moment, I'd not be able to take in one more molecule of oxygen.

I was about to protest that I belonged to no one, but his mouth came down over mine before I could guess at his intent. His kiss was nothing like any I'd ever suffered. It was at once masterful and commanding and vaguely repulsive. There was no emotion in it. Possession was all it held. I bit down on his tongue as he thrust it to caress my palate. I thought I tasted blood, and I expected him to pull away.

Instead, he chuckled into my mouth. His tongue came to life, transforming into a swarm of wasps that stung the insides of my cheeks and scored bits of flesh from my throat. I gagged, and he breathed into my mouth a taste of burnt sugar that scorched my palate.

When he finally released me, I had to gasp for air. Sputtering and choking on the welts of burning pain the wasps had inflicted in my throat, I scrabbled to escape. I fought him the way an old-fashioned heroine struck out at a villain, and I was that effective at getting away.

"Careful, my dove," he murmured, tightening his hold on me. "I do like a bit of violence with my passion. Too much struggling might bring out the beast in me."

His hooded eyes peered down into mine as he swung me in a circle and dropped me onto my feet.

"Of course," he went on, "you like beasts, do you not? One more little happy happenstance for me." He touched his finger against my lips when I wanted to protest. "Shh," he whispered. "Don't ruin the moment."

He beamed at me and gestured toward the room as he spun me around. One blink and the contents and decor changed. Instead of a plush and inviting bed-chamber, it was an armory filled with weapons. One more blink and it became a torture chamber.

Something lurched in my belly.

I thought I heard the distinct sound of pain echoing in the air currents. A shiver rode my spine until I hugged myself just to keep my teeth from clacking.

He took my hand, pulling it from beneath my armpit where I'd burrowed in for warmth.

"For us," he said. "I've brought many here in my eons, but never have I been so excited to show it to someone."

When I tried to pull my hand from his grasp, he tugged me harder so that my hand slipped with his beneath his arm. I fell against him awkwardly. "You are mad," I said.

His arm slipped around my waist. He ignored my comment. "We can try the lightest of tortures first," he said in a conversational tone that might have been him commenting on the weather. "Perhaps the whip or clamps. I wouldn't want to break you."

He ran an assessing hand over my side, poking my ribs as though testing a haunch of meat.

"With my pets, I don't have to worry about taking care. They are spirit you see, so the flesh does not come to harm, but you—" he pinched a bit of flesh below my ribs through my shirt, enough to make me jump. "Yes. Delicate. Fragile. We must take care."

At that, he shoved me so hard I stumbled sideways and fell with a crash against a table that had not been there before.

"That's being careful?" I said, rubbing the pain from where the corner had bitten into my shoulder.

He smiled and stretched, his arms snaking high over his head as he curled and uncurled his spine, his neck snapping with each twist of his head. A sensual sigh escaped him as he ran his hands down along his sides the way a stripper might.

"Take off your clothes," he said.

My mouth went dry as ash. I shook my head. There was no fucking way I was going to strip down to my bare skin. There was no way I was going to just play along with whatever mad fantasy he had in mind. He'd have to kill me.

His brow furrowed in confusion at first, then he moistened his lips.

"I see," he said, and in a heartbeat, his legs devoured the distance between us. I didn't see his hand flash out. I barely felt the way the neckline of my dress tugged against my skin, resisting for a second before it tore and gaped open, showing my lace bra.

"Purple," he said. "I prefer black. You will learn."

That was when the first true moment of terror struck. The instant I realized that if he did kill me, he'd have me here forever and the thought of the things he might do to me in all the eons of eternity sent fingers of ice tripping down my spine.

In terror, I dug my heels into the floor and used the leverage to ram myself backward. The table pressed into my back. Something fell from its top onto the floor next to me. Even as Lucifer dug his fingers into the waistband of my dress, my hand was scrabbling for whatever object had fallen.

I nearly lost contact with the thing—a vase, I thought. Heavy and cold, I rolled it beneath my wrist, found the lip with my fingers.

At the same moment I caught the vase in my grasp, he caught the hem of my dress. The material gave way, tearing audibly all the way down the seams.

I was already so freaked out, so drenched in fear adrenaline, that I was laughing right along with him, when the hot rush of air washed over my bare legs.

Too late, I remembered I wasn't wearing underwear.

A moan escaped him, one with a low-bellied growl that brought goosebumps out on every inch of my skin.

"You are beautiful," he said. "That skin. No scars. No dimples. Just pure, creamy flesh begging for my terrible touch."

"Touch me and you'll regret it," I said. "I swear I will fight you tooth, nail, and bone."

"I'm counting on it, my dove," he said and plucked me from the floor.

With ease, he draped me over one shoulder, and I nearly lost my grasp on the vase. Now that I could see better, I could tell it was an urn. Made of cold iron by the feel and heft of it. I could barely hold on to it as he strode with me further into the chamber.

I saw all sorts of equipment blur by and, with each step, I grew more and more desperate and terrified. By the time I caught sight of a very large sex toy strapped to what looked like a pommel horse, I was fighting like a badger and with about as much cunning.

"Stop," I said as I kneaded his back with several swinging blows. "Stop, I'll do whatever you want. I swear. Whatever it is. I'll do it. Just please please please put me down."

The pitch of my voice hurt my ears. I wasn't even sure why I was promising to be compliant, except I hoped it would buy me time. One second, one moment, one hour. I'd take what I could get.

"Why would I want you submissive?" he asked as he tossed me down onto a black leather couch. It looked very much like the one I'd sat in on first arrival, except this one was laid out with a black leather suit and high-heeled boots. I thought I saw a gag-ball peeking out from beneath the leather.

I bounced once, then came to a complete motionless rest.

"Submission is never as satisfying," he went on. "I'd rather you fought your way to acceptance. But there's no rush, my dove. We have a long time together."

I glared up at him. "Don't you fucking touch me."

He grinned. "How quickly we shift gears when it's time to deliver."

He ran a finger over my cheek, leaving a trail that felt like blood burning on my skin.

"Do you ever wonder why death magic is so powerful? Why black witches use it to power their spells? Why your mother tried so very hard to create a familiar out of animals she sacrificed to give you guidance and protection? How those poor creatures can gather together in the first place and juice up a ghostly creature that comes and goes on whim?"

He towered over me, reaching his hand for mine and tugging me to my feet. When he settled next to me, close enough that I had to strain against his hard chest, I gasped in surprise. He was made of fire, this one, so hot that I felt it through to my core.

He smiled with his entire face as I yanked my hand back. "Death has its own very powerful magic," he said. "Imagine the energy that is freed when the body expires. Energy isn't created or destroyed, merely moved. Now imagine a woman who can come and go on those energy currents like a goddess. Except—and here's where it gets truly exciting—she is mortal. Imagine the exquisite pain of the things she can experience under the right lover's hand. The rapturous taste of fear as she faces her own death at his touch, knowing she can reanimate herself and return to savor the pain again and again."

He shivered as though he were filled with that excitement he spoke of, and I realized the fullness of his madness.

I clawed at the sofa cushions, my fingers betraying my terror even as I leveled a casual glance at him.

"One might think that was the pinnacle of existence," I whispered, aware that his eyes had glazed over and that his chest was rising and falling a little too fast. "Except..."

I let the thought trail, not just because I had no true finish to it, but because I knew, just knew, he'd take the bait.

Those glazed eyes came to rest on my lips. "Except?" he asked.

I took my time getting to my feet, my gaze skirting over the various horrific paraphernalia behind him and all around us. There had to be something simple and painful, an uncomplicated weapon I could use to inflict pain and make my escape, that didn't require some sort of sexual position to be put to use. A blade. A sword. A—

Whip. A cat-o'-nine-tails if my memory was correct. It hung on a peg along with several other things I didn't recognize. If I could reach it, I might be able to hold him off. But for how long? What would it take to get out of his boudoir? I was beginning to believe such a thing wasn't possible.

I crossed my arms over my hips, hiding myself from his gaze as best I could.

"Except we don't know if I have that sort of power," I said, doing my best to look vulnerable. Breakable. "What if I can't do what you think? What if I'm just a mortal after all, a woman who traveled to your realm on the blood of her mother? Would you want to take the risk?"

He pursed his lips. "I think the pleasure could come from the trying," he said. "A test of my resolve. Of my control."

That wasn't the answer I was looking for. Not at all.

"And if you test yourself and fail? If I break?" I tried not to use the word die because really, I was already pretty freaked out. It took more resolve than I had to inch my way around him and do it in a way that made it look like I was merely considering things, working out the details. Negotiating.

"If you break, then I'll be disappointed, but happily fulfilled." He ran his tongue over his lips and as he did so, it split into three points. "As would you. And then I'd simply put your energy into my menagerie and take you out now and again much as I do the others." He shrugged. "They entertain me well enough. So would you."

A shudder ran through me. I was so close to the whip I could reach out and take it but he had followed me without moving, that head of his spinning on its axis to trail me much the same as an owl did a mouse.

"But then you'd be robbed of something you've wanted for longer than that."

His eyes shuttered halfway. Suspicious. "Explain."

I turned my back to the whip and slipped my hands behind my waist. "Persephone," I said, and his eyes lit up at the name. My heart did a little leap of joy.

"What of her?"

"She's yours, is she not? She fled your realm and abandoned you. Wouldn't you want to reclaim what is yours?"

His body spun to meet the direction of his head, and I knew I had him. I sidled closer to the whip and felt for its handle...just in case.

"You already said it," I said. "I can come and go in your realm at a whisper of magic. Who else could do that for you except my mother. But she's MIA, is she not? A goddess in mortal form unable to gather her magic to continue the bargain she made with you." I made a moue of regret, carefully omitting his part in her demise.

"Go on."

"If you test my sturdiness and I turn out to be disappointing, you'll have lost the one person capable of guiding Persephone back to you. You'll have enjoyed a few moments of pleasure—"

"Rapture," he corrected. "A rapture we would both enjoy."

I gave him a tight smile and side-stepped the comment by backtracking to the main point. "You'll have lost the chance to reclaim what is yours." I faced him, feeling the weight of the whip's handle against my palm. "I can be Persephone's guide," I said. "I can replace my mother for you and do her task."

"And when you die, as mortals do?" he asked. "What then?"

I shrugged. "Who says I need to die?" I asked. "Give me the same power you promised the cult who hounds me. I can continue your service for generations."

A sly, knowing smile laced itself onto his mouth. "Cunning," he said. "A bargain with the devil. How delightful. You would have me turn on my lovelies after we've come this far together? You are craftier than I gave you credit for, my dove. You are a match for me, truly."

I tried not to let the hope flare all the way from my chest to my face. I toed the floor casually as I waited.

He stuck out his hand faster than I'd have believed. "Indeed," he said, and as suddenly as the room had shifted to a chamber of horrors, it transformed into a sedate-looking office not unlike my mother's lawyers'.

He wore a business suit, his hair slicked back and curling handsomely behind his ears. A wide, toothy smile put a boyish look on his face. "Deal," he said.

I left the whip where it was and took his hand. "Deal," I repeated and tried not to think about how so many deals with the devil in literature turned sour.

In one fluid motion, he pulled my hand to his mouth. Biting down on his own wrist, he cut thorough the flesh hard enough to bring blood. Before I could prepare myself, he did the same to mine. A moan slipped through my lips at the unexpected pleasure of the pain.

Our blood mingled on our skin and pooled into a large drop that clung to the underside for a long moment before it dropped into a silver chalice he held below us with his free hand.

As soon as the blood hit the bottom of the chalice, the vessel shrunk and distorted until it was no bigger than a stone the size of my thumbnail. From its sides sprouted a silver chain that he looped over my head. The amulet settled between my breasts and he sighed softly as his eye followed it.

I looked down at the glow nestled in the mounds of my flesh and, for an instant, it looked exactly like the orbs of energy he kept in his walls. The chain looked like a serpentine coil of veins pumping energy in and out of the amulet, cycling and recycling energy in a kundalini circuit.

"The god of death aligned the daughter of a necromancer and the goddess of witchcraft," he murmured. "Our blood mingled will know the scent of death magic and you'll know it too. You'll taste it even as it responds."

I looked up from the energetic circulatory system to his face just in time to see his mouth descend to mine.

The kiss would have turned my legs to teabags if he'd been human.

He chuckled. "Maybe you're making the wrong choice, my dove," he whispered into my hair when he drew away. "Perhaps you should stay with me and become the queen of hell."

I forced myself to pull away, and in moving, the spell was broken. I looked up at him with clear eyes. Gone was the beautiful man. In his place stood a bright light I could barely take in without shielding my eyes. I winced and squinted through my fingers.

"Go," came his voice from the light. "Step into me and leave this place."

I advanced. Slowly at first, then faster. I wanted out. I wanted out very badly, and the need was so desperate I didn't care if stepping into his light would trap or free me. All I knew was I heard his voice echoing in my head as the light shrank around me.

"By the way, dove," he said. "Your mother is not MIA."

He grinned as he gestured toward the wall filled with orbs and throbbing veins of energy. "I know exactly where she is, although in her current form, she is useless to me except as an occasional plaything when I wish to play with a paltry bit of mortal energy."

# Chapter 12

Sudden darkness enveloped me then, leaving me casting around as though I had been dumped, sprawling and clawing, into a deep tunnel from a great height. I think I screamed. Something reached for me, touching my hair and then light exploded around me, peeling away the blackness as though it were a thick film.

I gasped. Air flooded my lungs with the sweet taste of rosemary and honey. I thought I tasted blood on my tongue. Confusion made it difficult to wrangle any words from my mind, but at last, something tripped over my lips.

"Layne," I said.

"I'm here." His fingers caressed my cheek, bidding my eyes to open for him. "I'm here, Brie. I've got you. Come back to me."

I drank in his face as it hovered over mine. His eyes searched my face, and the concern and love in his gaze warmed my chest. I hadn't realized how cold I felt. A shiver ran through me.

"Are you all right?" he asked as he noticed and gathered me into his arms. "You're cold."

Indeed, I felt his heat, a radiating thing that wrapped around me, full of vanilla and musk and that smell that was only him. Hell hadn't provided that sort of warmth.

"Hell fire is cold," I said without thinking what I was saying, but it was true. While Lucifer was hot, it didn't radiate into your core the way true humanity did. The fires of his realm lacked something, and I'd only realized it when I my body returned to earth.

I took a moment to look past him in order to ground myself. I noted we were still in the shower stall. I was soaked through and through, and the sexy black dress sticking to me. I plucked at the neckline, remembering how Lucifer had torn the dress off me.

"So he didn't undress me," I mumbled, half relieved, half confounded by the possibilities of magic.

"What's that?" he said with a nervous laugh.

I shook my head. "Nothing." I peeled myself away from him reluctantly.

"Here," he said, offering his hand when he saw me trying to get up and slipping in the stall. "Let me help you."

Whatever blood he'd spilled had obviously gone down the drain. The shower head was dripping, evidence that he'd run the water at some point to hasten its journey. Wet locks of hair stuck to my cheeks as I took his hand and let him help me onto the mat outside the stall.

He stood there, naked with goosebumps peppering his skin. The hard, tiny pebbles of his nipples blushed as he grabbed a towel and rubbed it over his chest.

He nodded at me. "I'm sorry," he said. "I should have undressed you before I turned on the water, but it didn't feel right to do that without your consent."

He gave me a shy look. The direction of his gaze led to my wet skirt, the fabric clinging to my legs.

"It's alright," I said, and then realized I should have said thanked him for realizing that sort of thing might need some consent. I looked down at myself ruefully, thinking that nudity wouldn't have shown any more than what I displayed with the wet fabric sticking to every inch of my body.

I shivered and when he noticed, he wrapped me in a dry bath sheet and rubbed my shoulders over the material, using a good amount of friction to bring blood to the surface.

I wanted nothing more than to sink into his embrace, but I needed to peel off the wet dress. I looked up at him. "Little help?" I suggested.

He grinned boyishly. "Don't worry," he said. "I've got you."

Without another word, he scooped me up, bath sheet, wet clothes and all and carried me to the suite. He arranged me comfortably at the edge of the bed and peeled away the towel that had begun to get damp and cold.

"I've been wanting to see just how wet you'd get in bed," he said, his gaze flitting over my lips. "I guess I've got my answer."

"You have a terrible sense of humor," I said, but moaned as he slipped his fingers beneath the neckline of the dress because his touch was at once hot and welcome.

"Keep that up and I won't be able to do what needs to be done," he said.

Through half-lidded eyes, I watched his expression as he pulled the edge of the blanket from the bed and used it to cover each inch he uncovered.

"And what is it that needs to be done, Mr. Garder?" I asked, with a catch in my voice.

He tucked a piece of the bedspread into my armpit. "What needs to be done is to get you sufficiently covered so you won't distract me."

I snorted. "And your nudity isn't distracting?"

"Not to me, it's not?" He raised an eyebrow. "Do you think you can control yourself long enough for us to discuss this thing we've done and where you went when we did it?"

I swallowed down a hard lump. I did not want to think about that. I much preferred the distraction of his body. I would rather lose myself in it until all thoughts of Lucifer were gone.

He took my silence for agreement and continued working the wet dress off me, all the time recovering me with the blanket. It took careful, attentive maneuvering, but he finally had me free of the fabric and sufficiently cocooned in the blanket.

I was warm. Too warm. And it had nothing to do with the plush hotel bedspread.

"You don't mind being naked while I'm completely covered," I said from beneath the thick shroud of fabric.

"My nakedness never bothers me," he said. "But I'm not completely naked. I do have a towel on in case you haven't noticed."

"Yes," I said. "You do. Why don't we make a deal?" I flinched at the word that spilled from me and hurried on before I could think any more about what that word had tied me to just moments earlier. "Let's agree to discuss this all another time, and I'll agree not to tear that towel off you."

"And after I thoughtfully waited for your consent to take yours off?"

In answer, I flung open the blanket and held his gaze. It dropped for one second to my breasts and lifted again to my mouth. "You are a nasty bitch," he said. "Just the way I like it. But I won't be dissuaded. At least not yet." Deft fingers trailed down my throat and that smile bled out along with the color in his face as they met the cold stone of the amulet.

"What's this?" His eyebrows knit together as he plucked the amulet from my chest and held it.

I swallowed anxiously. "A token," I said, searching for the best explanation. "The solid reminder of a promise and a threat."

Gold flared in his gaze at the word threat. "And who exactly will I be killing tonight over that threat?"

"No one. It's nothing," I said, pulling the blanket edges together again. The amulet looped over the top as he held on tight despite my securing the blanket tight to my throat.

I had to turn away from the heat in his gaze, so I studied the corner where Abbi was sleeping. Evidently, what we had done had worked at least. Score one for the nascent witch and her awkward grip of her power.

"Magic is strange," I said, and plumbed his grip to take the amulet from him. I dropped it beneath the blanket. When it settled between my breasts again, I let go an exhausted sigh and slipped off the bed.

He pushed himself to his feet as I stood. I was sure I felt the runes of my mother's magic charge as the amulet nestled into place. Death magic, I thought. I was still reeling from the information Lucifer had given me. The dizzying thought that my father was a powerful necromancer. The haunting reminder that the devil was the king of lies.

Once on my feet, I pivoted, my gaze seeking out my mother's familiar. Abbi lay beside the bed, her eyes alert and glowing. She looked solid enough to ride like a pony. I gestured toward her, directing Layne's eye.

"You did it," I said as I rushed the few feet to her side. I fell to a crouch beside her, his dark chuckle of pleasure dogging my heels.

"*You* did it, you mean," he said, and I felt him kneel beside me. His hand ran along the dog's fur. I half expected her to growl, but she merely grunted and laid her head on her paws as she regarded him.

Exhilaration tightened my throat, and I reached for his hand. "We did it. Thank you."

He squeezed my hand. I looked sideways at him. "Are you okay? You're not hurt?"

"From that little bit of blood?" he asked with a snort. "Not likely." He thumped his chest. "Me big werewolf. Me strong."

"Hardy har," I said at his ridiculous jape. "How am I supposed to know what effect it had on you. I mean, I was gone for long enough you could have bled to death."

"I doubt three minutes would have been a life-threatening time frame unless I cut into an artery, which I didn't."

"Three minutes?"

He pursed his lips thoughtfully. "Maybe I'm exaggerating, then. Let's give it a solid two."

"Sweet Jesus," I said. "All that in two minutes." I looked pointedly at his arm where he'd cut it. The skin was smooth.

"I only shifted enough to heal the wound," he said off-handedly, as though being able to manage that sort of power was a small task. I knew better.

He ran his hand once more over Abbi's fur. "And All what, exactly?"

We both sat on the floor on either side of the dog, and I told him what I could, omitting the parts where the devil tried to assault me. He listened patiently, waiting when I had to pause to gather my thoughts, especially in places where the terror still clung to me.

I was so glad to be back on Terra Firma with him beside me, my mother's familiar looking much better, that I didn't worry about the deal I'd made or the worry about how I was going to weasel out of it.

Instead, I leaned against him, letting my weight go. He didn't budge an inch, and I knew he wouldn't. Strong wasn't all he was. He was like an immovable and ancient stone. A force I could trust.

And he was warm. So warm. My body was starved for heat. His arm went around me and I turned into him, letting him hold me.

It didn't take long before the embrace changed. His hands ran over my back at first in comfort, but by the time it reached my waist, the pressure had increased. I was already straining for him, my throat aching with the need to kiss him. I was desperate to rid myself of the feel of Lucifer's hands on me.

"The dog," he said when he realized I was as ready for him as he was for me. "I don't think I can—"

"What dog?" I asked without looking where the dog had been. I knew she'd disappeared the moment I felt a cool breeze shiver over my hair. "You think the goddess of witchcraft's familiar doesn't know when she's not wanted?"

He chuckled as he claimed my mouth, and in time, he picked me up, letting his towel fall away. He carried me to the bed, spread open the blanket, and with patience and careful strokes, rid my body of the taste of the devil's breath. We lay together side-by-side afterward, naked and content.

I knew I'd sleep like the dead if I could crawl beneath the blankets. I was no longer afraid of what had happened here. It was an event, a horrible event, but one that was past. Whatever post-traumatic stress had been clinging to me, the magic I'd cast in the room had dispelled it.

Perhaps it was the certainty of the deal with Lucifer, perhaps it was knowing Layne's magic had helped Abbi, but I had the feeling it was the way we treated each other in the wake of all that magic that crafted a cocoon of safety, something I hadn't felt since my father died.

Layne fell asleep immediately. I lay beside him, with his arm around me, and I watched his chest rise and fall. I listened to the small noises he made as he dreamed. I savored the feel of his heat surrounding me, the smell of him, of us, and of the room itself.

I didn't want to move. I wanted to fall into a contented sleep as he did, but as my eyes finally fluttered closed, a new noise drew my attention. A shadow fell on the wall.

Under normal circumstances, I might have felt afraid, but I knew the sound of Abbi's breath, too. I knew the shape of her shadow. Her eyes bore into me from Layne's side of the bed, and I found it comforting. A night light to focus on instead of the shapes in the corners.

I knew I was drifting off to slumber when those eyes turned the same yellow as Layne's. Another shape drew up behind her, a three-headed shadow wearing one large crown. And when my fingers brushed against the amulet that marked my bargain with the devil tingled all the way to my elbows, I slipped at last over the threshold of consciousness into rest.

If I gave myself to Layne throughout the night, it was only because he asked it of me and I complied happily, snuggling into him afterward with a sense of rightness in the way we fit together.

# CHAPTER 13

LAYNE DROVE ME TO my shop the next morning after a leisurely wake up make-out session that put us both in languid moods and in need of strong coffee. Without encouragement from me, he pulled into a drive-thru and ordered two dark roasts and a ridiculously large and frosted donut with rainbow sprinkles.

"Necessary," he said. "I think my blood sugar dropped several points after that shower."

He bit down into it, and in doing so, took out a size-able chunk. Frosting dangled from the edge that remained.

"Your own fault," I told him. "You should learn never to walk naked to the shower where your girlfriend can see you."

He chewed the mouthful of cakey dessert without any hint of embarrassment and swallowed.

"My girlfriend should have been pretty damn satis-fied already," he retorted. "I gave it my all plus a few Viagra."

Dropping the donut onto the dashboard, he kicked the car into gear and pulled out of the parking lot. The donut sailed across the dash, threatening to spill over onto the floor, but he caught it just in time and tucked it neatly into his mouth as he drove.

I lifted one leg so the coffee balancing on my lap didn't spill.

"Most men wouldn't complain," I said. "Or run out on their ladies early in the morning." I eyed him over the console. "You think I didn't notice you escaping through the hotel door before 7 am? Were you scared I'd haul you back into bed?"

He snorted. "A man needs sustenance to perform like that, woman. Not complaining. Just commenting that my girlfriend is a sex addict." He grinned over at me. "And I can't believe I'm this lucky."

I decided the best retort was to blow on the rim of the cup and angled the visor mirror so I could check my handiwork from the morning. I wanted to make sure I hadn't dislodged the wig in my haste to get into the car. My skills were improving at fixing the wig and the prosthetics, but I didn't have Parrish's hand with goth makeup.

I decided, angling my face back and forth in the mirror, that I looked pretty much exactly like a sex addict right then. What I'd wanted to recreate as goth only made me look like a prostitute. My chuckle drew his attention, but I just patted his hand on my thigh.

"Nothing," I said. "Just glad the nymphomaniac in me has found a willing and able partner."

He mock growled at me, and we both settled into the seats, savoring the coffee when we could and keeping a keen eye on the traffic as we wandered around in our own thoughts. I wasn't sure about him, but by the time he pulled into a parking space a block away from my shop, I was a bundle of nervous excitement.

I fairly leaped from the vehicle and slammed the door accidentally in my excitement to get to my shop. The thought that I'd be back where I belonged, an imposter, maybe, but a happy one who could continue earning a living while helping those in need, didn't just make me eager. It lifted my spirits in a way they'd not been raised in weeks. I'd taken my shop and my work for granted.

It was as I winced at the sound of the door slamming shut and turned to apologize for the force of it, that I caught sight of a huge box on the back seat.

"Hey," I said. "You bought me something." I waggled my eyebrows at him. "Is it lingerie?"

His easy laugh lifted his eyes, that honey color casting its sweetness over the roof of the car.

"I'm not sure I want to think about lingerie purchases at this point after what I went through over the last purchase," he said. "But yes. I did buy something. Doesn't mean it's for you. Unless you count the coffee and donut."

"What?" I gaped at him. "That donut was mine? You ate it."

"Semantics," he said and ducked into the back seat to pluck the large box from the seat. When he came up again, he was holding his coffee in one hand and the box neatly balanced in the other. He had to use his hip to shut the driver's door.

I sighed theatrically as he rolled his shoulders and cranked his neck side to side so leisurely it had me huffing impatiently.

"Good Lord, you are slow," I complained. "You know I wanted to get there before nine."

Crossing my arms over my chest, with the coffee held in perfect balance, I tapped my toe on the asphalt.

He rounded the car, approaching me with a lightness in his step I'd not noticed in him before, or at least hadn't seen in him in what seemed ages. I'd put that hop in his step, I realized. Something in my chest warmed like liquid oil.

"Come on, old man," I said, waving him along faster.

He held out the box and coffee with a plaintive expression.

"Your shop will be there even if you pause to help an old man out with his parcels."

"Gracious," I said with a pout. "You didn't seem so decrepit last night."

"You think I was joking about the Viagra?" he said. "I'm nearly two hundred for Pete's sake."

"You are lying," I said. "We both know there was no time to pop any pills and wait for them to work."

He looked as though he wanted to hold his hands up in surrender. "You flatter me," he said.

I eyed him. He could be modest if he wanted, but I knew by the glint in his eye that it was all him.

I slid between his elbows and into his embrace. "I'm guessing that flattery is what drove you into the early morning air to go shopping." I plucked at the cover of the box. "Sexy toys?" I said. "Maybe a pair of fur-lined handcuffs?"

"Good God," he gasped. "Show your elders some respect."

This said with a hungry look in his eye as it traveled from my throat to my cleavage.

"It's cake," he said, the honey in his gaze grew sweeter until I was blushing to the roots of my hair. "I wanted you to have a nice re-opening, so I bought a cake to serve to your customers."

And because it was Layne, and we'd savored an intimacy that drove away all sorts of discretion, I reached up to clutch at the edges of my blouse and pulled the material back to show him the curve of my breast and pink of my nipples if he cared to look. Which he did.

"It's pretty hard to respect a man who does such dirty things to his poor naïve date."

He snorted. "Based on the things you did to me last night, I'd say the naïve party was yours truly." His gaze roamed hot over my face. "But give me one more chance, and I'll show you how disrespectful I can be. If you want those handcuffs, I can supply the real thing."

"Promises, promises," I said as I caught sight of a parking meter employee watching us from the other side of the street. I peeled myself away from his chest and pulled my blouse straight before plucking my coffee from the hood of the car.

I laughed and swung my purse over my shoulder in order to dig all the way into its depths and angle it toward the sunrise at the same time. I needed to find my keys.

"If you hadn't parked so far away, you might even now be testing out how disrespectful a gal like *me* can be," I quipped over my shoulder as the keys found my fingers and I pivoted to head up the sidewalk. "But alas, you are making me walk and so you'll have to wait."

I let him trail behind me, as I headed at a faster pace to the storefront. Seemed he'd decided to take his time, but I was eager. He couldn't hold me back with a sedate stroll. Not today. Not now that things were coming together. I had my shop back. I had my lover. Forcing me to slow walk my way to my life's restart was the height of punishment.

I dumped the empty coffee cup into the nearest trash and paused in front of the store. The windows looked the same. The door was still painted the same royal purple. I wasn't sure what I had been expecting. It wasn't like I'd been gone for years and sold the place, but being dead did strange things to a gal's psyche. I expected things to be different.

I was fitting the key into the lock when he shouted from behind me to wait. I paused, turning to see him stride up to me with a grin that made my heart jump up to my throat. I couldn't believe I wanted him again so soon.

When he closed the distance between us, I gripped him by the lapel and pulled him closer. The smell of his aftershave washed over me, making my knees weak with desire.

"I think there's a closet in there that needs a bit of work." I leaned on him heavily, almost knocking the cake box out of his hands.

"Careful," he said. "Don't want to ruin the cake."

"Fuck the cake," I said and twined my arms around his neck so that I could pull him down to me. He angled the box expertly out of the way so I could kiss him thoroughly, but when I tried to yank him inside, pushing the door with my hip, he held back.

"Oh, come now," I teased, my lips brushing against his. "We can make it quick enough you won't be that late for work." I nipped his lip with my teeth. "You can just say you were checking out a few dirty bits of evidence...which wouldn't be all wrong."

I was pulling him with me into the shop when his gaze flitted over my shoulder.

What I saw on his face made me freeze in place. I squeezed my eyes closed, my fingers tightening on the back of his neck where they'd tried to leverage him closer.

"Someone's in here, aren't they?" I rasped out, both terrified and confused by the expression on his face. Not lusty or angry.

It looked... amused.

Before I could turn around, the room behind me exploded in whoops and shouts.

"The cake," I said, a blush creeping its way up my neck. I unwound my arms from around his neck. "Fuck. I should have known."

An apologetic smile threaded onto his lips as he shrugged. "Surprise?" he said.

The next thing I knew, someone had grabbed me by the arm and was tugging me into the shop. I swung my head to catch sight of Parrish's red hair and green-eyed gaze.

"Seriously?" I said, but I wasn't mad. Not one bit. Just... embarrassed.

"You two can fuck later," she said with a broad grin. "We have a store re-opening to celebrate."

She tugged on my arm much the same as I'd done to Layne's. He let me go, and I let Parrish lead me into the middle of the shop proper.

The whole space smelled of hot coffee. Someone had decorated the place with a riot of different colored balloons and paper streamers, old-fashioned pull out fans and a homemade sign with awkward block letters that said: GET YOUR FORTUNE TOLD. Not classy. Not one bit. All cheesy, dimestore shit that made me tear up.

It was beautiful.

I spun in place, taking in all the decorations spilling over my space, my shelves, and racks, the pack members that I would never have expected to care enough to take time out of their workday morning to celebrate the opening of my shop. A shop that once belonged to the hated witch Brie and now was being run by Desiree, the woman Parrish had lost to Layne.

It was enough to turn my mind to spiral noodles.

"Hope you love it, babe," Layne whispered into my ear. I knew then that the decorations might have been Parrish, but the celebration was all Layne.

"Tell me you didn't order them to come here," I said, looking up at him. I kept thinking about those pack members: Charles, Emmett, Zach. Not all of them liked me.

Parrish snorted and answered in his stead with a swat to his shoulder. "This one? Hell no. It was me that threatened them into coming."

"Tell me you didn't," I said, gawking at her.

Layne took me by the elbow. "Don't listen to her. No one had to be threatened."

I swept the space with a glance. Zach stood beside the candle shelves. Charles and Emmet glowered out from behind the apothecary galley, while Parrish, now released of me, hovered near Ava.

I was surprised to see the secretary for my mother's lawyer there, but I was pleased. She was dressed in a prim business suit and clutched a styrofoam cup steaming with what I presumed was coffee. The tightness of her proximity to Parrish gave me hope for the two.

"Thank you," I said, taking in the room and feeling for a long moment that I belonged. At least some of the pack cared. I tried not to think that it wasn't Brie they cared about, but about the woman beneath the wig and makeup that they thought was Desiree. But did it matter? They liked me enough to celebrate with me.

"You deserve it," Layne said, leaning down enough to squeeze me tight to his side. "The shop needs it," he said louder to encompass the room. Anyone who doubted the reason they were there would take their orders from that comment.

He lifted his coffee cup to the air in a salute, and the others did the same. "You may not be the psychic Brie was," he said to me, and making me start at the use of my name in front of everyone, "but I'm glad she has someone to keep her legacy alive."

Everyone sipped from their steaming cups and cheered. It felt grand. I felt grand.

"The cake," I said. "Someone should cut it and pass pieces out. Do you have a knife?"

My gaze fell on Parrish, not because I expected it of her, but because she leveled me with a blank gaze that made me wonder what she was thinking. Then, as though nothing had passed between us, her expression shifted to the devil-may-care shifter I knew.

"Need a knife, ask a coroner," she said and with a flourish, dug down into her knee high boot to pull out a blade that she snapped open to an ungodly length. Even Charles's eyebrows lifted an inch from their usual spot.

With clomping, brash steps, she navigated the few feet to the counter and cut into the cake with a flourish. After she dropped the blade onto the counter—right over the top of the deep gouge the reaper had dug into my beautiful counter—she shoved her fingers beneath the pastry and scooped up the piece she had cut out.

She swaggered over to Ava, who stood watching her with a keen eye, and fed the piece to her bit by bit from her hand, all while holding her gaze as though no one else was in the room.

I felt the temperature in the shop rachet up and Layne muttered something about someone fucking later. I cut his comment short with a side eye. Ava wasn't ready for the ease of his friendship with Parrish.

As I pulled my gaze from Layne's, I caught Zach's eye. The hurt in his expression nearly staggered me. He turned away quickly and fiddled with the wick of a candle that sat next to him on the shelf. But I knew that look.

Someone was going to get hurt.

# CHAPTER 14

THE LAST THING I needed was for my shop to turn into a werewolf rumble. But I wasn't quick enough to stop Zach before he barreled past me toward Parrish and Ava like a man with a purpose. Jealousy and pain rode his expression so hard, I wasn't sure which one would win out.

"Count on you to bring a weapon that size to a celebration," he said to Parrish, ice in his tone. So I guessed pain won out.

"Darlin'," Parrish said in a tone that implied he was walking the razor edge of that blade. "I am a weapon."

Zach ignored her, proof he was spitting mad, and spoke again to Ava. "I'm sure that's just exactly the kind of thing that works to woo a sensible woman like your date." He tipped his chin at her. "You might want to reconsider what you're getting into."

"Maybe a woman like me needs to be her own weapon," Parrish purred, and I knew by the sound of her voice that she was using all her energy to keep things civil, but she was also doing her best to push back at Zach. "So many men just don't have what it takes." She licked her fingers of the rest of the frosting, and even I had to admit, it was a definite taunt. Sexual and intentional.

Zach's stubborn and defiant refusal to even look at Parrish signaled how he truly felt, and it didn't bode well for the peaceful treaty I'd hoped would smooth out the oncoming rush of argument. Beside her, Ava shuffled on her feet as Zach touched her wrist in a most intimate way that both dismissed Parrish, and had me shuffling my feet nervously in echo of Ava.

"You might be careful of a lover who calls herself a weapon," he said, leaning close enough that he didn't have to talk loud for her to make out every word. "That kind has a habit of turning on those who love her, looking for enemies where there are none." His fingers brushed Ava's wrist, too intentionally to be accidental. His words far too casual and playful to be anything but a warning.

I sidled up next to him as Ava's gaze darted around her. No doubt looking for an escape.

"Zach," I said. "I'm sure Ava is capable of deciding who she finds worthy of her affections and who isn't. It's not our business."

His fingers lingered a bit too long on Ava's wrist as he pulled away. "Sure she can," he said. "But sometimes we don't see the truth until it's too late."

Parrish pivoted enough to face Zach head on. "Are you talking in general terms or is there a specific and personal annotation to that little tale, Zach?" she growled, the yellow in her gaze rising enough to put the hairs on my neck on high alert.

Zach ignored her comment as he ran his hand along his hair, then stuffed his hands in his pockets. He rocked back on his heels. "Ava, is it?" he asked in a conversational way that belied all the threat of the last bit of discussion. "I've never known an Ava before."

Parrish edged closer to him so she could ease Ava further away from him. "What makes you think you'll know an Ava now, Zacharia?"

He spun his head in her direction, finally, and I knew the long form of his name irked him as much as the thought that she showed enough interest in a woman to bring her out to meet the pack. Because that was what this was all about, I realized. Zach saw Ava as a threat. He had decided to take it out on the woman he still loved so bitterly he couldn't let go.

"You promised never to use that name again," he said with grit in his voice.

Ava looked from one to the other. The poor girl. I needed to get her out of range before things blew up.

"Ava," I said. "I'd love to show you the shop."

Parrish grabbed for her hand and held it tightly to her side, keeping me from rescuing the poor woman. "She's busy."

I gaped at her. "I was just trying to help," I whispered but Parrish set her jaw stubbornly as she held my gaze.

I scrounged the room for Layne. Did he know what was happening? Did he even realize his small group of companions was about to implode right there in front of a human woman who didn't need any of this?

Charles was whispering something in his ear, keeping him from truly hearing what was going on around him.

I guessed it was up to me, and by the looks of it, I needed to do something fast.

I inched close enough to give Zach a big hug that he barely returned. "Shouldn't all good doctors be at their offices by now, or heading to the hospital to tend to poor sick folk?" I said to him.

"Who said I was a good doctor?" he quipped with a half smile that crinkled his eyes.

Parrish elbowed Ava in the ribs. "He's not joking," she said with a snort. Ava smiled up at her and leaned in close.

Zach's easy smile evaporated as he bowed his head slightly and angled his whole body toward me. "I'm on night shifts this week," he said. "I just got off."

Parrish snorted again. "In the shower before he left, I bet," she said and raised her coffee cup in his direction. "May Zach find a woman he loves as much as his own hand."

Beside me, Zach went rigid and though Layne was halfway across the room, I knew he did too. The very air changed and the only thing that could account for it was the tightness in Layne's shoulders.

One glimpse at Ava's face told me she was not sure what to make of the ribbing, and that the discomfort she felt meant she thought it was authentic retorts without a hint of jovial camaraderie.

I had to agree with her. I tried to cut Parrish off with a look but she just smiled down into Ava's face, beaming with her own sense of good humor without seeing or caring about the effect it had on Zach.

I thought he'd wave it off as just another one of Parrish's bad ribbing, but when she reached up and kissed Ava full on the mouth, flicking her tongue over Ava's lips, Zach's fists clenched at his sides.

"Ignore him, baby," she crooned. "He's never understood what the love of a good woman can do."

"I loved a woman once," he said, addressing Ava who directed her soulful eyes at him.

When he had her full attention, and when Parrish went just as rigid as he'd done, he put his hand alongside his mouth as though to let her in on a secret.

"But when the only way to that woman's heart was to offer her a naked woman on a horse, she can't be confused when he turns to his hand for loving."

Parrish sucked in a breath. Her face went purple for an instant. She flicked her gaze my way for half a second. I did my best not to give away my surprise, but I knew it was a bridge too far for her.

I knew in seconds the whole lovely morning could end up ruined, so I stepped in front of Zach, pushing him toward Layne, hoping the wolf within wouldn't take it as a sign of aggression and more of loving protection.

A scuff of dirt from someone's shoe caught my attention. I stared at it until Ava pushed by me because watching the changes on Zach's face was too painful. When Ava pushed by me, the tension in my shoulders released.

"I'm sorry," she said, leaning in. "I have to go."

She looked over her shoulder at Parrish who stood there, rigid and angry looking. She didn't even soften when Ava took her in. Ava sighed heavily.

"He loves her. Whatever she feels for him is too complicated for me to deal with." She fiddled with the cuffs of her prim suit for a moment, obviously aware that every eye was on her. "Goodbye," she said, and I wasn't sure if it was for me or for Parrish. I only knew she barely touched me as she brushed by. Her footsteps, tippy taps of high heels on my wooden floor echoed long after she left.

"Well, Zacharia," Parrish muttered. "There you go ruining yet another romance for me."

He leveled her with a harsh look. "You don't do romance, Beatrice," he growled. "Just people."

"You're a bastard, you know that?" she said. "A real hateful, vindictive prick."

He gawked at her for one long, agonizing moment, then before Layne could stop him, he bolted. He was out the door in moments and Parrish watched him go with a glower.

The excitement I felt at coming to my shop drained as though I was a bucket with a rusty bottom. My fingers sought my temples, and I rubbed the pressure points till my jaw released enough tension to finally speak.

"I think you should all leave," I said, my head hanging to toward the floor. "I've celebrated enough for one day. Thanks, but I think it's best if I am just left to get things rolling on my own.

The murmur that ran through the room didn't matter to me if it was assent, argument, or surprise. I just wanted them gone. My heart ached for Zach, and it ached for Ava.

Layne's fingers found the back of my neck before I knew he'd drawn near. "Are you okay?" He kneaded the muscles, releasing knots that I hadn't realized I'd tied into my neck with the tension in the room.

I sighed heavily, his fingers easing more than just a few knots. "I'm fine."

"You don't sound fine," he said and pulled me close. He dropped a kiss on the top of my head and I had the feeling by the look on Parrish's face as he did that, that he'd sent a meaningful look her way. It didn't take too much imagination to figure out what that look said to her.

She rolled her shoulders back. "He had no right," she argued, and Layne held up his finger. Instead of clamping down on the words still rolling from her lips, she forced them out. "He didn't, Layne, and you know it. He's not had any right for a century."

"You provoked him and you know it."

She sucked the back of her teeth. "He's too easy a target," she said, but she sighed and crossed her arms. I knew she was regretting urging him to spoil into an argument.

Layne pulled me all the way into his chest, wrapping both arms around my shoulders as he spoke. I inhaled his scent and let it calm me. It was just an argument. Nothing more. It didn't mean Zach would do something foolish.

"You accepted that gift of his and you rubbed it in his nose and he has a right to feel hurt and betrayed."

She snorted. "He needs to get over it."

As much as I hated the thought of leaving his arms, I pulled away to spin toward Parrish. "You need to be more sympathetic. He's hurt. I'm afraid for him."

She ran both hands over her hair, then flapped her arms down by her sides. "What?" she demanded. "You think the poor fragile doctor will hurt someone?" She blew her lips. "Zach doesn't have it in him."

I took a step toward her, unsure how she could be so blind that she couldn't see it. "He still loves you, Parrish. If you don't care for him the same way, that's one thing, but to poke a bear no matter how long it's been sleeping is suicide."

I heard the prescience in the comment, and my hand flew to my throat in reaction.

"He's not going to hurt anyone," she said, noting my fear. She planted her feet stubbornly as she crossed her arms over her chest and glared at me for daring to question her. "I thought you were on my side." Her gaze flicked past me to Layne. "You too. So much for my alpha siding with his own pack."

"Really?" I said. "You really don't see how truly hurt he is? I'm not worried about him hurting someone else. I'm worried about what he'll do to himself."

Her brow furrowed, and the green of her gaze lightened to a honey yellow.

"He won't do that."

I shook my head at her. "You're an astute woman, Parrish," I said. "You are great at reading people. You don't see it because you don't want to see it. All those emotions he has felt for you all these years—decades, if that is what it is—they're a pressure cooker. Fix it."

"So you're going to play dominant wolf with me? Pull rank because you're fucking the pack's second?"

I noticed Layne avoiding my gaze, even avoiding Parrish's, and I didn't think it was cowardice. Something was happening here, something he expected her and me to work out and was wisely staying clear.

"I have no rank to pull, Parrish," I said. "I'm saying it as a friend. If he does something to himself, you'll not recover from the grief. Fix it between you for your sake."

She swallowed, and her mouth twitched. I'd hit a nerve, and I knew it. She ribbed him out of some long-ingrained desire to push people away. Zach had gotten too close and she couldn't bear letting herself vulnerable. She didn't love him the way he did her, but she still loved him.

Finally, her shoulders sagged as the righteous anger drained away.

"OK," she said as a long, hissing sigh left her. "I'll go to his apartment tonight after work. Check on him."

"Make sure you do," Layne said, and the command was clear.

"Right," she grumbled. "I'll be the good submissive pup."

"Fuck you," Layne said with a laugh. "The last thing you are is submissive."

The dread I felt for Zach didn't exactly evaporate, but I felt better. I scooped a slice of cake and slip it onto a paper plate with a napkin over the top. "Here," I said, passing it to her. "Might as well eat the cake you're having too."

She hadn't but touched her fingers to the plate when something over her shoulder caught my gaze through the window.

And what caught my eye made the breath in my throat suck back in. And right at that moment, the amulet tucked between my breasts heated up and burned hot enough that when I dug beneath my shirt to grab for it it burned my fingers.

# CHAPTER 15

OUTSIDE MY SHOP, STARING inside, a witch drew runes in the air. I didn't recognize the spell she was casting, but I recognized Honey, and I knew the smell of danger that electrified the air as I caught her eye.

"Honey," I said, and the way her name gushed from my mouth, I was afraid I'd lost all the air in my lungs.

I didn't have time to react further. Both Layne and Parrish swung toward her and loped across the shop so fast, Honey didn't have time to widen her eyes in fear before they reached the door.

She was still mid-rune when Parrish yanked the door open. Layne's fist closed down on Honey's wrist and the witch was pulled inside the store so quickly that the woman on the street who had been walking by, got caught in the draft and stumbled.

I managed to force myself across the space to offer the woman a tentative smile through the door before flipping the sign from OPEN to CLOSED. I twisted the lock, listening hard for the click that indicated it was barred, because I needed to know, to be sure, no one could get in, wandering in or forcing in didn't matter.

By the time I spun back around, Layne had wrestled Honey all the way across the shop and was tossing her behind the counter.

It had all the hallmarks of an abduction, I realized as I saw the bristling mess Parrish was in as she barreled her way behind Layne. I turned to mouth an "It's all right," to the woman who stood there over my shoulder.

She furrowed her elegant brows and lifted a shocked hand to her chest, but I smiled all the brighter and tossed up my hands with a rolled eye toward the ceiling as though we were just all old friends and one of us had been being naughty. Like a kid who'd bolted past a garden gate and needed a good scolding.

My heart hammered behind my voice box as I waited to see if she'd buy into the act. Behind me, Parrish's growl became decidedly feral. Some sort of squeaking sound was coming from behind the counter, Honey, I realized, fighting her way to yell through someone's—Layne's—meaty hand over her mouth.

My foot slid behind me to take a step back, but I couldn't pull my eyes from the stranger on the street. Not until I could gage if she was going to call the cops. Then I laughed. The cops were here. There was nothing to worry about, right?

A hitch of breath and the woman on the other side of the door finally made a swirly motion with her finger toward her temple. I repeated it with a lolling tongue and forced a laugh. She waved. I waved.

The tightness in my chest only let go when she continued down the street.

I spun on my heel. "Tell me that bitch is tied up like a pig," I growled as I barged across the floor.

Neither Layne nor Parrish was visible, and I had to guess they were both behind the counter, pinning Honey down. I could hear the sounds of struggle. Parrish swore like a sailor.

"Fucking bit me, the bitch," she ground out, and by the time I rounded the counter, Honey was pinned flat on her stomach.

Her hands were stretched over her head, caged by one of Parrish's hands to the floor by the wrists. Layne's knee was on Honey's back and his face, his expression lacked any human emotion. He was all animal right then, in a way that made my spine try to shake free of my skin.

Honey couldn't see him, but I doubt she needed to in order to understand the very real danger she was in.

My gaze slid over the way her ribcage refused to move beneath Layne's weight.

"You're going to kill her," I said flatly. "She can't breathe like that."

"Fuck her," Layne said just as emotionless, but there was something odd in the way it sounded. Growling, more animal than man. At the sound of it, Parrish's expression lit up with hateful humor.

"Yeah. Fuck her, the bitch." She leaned down to peer into Honey's face. "You hear that, bitch? You are so screwed right now."

My breath wheezed out of me the longer I looked at the witch who had nearly killed me. I sagged against the wall. My mouth went dry. I had to suck the back of my teeth to get enough saliva to speak.

"Let her go."

Layne's head snapped in my direction. I knew the expression of rage in his face so acutely I felt it in my chest. I felt the same. But killing her now would be foolish.

"You're a cop, Layne," I said. "You can't do this."

"The hell he can't," Parrish cut in, and I realized she was speaking for him because he couldn't. His animal had him in its grip tightly enough he was doing all he had to hold on to his humanity. "She nearly killed you, Brie." Parrish's eye flicked to Layne, and he took a hard breath, suggesting I was right. "She doesn't deserve to live."

I crouched down beside Layne and put my hand on his back. The hard knot of muscle twitched. "You can't do this, Layne," I whispered. "She's not worth it."

From below me, Honey made a ragged sound.

"Shut up," Parrish told her, then lifted her gaze to mine. "Layne doesn't have to kill her."

Meaning she would. Lord have mercy. I shook my head as Honey made a pitiful attempt to struggle and ended up coughing the last bit of air out of her lungs. Her head turned to the side, and I caught a look at her skin. Pale. Her lips were losing color.

I shoved at Layne. "Stop," I said. "Just stop it right now."

I wasn't sure what I expected of him. After the violence I'd seen him capable of, after the animal I'd seen fighting with the reaper in the dark, I guessed I assumed when he killed, it would be a terrifying, predatory horror, not this cold and quiet murder.

The instant I realized Honey was going to die, something snapped inside.

"Fuck you, Layne." I put my weight into it, pushing him as though he was an immovable stone and he was. He was the rock, and I was Sisyphus, except I couldn't budge him one bit.

"We need her," I said in a small voice, the last of my own breath going to the exertion. "Damn you, Layne, we need her."

All of a sudden, the resistance leaked away, and he moved so fluidly, I didn't see him shift off Honey's back until he pulled me along with him and held me in his embrace. We stood together and looked down at Honey's face as Parrish flipped her over. The witch lay sprawled with her arms limp to the sides.

"Air," Layne said in a grating voice and immediately, Parrish kneeled over Honey and breathed into her mouth. We waited for a full twenty seconds before the witch's chest rose in a sudden gasping motion.

My head fell against Layne's chest. "Thank sweet baby Jesus," I said.

Honey's eyes flew open and her palms scrabbled against my wooden floorboards as she fought for purchase to push herself upward. With a speed that surprised me, Parrish's hand clamped down around her mouth, giving her enough space to breathe through her nostrils.

They flared as Honey sucked in air.

"You understand what you have to do?" Parrish asked her.

Honey nodded.

"You're alive because of Brie, you understand?"

Again Honey nodded and a humorless grin stole across Parrish's face. "Give me one indication that you are going to raise trouble, and I swear, I will gift you to Layne and watch him chew your stomach out." She shrugged. "Me? I'm a leg gal."

Honey swallowed and Parrish peeled her hand away. The icy hardness of the witch's expression didn't melt one bit as she flicked her gaze to mine. I eased away from Layne to approach her.

I bent over her and inhaled. I smelled sulfur. "You were casting magic," I said. "You recognized me."

I sat back on my heels and waited for her answer. Not that I needed it. I knew she had been, just as she knew I was Brie and not Desiree.

"Well?" I said.

Honey glared at me with a lifted chin. "I wasn't casting black magic," she said. "I was casting to protect myself."

Layne grunted, catching her attention.

"Last I checked, you were the danger here," he said, and then with half-shuttered lids that did very little to soften the flare of anger in his eyes, said, "At least you were until you threatened my mate." He grabbed her by the elbow and yanked her to her feet. "Now, I am the threat."

One hand drove itself into the yielding flesh of Honey's throat, hard enough that she gagged. I dropped my fingers onto Layne's wrist.

"Not yet," I said. "I'm not done with her."

Layne grunted as he pulled his hand away. "You're one lucky witch that my mate is compassionate. Me? Not so much."

Parrish shoved Honey toward Layne. "Thank your lucky stars his mate is compassionate. He would have killed you and I would have let him."

Honey shrugged her arm out of Layne's grip, only possible because Layne let her go. She faced me.

"It is you, isn't it?" she asked. "I wasn't sure at first."

I crossed my arms over my chest as I regarded her, electing instead to ask the questions not answer them. "Why were you casting a protective spell?" I asked. "Desiree would have no reason to hurt you."

One caramel colored eyebrow lifted. "But you're not Desiree, are you? You are *her* daughter."

*Her*, emphasized and hushed sounding as she uttered the pronoun, and obviously meaning Hecate. I noticed she didn't want to say the name aloud. I waited, my fingers tightening around my arms, acutely aware of the two wolves who caged the witch in front of me between them, both of them looking so predatory the hairs rose on the back of my neck.

Honey looked from one to the other before dropping her gaze to her feet. "I've left the coven," she said in a small voice.

Parrish let go a guffaw and dropped her head back on her neck. Layne didn't move a single inch. Instead, he watched her with the sort of attention a hawk does when it's staring down the entrance of a mouse hole.

If Honey noticed, she was doing pretty well with managing to look confident. I studied her for signs of insincerity, but couldn't detect one. At least, not a clear one.

"They kicked you out," I said, careful not to let any sympathy slip into my tone. This woman had done horrible things, and I hadn't forgotten it. "You failed and now they've cut your ties."

I canted my head sideways, looking for evidence I was right. A wrinkle to show some aging, a few gray hairs, crepe skin on her throat. I found it in the skin on her hand when she crossed them in front of her hips.

She lifted her chin. "They used me," she said. "I was the youngest in the coven. They exploited that, used me to do the blackest magic so they wouldn't get their hands dirty. Bastards the lot of them. They promised me I'd be the first to taste the power in return for shouldering the load."

Layne had started fiddling with something behind his back and I realized he was pulling out a set of handcuffs. I held up my hand to stay him.

"She has to go to jail," he said to me. "If you won't let us end her, she has to pay somehow."

"Jail?" Honey said with a disbelieving laugh. "You are such a small thinker if you believe you can just try me and jail me. On what grounds? What proof?" She snorted. "Look for my identification, detective. See if you can find a twenty-eight year old woman who goes by my name in any records or census in the last ten years. Or twenty, for that matter. No one will believe you when you try to take a woman to court who died fifty years ago."

He shrugged and snapped one cuff on her wrist. "Fine by me if you don't exist. Just makes your death that much easier," he said with a heart-stopping grin so full of camaraderie I gasped at how cold he could be.

"Hold on," I said. "No one is killing anyone—at least not yet." I leveled Honey with a cool look to rival Layne's. "What Layne is saying—in case you don't understand—is that you are already dead so no one will miss you if I agree to let him tear your throat out."

She swallowed hard. "But then, how will you get to your mother's power sources? Her vessels? Her bones?"

My mouth went dry. "Her bones? You know where they are?"

The perfect bow lips spread out in a taunting smile. "Of course I know where they are," she said. "I'm the one who killed her."

# CHAPTER 16

There was something eerily terrifying about a woman who would confess with a bright smile to killing another person. Knowing this woman had killed, felt pride in it was bad enough. Knowing she'd killed my mother, a goddess, made her even more terrifying.

Had I not been surrounded by two werewolves ready to bring her down with a mere movement of her pinky finger, I might have backed away. As it was, both of those wolves would die for me and I knew it as acutely as I knew my own heartbeat.

That lent me the courage I needed to step closer to her. I was an inch from her face, so close I could smell the liquor she'd downed before showing up on my shop's doorstep.

"Only a fool admits to killing a necromancer's mother," I said and was rewarded by a widening of Honey's eyes. She hadn't realized it, I guessed.

"That's right," I said and took her hand in mine, laid it down on my chest where the runes, still invisible to the naked eye, thrummed beneath my skin, sending whispers of power to my fingertips. "You thought I was just a simple vessel?" I asked her. "You think the goddess of witchcraft would put the better part of her own power in a mortal container while a weak coven tried to drain it from her mortal body?"

I shook my head to indicate how foolish I thought she was. "My mother was smarter than that. You think to play chess with a god?"

She tried to pull her hand from mine but I tightened my grip, held her fingers with force against my skin. I wanted her to feel the burn of the power. I wanted her to know what she'd awakened with her greed.

"I've met your master," I rasped, and at that her gaze widened even more. I nodded at her as a gloating, victorious smile stole the muscles of my mouth. "That's right. I've been to Hell. I've met the angel of the morning. He has broken ties with your coven and made a bargain with me."

"No one bargains with Lucifer and lives to see it fulfilled," she said, but her gaze skirted to Layne as though he could confirm it. Whatever she saw in his face made her sag inward. She might have fallen except Parrish hung so tight to her side that she bolstered the witch. She dragged her hand from mine finally, and I let it go.

"He's a liar," she said. "And he always wins." She hugged herself. "You'd be smart to remember that. If he broke our bargain, what's to say he'll keep yours."

I shook my head. "Doesn't matter what happens to me," I said, and it was true. Once I'd realized exactly what kind of power ran through my veins, that the power wasn't mine, I'd known I wouldn't survive bringing my mother back. I'd made my peace with it. "What matters is that you're going to help us bring the coven to its knees."

She nodded. "I'll take you to the casting circle where her bones are. Tonight. We can go tonight. Before three AM."

"What does she mean?" Parrish asked me as she threw her hands up in the air in frustration. "Why won't it matter? What bargain?" She breathed out a loud and long sigh. "Hell, I'm so fucking far behind on the scuttlebutt I'm going to have to pick up a brochure."

I stepped back and directed my gaze to Layne's face. "Do you have a safe place to keep her until midnight?" I knew the significance of the time. The witching hour gave force and power to witches. It also thinned the veil between life and death. She didn't want to give me any more power than she had to.

Layne snapped the other cuff around Honey's wrist, cutting off my thoughts. "I'll take her to the safe room at the pack house." He jerked his chin at Parrish. "Call in sick today if you can. Stick with Brie. If one witch found her, we can't be sure another won't."

Parrish nodded, but she kept her eye on Honey. "It's been slow lately, no doubt because these bitches haven't killed anyone lately, so that won't be a problem." Her eyes flashed yellow as she regarded the witch. "But trust me, you make one stupid move and I'll make sure there's nothing left of you to examine."

Honey held her gaze, and I had to admire her courage under that stare. I rolled my shoulders and shook out my hands. The taste of expectation clogged up my throat. Tonight, after all these weeks, things might come to a head. It was terrifying and exciting at the same time.

Layne caught my eye and leaned down to kiss me. He tasted of coffee. He hovered over me for one instant, telling me with his gaze that he loved me. I swallowed down the clump of desire and emotion that rose to meet him.

"I love you," he whispered. "We end this. Tonight."

I nodded, and he withdrew, yanking Honey not unkindly by the elbow as he perp-walked her out the back of the shop to the car, mindful of potential customers seeing them and making assumptions that might hurt my business.

I blew out a long, awed breath and pivoted on my heel to survey the shop. Crumbs from the cake on the counter had spilled to the floor and the heady scent of coffee hung in the air. I chewed my lip thoughtfully.

"I know that look," Parrish said.

My eyes found her sidling up to the counter and cutting another slice of cake. She popped a chunk of it into her mouth and chewed as she watched me with a narrowed gaze. She licked a bit of errant frosting from the corner of her mouth and held up her finger. "You are either going to do something stupid or you are going to get me to do something stupid. Either way, I'm all in."

"No one knows I'm open," I said. "We haven't even had a customer walk by."

"So?"

"So, we could just not open."

"And then what?"

I shrugged. "Are you sure you're all in?"

She broke off another piece of cake and was aiming it for her mouth when she stopped, wary. "Exactly what do you have in mind? Because if it's got anything to do with magic, I will fight you tooth and claw till Layne comes back. Because that would be too stupid even for me."

I shook my head. "It's not magic."

My arms found my waist, and I hugged myself. Now that Honey was gone, I expected the dread to lift. It didn't. That meant something else bothered me. I knew exactly what it was.

"I am going to Zach's," I said. "But I don't know where he lives."

She held up her hand. "Oh fuck no," she barked out. "I draw the line at that kind of stupid."

"Parrish, something's not right. We have to check on him."

"You heard him. He's gone to work."

I cocked my head. She knew as well as I did that he'd said he was on night shifts. But I called her bluff just the same. "Then his empty apartment shouldn't scare you."

"I do not scare."

"Prove it. Call him."

She glared at me but took out her phone. I heard the phone ringing on the other end, and ringing. And ringing.

My heart did a little flip-flop as I watched the emotions flicker across Parrish's face. In the end, she tapped the phone off and gave me a look that made my heart feel as though someone had reached in and squeezed it.

"I think it's time we checked on him," she said in a tinny voice.

"Should we go to his apartment?"

"He doesn't have one."

"He lives somewhere."

"Yeah," she said in a strange voice. "He certainly does." She gestured at me to follow her.

Where Zach resided was nowhere around the pack house or the manse. It took ten minutes to motor to an older part of the city, where nineteenth century houses and brownstones lined the streets and formed various cul de sacs.

There in the center of the city, surrounded by brick buildings and walkups squatted an old style bungalow with a veranda better suited facing a lake or hunched into the embrace of a mountain landscape. It was out of place where it was, and so quaint it made a wash of unexpected nostalgia ripple through me.

I pictured a swimming hole out back and wicker rockers on the porch and a stone fireplace on the inside. The longing I felt looking at it didn't make any sense, and yet it made all the sense. The facade evinced a feeling of days gone by, of jams cooling on counters and pies on windowsills.

"Shit," I said, pushing open the door of her car. My shoes crunched on gravel as I stepped out. "This is something."

She huffed as she slammed her door. "Yeah. Our good doctor longs for his childhood home. No matter how much money he makes, he keeps this old shack."

She ran both hands over her head, scrubbing her scalp beneath the auburn tresses until her hair fell forward over her shoulders and around her face.

"I secretly think he had it moved here, but he swears he just had a contractor build it from pictures." A heavy sigh escaped her. "Well, no time like the present," she said.

She outpaced me as she headed toward the porch lined with rhododendrons and azaleas and a host of rose bushes long gone to hips and buds. An old-fashioned wooden plow graced the middle of the garden on one side of the front door, and on the other, the gardener had placed a huge wagon wheel.

She paused at the bottom of the wide stoop and stood there for a long moment, staring at the facade with her hands in her pockets until I thought she might actually kick at a pebble like a kid in a movie.

Eventually, though, she bounced on her toes and dropped her head back.

"Fuck, I hate this," she said. "You go in. I'll wait here."

I nodded at her. "Hopefully, he'll be drinking himself out of his rage and into a coma."

The look she gave me suggested she had very little hope of that.

I sucked in a bracing breath and strode purposefully up the stairs. I looked back at her over my shoulder and she gestured at me to keep going. I stomped on the veranda. On the corner, facing outward, he had indeed placed an old-fashioned wooden rocker. My throat ached as dread began a dance up my spine.

One sharp rap on the door echoed back at me the way only an empty house can do. I paused to listen for footsteps inside. In my mind, I imagined a wood-burning stove, a large picnic table clothed in checkered material. A stone fireplace crackled with dry logs beneath an oak mantle.

I expected wooden floors and slippered feet scuffing along to meet me. Through the screen door, I'd catch a glimpse of a man sauced from too much booze with a drawn look on his face as he realized he'd have to make chit chat conversationally with a visitor.

The picture in my mind was so clear, I was sure I heard those scuffing steps. I waited a moment longer, knowing he'd open the door. It was Parrish's voice behind me that swept over me, startling me.

I jumped at least an inch off the porch floor. She didn't even chuckle.

"Something's wrong," she rasped over my shoulder. "Fuck, Zach. You bastard."

She didn't bother to knock then, just dropped her hand over the doorknob and twisted. Something broke inside the gears and with a hitch in her breath, she pushed open the door.

Inside, all the lights were blazing. The open concept layout showed nearly every bit of detail in the harsh light. Almost too much detail.

From where we stood, we could see everything but the bedrooms and bath. The wrought iron chandelier I didn't expect to see, with eight bulbs hanging over the shaker style plank wood table, gave off too much light.

A propane fireplace whose mantel lined with LED candles set in various pillar stands stood cold and dead of flame, but the candles all flared with a yellow glow. Each lamp on the tables was lit. Every under cabinet LED glowed.

"This has to be encouraging," I said to Parrish. "I mean, if he was planning to hurt himself, he wouldn't turn on every light, would he?"

She rolled her eyes. "Drama queen Zacharia, you mean? Who the hell knows?" She was already heading across the room to the right where it looked like a hall hunkered in the middle of the whitewash cabinets.

"Zacharia," she shouted. "You better fucking well be drunk on your bed, you bastard. And you better not be fucking naked because I'm coming down there."

I followed her, the dread toying with my gooseflesh. She hadn't bothered heeling off her boots, so I didn't either, and the sound of our footsteps on the oak floor was too loud. I took to wringing my hands like an old-fashioned schoolmarm.

She had made it as far at the mouth of the hall when I saw him. I grabbed her by the tail of her shirt. "Parrish," I whispered.

She halted, looked at me over her shoulder. Whatever she saw in my face made her eyes go wide.

"What?" she said. "What is it?"

I pointed to her right where Zach was sitting on the counter watching us. A pistol rested in his lap. The barrel was still smoking.

"Don't go down the hall," I said, my eyes glued to the tendril of smoke rising toward his chin.

"Fuck that, Brie," she said. "We need to know if he's OK."

"He's not OK," I said, jerking my chin in the direction my finger pointed.

I felt her go rigid.

"Don't," she rasped out. "Don't fucking say it, Brie."

I considered arguing with her, but she was already tearing down the hallway to where she obviously knew his bedroom was located. I thought about warning her, but she was already shouldering her way through the bedroom door, splintering it with the force of her weight.

But it was no use saying anything then. She'd find him as I expected him to be.

The ghost on the counter caught my eye and pointed the gun at his temple.

I screamed right about the same time Parrish did.

# Chapter 17

Zach was dead. Because of the gun the ghost had clutched in his hand, I expected Zach to have shot himself. That wasn't the case. At least, from where I stood in the doorway of his bedroom, I couldn't tell if he'd shot himself. There was no blood. I knew that. If he'd shot himself there would be blood everywhere, wouldn't there?

He lay on his bed, half propped up by four firm pillows. His arm lay slack at his side with an apple rolled an inch away from his curled, open fingers. Choking. He had choked to death, not shot himself. I wasn't sure if relief was the right emotion, but I felt it anyway, and it clung to me like a wet blanket.

Parrish had already made it to his side and presumably had already checked his vitals and was now thrusting her fists into his abdominal cavity. I raced to the bed, a dreadful hope making my stomach hurt with each aggressive thrust she performed.

"It's not working," she said and abandoned her maneuvers to lean over his head. Without a single bit of compassion or sympathy, she dug into his mouth with her fingers. I winced and gagged reflexively. Sweat broke out on my forehead and heat rushed over my skin, flushing it.

"Don't you fucking puke, Brie," Parrish said absently as she plumbed as far into Zach's throat as she could. "I don't have it in me to deal with that right now."

My hands flew to my mouth, clamping down on whatever would rise, and I staggered backwards until my back met the door. Turning, I fled down the hall to another doorway. Praying it was the bathroom and not a closet, I twisted the knob.

I vomited into the bidet, a stream of still warm coffee, then cream soured and clumpy. With my palm against the rim, I leveraged myself back onto my feet and stared down into the bowl. From beyond the doorway, I could hear Parrish muttering to Zach, then the grunting sounds of her exerting herself over his abdominals again.

It was too late. I knew she knew it as well as I did. The pallor of his skin had been too gray. He'd been lying there for too long. There was no coming back from death, even if Parrish did manage to get the hunk of apple out of his throat.

I wiped my mouth with the back of my hand and flushed the bidet. I ran some water in the sink to splash onto my face and clean my tongue. The mirror over the sink was homemade, I noticed, with reclaimed wood that had a distinctly gray appearance. Gray. Like Zach's skin. My stomach started to rebel again as my mind untapped the image of him lying on his bed again.

"Don't do it," I mumbled to myself. "Don't you puke again, you idiot."

I pulled in a breath to steel myself, then ran a bit more cold water from the tap. I was bringing my cooled fingers to my face to tap over my eyes when I caught sight of a shadow in the mirror. How Abbie was able to fit into the space behind me, I didn't question. She wasn't exactly corporeal and being born of magic, she wouldn't have to answer to the rules of time and space.

But the fact that she was there, with her eyes boring into mine, meant there was more going on than what it seemed.

I pivoted to stare at her, but she evaporated. I felt her eyes on my back the whole way to the bedroom. I knew what Parrish was going to say even before she said it. I should have realized it the moment I'd seen my mother's familiar.

"Bring him back, Brie," she said. "Bring him back."

She was standing by then. Her hands hung at her sides. The usually lively face, with its quickness to smile, had gone blank. Her expression wouldn't even contort into the familiar leanings of grief.

"You're a witch," she said flatly. "I've seen you raise the dead. Bring him back."

My gaze flitted to the body on the bed. Without the flush of life beneath his skin, Zach looked plastic. At some point, Parrish had flipped him over to thump on his back. A hunk of red apple lay on the bed beside him and from his angle, he looked up at me with a crooked tilt to his neck.

"I can't," I said. "I can't bring him back. He's dead."

She prowled toward me then, and the way she moved forced my feet to backstep. "Isn't that what necromancers do, Brie?" she said. "I saw what you did with the dogs and birds and the owl, for fuck's sake."

"This is different," I said, wringing my hands as I stole glances at Zach. "Those were small animals and it just happened. I didn't *do* anything."

"It can't be much different. They were dead God knows how long. He's just been dead a short while."

The way her eyebrows knit together, I could see she was struggling to keep her calm.

I shook my head at her. "I don't know how."

It was a lie. I knew how. Even as I said the words, I knew I understood exactly how to bring him back. Spells reeled themselves off in my mind. The runes on my chest burned. Something about a deal with the devil and realizing my father was a necromancer had loosed the knowledge into my psyche.

"Don't lie to me, Brie," she said and her eyes flared yellow. "This is Zach. He would help you. He has helped you. You can't just let him die."

"He's already dead, Parrish," I whispered. A shadow deepened near the corner of the room, catching my eye. Abbi again. I tried not to look at her. "I can't do this."

One more step, a threat veiled in the movement. "He doesn't have to stay dead. What is all that power for if not to use it for good? Zach deserves it. You know he does."

"It's not as easy as all that." I thought of all those I'd seen in the underworld, the souls contained in orbs for Lucifer's playthings. His menagerie. Did everyone go there at death? What if Zach was there, meeting Lucifer, discovering all the lovely things the devil wanted to do with his soul? The thought of it shivered through me. Could I let that happen to him?

All that was racing through my mind when Parrish's hand clamped down around my wrist. "I would never hurt you," she whispered, but her eyes were all manic, which made them look even more frightening in that deadpan expression. I realized she was trying to convince me because I saw how frantic she was. My face must have worn all the doubt and fear of that knowledge.

"You know what my last words were to him," she said. "He didn't deserve that. I can't have that be the last thing he ever heard from me."

I didn't know what to say. The truth was, she'd said it with every intention of hurting him. Now she couldn't take it back, and while I felt for her, I knew there was nothing I could do to change it.

"You told me what you saw in Lucifer's world. All the creatures he collects, both human and inhuman. Mortal and monster. What if Zach is there, Brie? What if he is there right now, suffering, and you could do something to change that?"

Abbi lowered her head as though watching me for my response. I tried not to look at her as I thought about the possibility that Zach was even then facing off against Lucifer. A chill swept over me.

"I'll need grave dirt," I said as the words burst from me.

I sank onto the bed, far away from Zach's body, angled toward the door instead of the dresser mirror so I didn't have to look at him. My mother fashioned altars in our basement, burned entrails and sacrificed puppies, but was it to raise the dead or to create vessels to store her power? I really didn't know. I did know, however, that raising the dead as a mortal was going to be much harder. I'd need every powerful talisman I could muster.

Parrish didn't seem to notice my hesitation. She straightened up, her posture rigid with alert and hope.

"I can get that. What else do you need?" She turned away from me and started rummaging through Zach's end table drawers. She lifted out a brush and held it up at me. "Hair? Toenail clippings?" She shook the brush in my direction. "What?"

"I'll need a blade." I thought about the way I'd had to cut into my runes before to access my magic. So much of it all seemed to stem from blood as well as intention. "And a basin or something."

She quirked her eyebrow. "A basin?" then her face lit with realization. "Oh, you mean for the blood."

She shivered visibly, which I thought strange thing for a werewolf who dealt in death for a living. Then she braced herself, a movement so instinctual I didn't think she could control it.

"You'll take mine," she declared. "If you need blood, mine is filled with magic. The kind he needs." She tossed a look at the bed. "And if it works, I want it to be my blood that brings him back."

I nodded. "Good idea. I think that may help." I sighed and pushed myself off the bed to pace the room as she headed out to the kitchen.

Abbi fell in step behind me and trailed me with every step. I knew Parrish hadn't seen her, and I didn't want to alert her to the dog's presence since she was already freaked out enough. Pacing helped calm my nerves.

Instinct told me casting magic this time would not end me back up in Hell or into the shadowy place I'd visited before.

There was no way I could know it, but I trusted that instinct. Before I'd gone into magic naïve and ignorant. Now, I knew exactly what prices needed to be paid for using any power. Magic always came at a cost. My mother had paid it dear, losing her lover and her own power in the process, and she was a god. I was merely mortal, but I had something most mortals didn't. I had a bargain with the devil.

A mere drop of blood and a whisper to my magic, he'd said. Energy did not disappear, it merely shifted, moving in currents invisible to the naked eye but gifting to us a promise of magic if we knew how to take it. I could dance on the currents of death and cross to his realm the same as my mother could. And because I held her magic, I could access the realm of death without entering it.

I just had to figure out the best way to do it.

Those were the things that I knew as I paced. Things Lucifer himself had given me along with that amulet when we'd struck a bargain. That was when I realized the most important ingredient in the spell, something Lucifer himself had given me. Not just a talisman of promise and bargain, as I'd told Layne, but a vessel powerful enough to hold a human soul.

Persephone's soul, I realized. That was why Lucifer had given it to me. A vessel capable of ferrying a human soul, her soul, to him.

I spun on my heel, excited now. I reached for the stone and clutched it. My blood and Lucifer's created the stone. God of death aligned the daughter of a necromancer and the goddess of witchcraft.

The stone warmed in my touch the way it had back in my shop. Between my breasts it was as warm as my skin but it was warmer now, warm because Zach had just died and his death energy danced on the currents of the air I stood in.

Abbi made a sound like a low throated huff of a bark that drew my attention. Her head was lowered, her hackles raised.

"You have a better idea?" I asked her. "I have to figure out how to raise you, anyway. This is a good test."

She yipped at me, and I decided to take it as agreement. By the time Parrish came back into the room with a basin and a razor blade still in its paper sheath, I had already taken off my clothes and was standing in my bra and panties. I'd pulled a blanket from the bed and draped it over the floor.

"No sense getting blood all over his nice carpet," I explained when Parrish's eyebrows raised half an inch. "Do you have the grave dirt?"

"Right," she said, holding her arms out the sides. "Because I carry shit like that in my purse." She held her arms out to her sides.

I chewed my lip, thinking. "Do you think you could carry him out to the backyard?"

"No," she said. "I am not doing that."

"Come on, Parrish," I said. "A grave is a grave. We don't have the time to go to the cemetery. Dig a hole in the backyard and put him in it."

"I'm not going to bury Zach in his yard." She crossed her arms over her chest. "It's midday, for fuck's sake. Someone is bound to call the cops."

"You're the medical examiner and Layne is the cops," I told her. "I'm going out there in my underwear. Do you want me to raise him or not? We don't have a lot of time here."

I stared at her. "Besides, it is midday. Most people will be at work."

Her fists clenched down at her sides. "Fuck," she said and pivoted on her heel and stomped down the hall. I heard her close the back door with a muttering curse. I waited for maybe ten minutes before she stomped her way back.

I had Zach covered with the blanket I'd draped over the floor. The amulet had grown cooler the longer we waited, and I knew time was growing short. The fact that I'd seen his ghost in the kitchen had bolstered my hopes that he was still lingering in the here and now, but the coolness of the amulet worried me.

I decided not to tell Parrish, and she lifted him from the bed with no effort and muscled her way through the bedroom door and down the hall to the back door. She turned to look at me over her shoulder before she pushed her way through that, too.

"I'm not burying him deep," she said. "I don't want him suffocating in there."

I smiled. "It doesn't need to be deep. It just needs to be a place where he's buried. We'll just toss a bit of earth on him, enough that we can call it a grave and gather it back to form an altar."

I stopped mid-thought as I stepped out onto the back porch and saw the loveliness that was Zach's back yard. Apple trees stretched up to the crystalline sky, forming a small orchard in the half lot that remained in the back of his house. Tall cedar fences lined the perimeter with ivy weaving a mat of green foliage. Flowers of all sorts, hostas, and pots of vegetables seamed the fence.

And there, close to the house in a garden all its own rioting with color, Parrish had dug a man-sized hole.

"It's only about a foot deep," she said and hitched her burden higher.

"It's perfect. Just enough."

She tread reverently toward the hole and bent to lay Zach almost tenderly into the space in the earth. There was a quick arrangement of the end where his head was, as she did her best to make it straight. She shifted his shoulders, his torso, beneath the blanket and patted the spot where his belly would be. Then she stood back. With a swallow, she placed her hands on her hips.

"Don't want him to freak out because he's facing down," she said with a glance darted in my direction. "You know, for when he comes back."

When he comes back. Not if. She was sure he would make it. She was certain I had the power.

It seemed we were about to find out.

# CHAPTER 18

ZACH'S GRAVE SMELLED OF lavender. The fragrant herb grew in swaths of purple all around the plot Parrish had selected. I decided she must have some bit of witch in her to have picked a spot that would naturally repel evil. I kept those thoughts in mind as the fragrance washed over me. Then, I clutched handfuls of his grave dirt and knelt to draw the Hecate wheel on his chest.

Parrish had been worried we'd have to cover him with earth, but that wasn't necessary. He only needed to be resting in the hole for it to be become a grave. At least, I banked on that technicality.

I decided not to remove him once she put him in it. No sense taking any chances. Busy with drawing the symbol of my mother's power, I sent her back into the kitchen for salt. I had no sulfur or brimstone, so the salt would help me form a protective circle. Again. Just in case.

I was hefting myself up from the grave when she came out with a box of table salt and a handful of white taper candles.

"Pictures online and in movies all show witches using candles," she said with a lift of one shoulder. "And you sell them in your shop."

I nodded at her. "Great call." I took the elbow she offered to me as leverage to haul myself onto level ground.  I planted my hands on my hips to survey my work. "Let's hope it's enough."

I stood beside her, both of us looking down into the grave at Zach's shape beneath the blanket. The Hecate wheel on his chest didn't look too warped. The length of the hole wasn't quite big enough for Zach to lie flat, and his knees bent a bit to accommodate him, but all in all, it was a decent grave. A good enough tableau to appease whatever power I'd have to call upon to do this thing.

"Maybe you should get in with him," I said to Parrish as I considered the finicky need of ensuring the blood she offered made it directly onto the symbol.

She made no complaint about the tight space, the awkwardness of her feet trying to balance her large form as she found uneven ground inside the hole. I waited until she had found a position near the symbol, straddling him with both feet planted on the sides of the grave. She had to steady herself with her palm against the top of the grave to keep from pitching all the way over. She nodded at me when she felt ready.

Magic was a personal thing, I gathered. Some bits were complex and expected, but spells were individual to the witch casting them, steeped in ceremony, ritual, and language.

I'd set my own sort of magic, it seemed, when I'd used my own blood to power the magic inside with the runes. I hoped the spell I crafted would be enough to call the magic for raising the newly dead.

I took my time drawing the casting circle even though I knew Parrish had to feel uncomfortable. Each step, I focused on my memories of my mother as she cast her spells in the basement of my childhood home. I pulled those things to me like a shawl and hoped that the faintness of the memory, the mispronunciations, the shade of half spells, would be enough. I hoped the intention of the spell mattered as much as the words.

Looking over the shape of the salt circle when I was done, I identified pretty quickly the points where the candles needed to go because small areas glowed as though the lines of power beneath the earth had lit up.

Parrish watched me with a keen eye as I placed the candles into the earth in seven places.

I halted outside the grave at a spot even with Zach's chest. Parrish shifted her left foot, splaying it out to the side as she dug her shoulder into the wall of the grave so she could hold herself up without using her hands for support.

She nodded at me, and I held the razor blade out to her. By the time I straightened back up, a hulking shadow with glowing red eyes had begun to form at Zach's head. Abbi. Watching us with that surreal gaze, her head lowered the way a dog does when it sees something interesting.

"Fuck me," Parrish whispered as her gaze swept over the space where the dog was becoming more corporeal.

Abbi gave her a baleful stare that Parrish couldn't return. Instead, the werewolf flicked her eyes to me.

"Alpha," she said, and I understood what she meant. The energy of the dog was not a submissive one, not even dominant. Abbi was the height of dominance in Parrish's eyes, and it stood to reason that Hecate's familiar would have alpha energy to a werewolf.

"Ready?" I asked.

Parrish held my gaze so intently I couldn't bring myself to look away. It wasn't that she was bracing herself for what she had to do, but rather, she was giving me the support I needed to hold fast as the spell began. The fortitude to continue no matter what happened.

I appreciated it. This was more than raising a few small animals. This was resurrecting a soul back into a body that had begun to decay. The magic had taken so much from me in the past. I'd ended up in the hospital, nearly died, gone into fugue states as I touched the energy of my power.

This time, I was doing far more, and I was doing it intentionally. It wasn't out of curiosity but compassion that I was doing this thing. But how it would all unfold was still uncertain.

Parrish lifted her arm, holding her palm facing the clouds, her wrist directly over the Hecate wheel. She waited until I clutched the amulet and squeezed before she cut into her wrist. We'd talked about this. She would bleed, but she would heal. She would know the moment she needed to shift if the cut went too deep.

But she was a coroner, so she knew the smartest places to score into skin to bring enough blood without putting her in true danger. At least, that was what I hoped.

I dropped my head back as the first pitterpats of blood struck the dirt on the symbol. Beneath my breath, I called out to Hecate, goddess of witchcraft to guide my spell. I dug my bare toes into the earth so I could connect with the energy of the world's magic. The candle to my left whooshed into life, a breeze swept up from the circle, moving my hair.

The casting had begun. There was no way back now. I felt the tension of the moment trying to choke me. I fought the pressure, held myself erect as a force around me tried to push me out of phase and into the grave with the both of them.

The magic did not want to be used. Necromancy was a dark art. It was unnatural. The pressures of forcing the energy to my shape, of pulling it toward me was great. I wasn't sure I could withstand it.

I dropped my head level so I could watch Parrish, watch Zach, watch for the moment that I knew might trigger the energies tugging at me to funnel into one small area over my chest. I wasn't sure I'd know the moment, but the way Abbi was shuffling her feet, her hackles raised on the back of her neck, the way her tail went straight out behind her, I knew the instant was near.

Time drew out like a string of warm taffy. Parrish held her arm over the symbol, letting the blood drain onto the dirt. It sizzled where it fell. Parrish weaved and swayed, the effort of holding herself in position, the loss of blood showing in her face. If things didn't happen soon, she'd collapse, and I'd have two dead werewolves in one grave, and a hell of a lot to answer for when the cops arrived.

Just when I'd begun to despair that I'd harmed Parrish for nothing, I felt a hot knife of pain razor through me. I cried out. My body arched painfully backward, and I nearly lost my footing. My grip on the amulet slipped for one second, and I was terrified I'd lose contact altogether. I let myself fall onto my side so I wouldn't let go.

My face mashed into the grass. The fragrance of lavender climbed my cheek to my nose, tickling the senses that had detected a note of brimstone in the air.

"It's coming," I gasped out, and no sooner had the words left me, then the amulet burned hot, shooting shocks into my fist and down my arm. I held on for dear life, knowing this moment was the one I'd been waiting for. The amulet was testing my resolve. I squeezed all the harder, even though my fingers wanted desperately to let go.

Abbi stomped her feet. Her low growl met my ears. Parrish might have gasped or swore, I wasn't sure anymore. All the surrounding sounds had begun to meld together into a cacophony that sounded very much like people shrieking in agony.

But I held fast to the stone, and I held it out before me as I rolled onto my stomach, half hovering over the grave. I kept hold of Parrish's gaze with my own. Whatever she saw in mine put a look of horror on her expression, but I didn't let go. I felt the wig fall to the side of my head. Nausea rose up into my throat.

When the amulet finally cracked out a splitting sound reminiscent of lightning hitting tinder, a scream tore from me, soundless and painful.

Fire leaped from the stone and through my fingers. It shot toward the Hecate wheel. It lit the blood on fire. Parrish pulled her arm back to her chest fast enough to cut off the flame as it tried to follow the line of blood from the symbol to her flesh. But the symbol burned.

Abbi fell to her belly, her muzzle on her paws. She whimpered.

Both Parrish and I stared at the fire as it consumed both the blood and the grave ash. With my heart so far up my throat that I could taste blood, I stared at the magic as it consumed the offering. My palms dug into the dirt around the grave. Nothing moved beneath the blanket. The symbol disappeared. Parrish sat awkwardly on her side of Zach with her arm cradled against her chest.

But the air was so still it felt as though the world had been buried beneath a landslide of energy. And still nothing moved beneath the blanket.

We'd failed. Zach was gone.

Tears slipped down Parrish's face and streaked her mascara as she stared at the lump of man beside her. She dropped her head back and howled. Abbi howled with her.

I was about to climb to my knees when I saw the faintest bit of movement. At first, I thought it was the waver of heat as it climbed from the flames, but then the flames sort of...paused...and I saw Zach's head beneath the blanket move to the side.

"Parrish," I said, in warning.

That was all the time I had before the flames roared to life and caught the fabric of the blanket.

What was beneath it started thrashing madly then, and a shout escaped me.

Parrish reacted faster than I could. She fell on the fire with her entire body, rolling and grabbing for the edges of the blanket as she went. Stop, drop, roll. The blanket covered her as she rolled, moving nowhere in the tiny grave but spinning in place as she pulled inches of fiery blanket around her. The blanket tore, giving her space to spin enough to peel it away from Zach. Enough to smother the blaze.

Before I could react to help, a mass of limbs tangled together in the grave as both she and Zach wrestled to find their way out from beneath the scorched blanket. The stink of burned hair clawed its way into my nose. I made a grab for the nearest hand and pulled.

Parrish's, I realized. She was too weak now to do more than cling to me. And I was too weak to holds her. I fell on my ass, letting go of her grip in the process.

It was only because Zach had managed to extricate himself from the fabric and was shoving at her backside, pushing her out of the hole that she was able to claw her way to completely free of the grave.

She lay on her back, facing the sky. Zach fell over the top of her waist, face down with his nose in her belly. They both heaved for air and energy for what seemed a long time before she shoved him off her.

"Get your damned hand off my crotch," she lamented and rolled onto her side as he heaved himself onto his hands and knees.

I couldn't move. I was aware I was lying there on my stomach watching it all happen, but the relief and the shock paralyzed me. It was only when Zach sat up that I found the strength to do the same. He reached his hand out for Parrish's and she took it begrudgingly.

A moment later, both of them were sitting, hanging over their knees, looking at each other.

"You look like a scorched ham," she said.

His hair had burned off in the fire, so she wasn't too far off.

"I feel like a scorched ham," he said. "What the hell happened? Why were we wrestling in..." he sent a confused look toward the grave. "...a hole you seemed to have dug in my lawn that has literally ruined the mother of thyme I planted this spring."

She sent him a scathing look. "Because you killed yourself, you fucking idiot. We had to bring you back."

It took a moment of confusion as he sorted through all the things his memory might have held, the moments he'd found himself wrapped in a blanket in a hole in the ground, and pieced it all together into an inescapable conclusion.

The truth of it had to have hit home in a way that made him feel sick, but then his brow moved in a way that suggested if his eyebrows hadn't burned straight off, that they would have shot up an inch.

"Killed myself?" he snorted. "I was eating an apple in bed. I must have choked."

"Either way," she said. "Brie brought you back to life." Her eyes shone with admiration and relief as she directed her words my way. "She's a fucking god."

My fingers rose to my temples. "Apparently pulling out the god molecule gives a witch a really bad headache."

She tittered and looked down at her wrist, still oozing blood but clotting nicely. Zach laid his hand down on it and I could see he was exerting pressure as she lifted it above her heart. "You'll be fine. No need to shift to heal it."

She snorted. "Says the man who isn't bleeding."

His eyes were glassy. "Are you that much of a pussy you can't stand the pain of a little cut?"

She didn't respond to the ribbing, which was strange. Instead, she held his gaze for a long time. Some communication passed between them, words that needed no voice.

After a long time, he licked his lips, wetting frays of skin that had split his mouth.

"On second thought, maybe you should shift," he said. "You don't look so good."

She fell back onto her haunches with a nod. "I think you're right. I feel strange."

"Probably the magic and the blood loss," I said. "I don't feel quite right either."

I rubbed at the spot where the headache seemed to be trying to tunnel into my skull. The pain was almost enough to dampen the sensation that I felt as if half of my body wasn't quite my own. It didn't respond as quickly as the other side. I tested it by squeezing first one hand into a fist and then the other. I shook them both out when I noticed Zach squinting at me.

"I'd like to thank you, Brie, but I think that will have to come later. Neither of you look so good."

I waved him away and pushed myself to my feet, an echo of movement I saw in Parrish as she struggled to rise to hers. Zach let her use his body to leverage herself up and held onto her as she weaved on her feet.

"Shift," he said to her, his brow furrowed with worry. "You need to shift."

She blinked owlishly at him. "Too late," she said.

Then she collapsed into a heap.

# CHAPTER 19

PARRISH WAS DEAD. I had killed her.

That was the thought that whispered across my mind as Abbi leaped for Parrish the moment she fell. The growl that erupted from her sent chills racing up my spine.

I didn't know how I got to her before Zach, or what the moments in between taking a step and feeling for her pulse held.

All I knew was that I couldn't feel any reassuring thrum beneath the pads of my fingers. I was leaning down to her mouth, my ear straining for the sound of her breath, when Zach shoved me roughly aside.

"Doctor, remember," he growled. "Give me room."

I relinquished my spot to him so he could lean over Parrish. I watched him testing her vitals with a pinched expression that grew ever more alarmed the more he worked on her.

"She's dead," I said flatly. "I killed her."

His fingers ran down the length of her neck to touch down on her wrist, then it moved to her temple, then he laid his palm flat beneath her ribcage in the center of her body. "Not dead," he rasped out. "Breathing, pulse faint but there."

I was already pulling out my phone to call an ambulance. He caught my wrist. "Don't," he said and shook his head.

"But she needs help." I yanked my hand from his. "You don't get to make this call, Zach. She died trying to save you. If she's dying, I won't let you just let her slip away."

He grabbed both of my wrists then, and I fought him. Abbi growled from behind him, baring her teeth at me. AT me. That just made me fight all the harder.

I tried to bite his wrists and failed. "She needs help. You've gone mad. I know you're mad at her, but you can't just let her die."

He wrestled me until he'd pinned my arms against his chest. Abbi loomed over his shoulder. If he knew she was there, he made no signal. "Brie," he said. "I love her. I'm not about to let her die."

"You better not, Zach," came a low-throated, masculine voice from the porch. I knew we both realized who stood there.

I scrabbled backward, crab-walking until I was out of range of Zach's reach.

"Layne," I said, relief swelling my voice. "Thank God." He could fix it. He could make Zach call for help.

Zach crouched with one knee bent and a foot planted in front of him. His hand strayed toward Parrish's chest and flattened down on her ribcage.

"Don't come any closer," he said to Layne. His eyes flashed yellow. "I don't want to fight you. Not now. Not now." His expression sagged with exhaustion.

"If you feel attacking your alpha is the right thing to do in this moment, Zach," Layne said calmly. "I'll not hold it against you, but know you won't win."

Zach nodded. "I'll die to protect her. You know this."

Layne took one more step down the stairs of the porch, crossing one ankle over the other in a leisurely stance that looked anything but casual. "I know she's your mate, Zach. I know you'll kill anyone that comes near her, but she needs help."

Mate? The sound of the word had me reeling. How could they be mates when Parrish didn't even like men? Did that explain why she was so angry at him all the time, angry because the fates had given her a male mate and not female? I couldn't even fathom the injustice of that.

Zach moved slowly, deliberately, with his eye on Layne as he scooped beneath her knees. He stood just as slowly, but not out of exertion. Parrish looked very light in his arms. It was more that he was watching the both of us so warily that he was afraid to move too fast.

Layne watched him without moving, but his eyes had that same yellow glint.

"She needs help, Zach."

"I know this," Zach said as he hoisted her higher. "Who better to care for her than a doctor, Layne? Wouldn't you be hiring me to look after her, anyway?"

Layne sighed. "I would. You know this. But you don't look exactly sane right now. I won't risk her life for your feelings."

A surge of power washed over the back garden. Zach bowed before it, and his knees buckled, but he did not relinquish his hold of Parrish.

"She's not dying," he said.

"She is," Layne insisted. "She needs to go to the hospital." He directed his gaze toward me. "Call," he said.

I hesitated. Not sure why, but I trusted Zach in that moment and not Layne. "If she isn't dying, Zach," I said. "Then what's wrong with her?"

He swallowed hard and looked from Layne to me and to Parrish before he spoke. A bead of sweat ran from his flushed and naked pate down along the side of his nose. "Hell fire is cold," he said in a tight voice.

My back went clammy at the words. I'd said them myself. "Hell fire?"

He swung his gaze to mine and nodded. "I touched it. For a long time I was trapped here," he directed a look toward his house. "In there. Out here. I watched you and her, I think. I heard you."

His face pinched into a confused look. "Nothing was real, and the words made no sense, but I was here." He closed his eyes. "And then I wasn't. It was dark. Cold." When he opened his eyes again, they had gone a brilliant molten yellow. "She's where I was when I touched the icy flame of hell. Not alive, but not dead."

I inched closer, my breath caught in my chest. "What did you see, Zach?" I whispered. "Who did you see?"

He looked surprised. "I saw you," he said, and then his legs gave out and he sank to his knees on the grass.

Layne took the moment to approach. He crouched in front of Zach with his arms out. "I'm not going to hurt her," he said. "You know this. Your wolf knows this."

Zach nodded soberly as he held Layne's eye. He didn't fight when Layne took Parrish from him.

"It's OK," Layne murmured to him as he collected her from Zach and held her close against his chest. "I'm just taking her so you can gather your strength." He waited until Zach laid his palm on Parrish's forehead before he eased away, slowly, his eyes on Zach's the whole time.

"We'll take care of her together until we can find out how to get her back." He looked at me. "She sent me a message. Telling me to get my ass over here. I came as fast as I could."

I shook my head. "It wouldn't have changed anything," I said. "The magic has its own mind."

He started for the porch and I followed, not sure what else I should do and feeling as though Zach needed some space.

Layne spoke to me over his shoulder. "He was dead? You're sure?"

Meaning had I really resurrected him? "Yes. Parrish was one hundred percent certain."

I thought it relevant to explain she had made that declaration as a professional. Just like Zach was. If he said she wasn't dying, I tended to believe it.

His footfalls on the steps echoed back at me and I hurried along to outpace him so I could open the door.

"Put her in my bed," Zach shouted at us. "It's the most comfortable."

I looked back at him, the way he sagged onto his haunches. The bald and scorched face without eyebrows gave him a strange appearance that was only accentuated by the deadpan, exhausted look on his features. He followed us with his eyes, unblinking. I thought he might collapse the moment we got inside.

I eyed Layne as we entered. "He seems sure," I said.

Layne twisted sideways so he could handle her without knocking her head or her feet into the walls of the hallway. "I believe him, but I'm not about to leave her here with him alone. I'll call Emmett to come help."

"I can stay," I said, and he swung on me. And in his eyes was a hard glint of anger.

"You look like you're about ready to collapse too, Brie. Whatever you did out there, it's not... it's not right."

I worried my hands, one over the other. "You would rather I let him die?" I snorted. "I'm not that kind of friend, Layne. You weren't here. You didn't see..."

He pushed against me so suddenly, using the weight of the woman in his arms to cage me against the wall.

"You're all I care about, Brie. My pack, my life, my father. All of it is nothing to you. Have you taken a moment to focus on how you feel? Because you look like you're about to come apart at the seams. Hell, one of your eyes doesn't even look like yours. You think Zach is mad with worry over his mate? Try reaching for our bond and seeing how I feel."

His voice was a ragged sound that tore from his throat. He was so close, I could smell the worry in his perspiration, the faint scent of spearmint gum coming from his pocket.

"I don't want to be more important than your pack, Layne," I said. "They're family. They're who you are."

He shook his head. "I'm nothing without you. I told you I wouldn't let anyone hurt you ever again, and that included you, Brie. You should have called me. I should have been here."

"There wasn't time."

He leaned against me, the woman between us, keeping us from touching but both of us needing the intimacy.

"I'm not sure I'll be able to handle that sort of compassion," he said. "It's going to be the death of me."

A long moment passed between us as we gathered ourselves. Zach came in from the back porch and nudged Layne.

"I can take her now."

With a short nod, Layne passed her over, and we followed him into his bedroom. I scrabbled for the clothing I'd discarded on the floor and pulled it on as Zach laid Parrish on his bed, taking the time to arrange her legs and arms comfortably. He fluffed the pillow behind her head. When he looked our way again, his face was set with a determined look.

"Do you smell it?" he asked, directing his question to me.

I canted my head at him, curious.

"You smell it, don't you, Layne?"

I peered up at my mate and watched his nostrils flare as he drew in a long, sensory breath. He held the air in his nose for a moment, then nodded. "Sulfur."

"Brimstone," Zach corrected him before directing his next words to me. "You're probably too close to the magic to catch it," he said. "You being the caster and all, but there's a faint stink of brimstone all around her. Around you."

I stepped closer. "It's typical," I said. "Especially when calling to darker magic."

He shook his head as he lifted Parrish's wrist, touching down on her pulse with his fingers. "Not like this."

Layne nudged me with his elbow. "Care to explain what he's going on about?"

I crossed my arms as I studied Parrish. "Sulfur and brimstone are very close in nature, but while the one is used for protection, witches or other spell casters turn sulfur into the darker element of brimstone with their magic. It's an element associated with protection...needed for black powers."

"Like what comes from Hell," Zach said, tucking Parrish's hand next to her. "You've smelled it before, haven't you, Brie? I've smelled it. You should recognize it the same as I do."

Something inside me cracked. He was right. I should have recognized the signs. We'd brought him back alright, but at a cost.

"I need you to reverse it," Zach said. "The spell. I can't live knowing I swapped my life for hers." He looked down at her and brushed her hair back so gently it hurt to watch.

My knees went to water, and I clutched at Layne until the strength came back.

Mouth dry and heart hammering away in my chest, I found the strength to inch toward the bed.

"Energy doesn't go away," I murmured as I sat on the bed next to Parrish. I took her hand in mine. It was still warm, evidence that she wasn't dead. Zach was right. Hospitals would do nothing for her. She needed something medicine couldn't give her.

I lifted her fingers to my nose and breathed in the smell of her. Brimstone. It clung to her fingers, her wrist, and when I let my nose travel up her arm, it was in her elbow and shoulder.

I turned my gaze to Layne. "He's right, Layne," I said. "No hospital is going to help. Not now." Tears stung the backs of my eyelids. "Death magic is powerful," I said. "But it's still magic."

"You brought me back," Zach said. "And I'm grateful you cared enough—"

"It was Parrish," I said, cutting him off. "She wanted you to live. She begged me to do the spell."

His eyes shone with unshed tears, and I saw how hard it was for him to swallow. He pulled his gaze from mine to study the woman lying on his bed.

When he spoke again, his voice was tight, as though he could barely work his throat muscles. "She loves me," he murmured, looking down at her. "Not the way

I want her to, but she loves me. That's enough for me, I think. I can die knowing that."

He squared his shoulders and faced Layne. "I'm sorry," he said.

And in the next moment, Zach, the mild-mannered doctor, leaped for his alpha, his clothes tearing as he shifted into his wolf.

# CHAPTER 20

ZACH WAS STILL CHANGING by the time he slammed into Layne, his hands sprouting claws an inch long. His teeth snapped as he aimed for Layne's throat. With a quick pivot, Layne managed to avoid the bite and was circling his pack member.

"Brie, you need to leave," he said.

"Don't hurt him."

"I'm not going to hurt him, the fool, no matter how hard he tries to make me."

I understood then what Zach intended. He wanted Layne to kill him again in the hopes it would free Parrish from the spell. That he could swap his life for hers, reverse the magic or force me to do the spell again.

But turning fulling into a werewolf obviously took time under a moon that wasn't full and it always looked painful.

"He can't shift the whole way," Layne said. "Not under a regular moon. And it's going to hurt to force his wolf out. He doesn't have the alpha energy to control it."

"That's a good thing, right?" I said, dodging out of the way as Layne tried his best to cage Zach against the wall.

"It might be good if he wasn't so damned determined to die. He'll use the pain to get the wolf really mad. I'm not sure I can hold him off alone without hurting him." He grunted as Zach slammed into him from the side.

He couldn't look at me. He was so engaged in fending off a snarling, half-transformed werewolf. Zach was a handsome man as a human. As a wolf, I expected he was beautiful. But as a creature that was neither, he was grotesque.

He was also strong. Not as strong as Layne, but with the latter doing his best to avoid hurting him, Zach had the advantage.

"Don't hurt him," I said as Layne ran the both of them into the wall.

"Brie, I'm still inclined to go feral. The wolf in me, the alpha, it wants to put this pup down."

That couldn't happen. Because if it did, and Layne killed Zach, I wasn't even sure if Zach died that I could do the magic again. While I'd brought him back to the land of the living, it had taken much of Parrish's life force to do so. What would the price be to bring her back? Presuming I even could.

I wouldn't risk it. That's what Abbi was trying to avoid. She knew the spell would take something dear. Magic, and especially black magic, always cost. I was a fool to think otherwise.

Zach would be sacrificing himself for nothing.

I had to stop this foolishness.

The only thing I could think to do was remove the reason Zach was fighting. My gaze darted to Parrish and my heart ached at what I was about to do. I rushed to her before I could change my mind.

I grabbed the pillow from beneath her head and laid it atop her face. Telling myself it would be alright, I exerted just enough pressure to feel her nose beneath the cushion.

Then I cleared my throat of the cottony ache that all but closed it up. Took a deep breath. And yelled Zach's name.

I had to shout twice before his gaze swung my way. His face went white, the half-formed snout with its thick pointed teeth crinkled. The eyes half-yellowed with wolf's rage swirled with hazel hues.

"Stop or I'll kill her," I said.

I expected him to charge me, but I didn't expect him to be so fast. He either got by Layne or Layne let him by. Either way, he was halfway across the room before Layne caught him by the waist and held him immobile against his chest.

Back to, Zach struggled and snarled, but he was unable to free himself from Layne's strong grip. Layne's eyes found mine. "Smart," he said.

I nodded mutely, chest sagging in relief. I pulled the pillow away from Parrish's face, but I held it aloft, ready to drop down again at any moment.

"We don't have time for this, Zach," I said. "I have to meet a witch and Parrish won't be able to return to us even if I did the spell right now."

Confusion crossed his face. He stopped struggling. I kept talking.

"I don't feel like myself," I told him. "That spell... it took something from me. It worked, yes. We were able to resurrect you, but I don't know if I can do it again. Not so soon. And I don't even know if the magics *can* be reversed, if it will let me use your energy again to affect her."

The snout slowly pulled back. His arms hung limply at his sides.

"Keep talking," Layne whispered in a hushed tone. "It's working."

I swallowed and laid the pillow on Parrish's chest. "I need more," I said. "More information, more understanding. More time. I'm not ready to perform this kind of magic. It's clear from the splitting headache, the fact that Parrish is dead and not dead, the way I can't seem to move my body anymore... the magic takes more finesse than I have right now. You don't want to die for nothing."

He sagged against Layne's chest. Intelligence came back to his gaze.

"Keep her alive," I said to him. "Keep her alive until I can figure this out."

"And then you'll kill me?" he asked, his eyelids going to half-mast. "Once you figure out how to do it without hurting someone else, you'll sacrifice me to save her?"

I swallowed hard at the inference, but I nodded. "I promise. If I can figure it out, I'll use your energy to bring her back."

He hung his head for a long moment, but then a heavy sigh escaped him. "Let me go, Layne," he said. "I'm sorry."

Layne released his arms, and his voice, when he spoke, was soft and compassionate. "I understand," he said. "I know the pain of losing a mate." His eyes darted to mine. "I won't hold it against you; my wolf understands better than you know."

Zach trod across the floor, naked, to pick up his clothes. He bent to scoop his shirt, his pants, and was pulling them on by the time he reached Parrish's side.

"She told me once how badly it hurt when her Vi was killed. I always thought I understood. I loved her, you see. I thought I could understand that kind of pain. But I couldn't. Not till now. It took losing her to really comprehend the grief, to really see how she went feral for so long."

He smoothed Parrish's hair back from her temple. "Go to your witch," he said to me. "Do what you have to. I'll stay with her. She's safe in my care." He looked up at me. "But if you discover a way to use me to bring her back, you will do so as soon as you can."

"I promise," I said.

He dismissed Layne and I both with a glance back to Parrish. I didn't need for him to tell us to leave. His dismissal was in every inch of his posture as he leaned over to check her vitals again. He was pulling a soft fleece blanket over her when we left.

"Do you think you can kill him?" Layne asked me when we reached the end of the driveway. He reached for my hand and I let him take it, happy to feel the warmth of his palm against mine. "I mean, really kill him if it means bringing her back?"

I squeezed his hand. "His isn't the first promise I've broken," I said. "And he's not the first person I've lied to. God help me, but I won't keep that promise. I'll have to find another way."

I sighed heavily. One more burden to carry when I didn't really know how I was going to handle all the others I was balancing. I released Layne's hand because it had become too present in my grip. Too honest. I had never been a good person, but lying to Zach and knowing I had made a promise I wasn't going to keep bothered me more than I wanted to admit.

More than that, I knew Parrish wouldn't want that sort of sacrifice.

"She'll go feral," Layne said, as though he'd picked up my train of thought. His hand I'd released had gone smoothly to the small of my back as he guided me to his car. "She's tough, that one, but even she won't be able to live with the guilt. She cares for him. She doesn't love him that way and never would, but she does care. His patient acceptance of her taunting drove her near crazy."

"He won't be able to live with it either," I said and peered at him over the roof of his car.

"At least we won't have to worry about him doing anything rash until there's no hope for Parrish." He tapped the roof four times, a sentimental echo of his friend's habit.

"Why do you think that is?" I asked. "If she cared so much, why try to hurt him so often?"

"It's a complex relationship between two complex people. If you knew their history, it might explain things, but it might be enough to say the gods can be cruel. They gave her a mate she couldn't love and him a mate he loved too much. She deals with it the only way she knows how. You might not realize this, but she has a habit of pushing people away when she thinks she cares too much." He buckled himself in and cast an eye in my direction as I pushed into my seat.

"I'm pretty sure I've noticed that trait."

"You, however, you she let get close. I'm not sure how I feel about that."

I chuckled. "I don't think you have to worry about her wooing me away from you. Maybe she just doesn't care about me as much as you think."

"Believe that if you want, but Parrish loves you. The wolf in me knows it. The wolf in her knows it. But we also know you are *my* mate. She'll respect that."

I looked out the window at the house and the pretty verandas with the flowers and shrubs enveloping it in a homey atmosphere, and I imagined her lying on that bed with Zach tending to her. In my mind, I could see again how distraught she'd been over Zach's death. She didn't love him that way, no, but neither did she love me that way.

Layne was wrong. How she felt about me was like the way she felt about Zach. I doubted anyone would touch Parrish's heart again the way Violet had. I was pretty sure she felt that to feel that way about any other person would be a betrayal.

Parrish was a one-woman, woman. Loyal to the core, she felt things deeply. Perhaps too deeply for her own sake.

"She'll be OK, won't she?" I said to the window because I couldn't bear to look at his face when he lied to me. I'd see the truth, and I wasn't ready for it.

From his side of the car, all I got was silence, so I expected he didn't want to lie to me as much as I couldn't bear to hear the truth.

I laid my hand on his thigh and felt the muscle move beneath my fingers. The last few hours were hard, and we both knew how hard the next few would be. My head ached as though someone had taken an axe to it. I lifted my fingers of my right hand and did a few simple, dexterity gestures. Each one was like I was trying to do them with my toes. Even the right side of my body felt a bit numb.

Anxiety, no doubt, and the aftereffects of the dark magic. Perhaps it didn't matter that my father was a necromancer and my mother was a goddess. I was still mortal and unversed in casting when it all came down to the end. What inherent nature took over where expertise left a gap, had probably left me with a lot of energy reserves depleted.

Not the sort of thing you wanted to have happen to you when you were about to face a crafty, ambitious witch.

I watched the streets go by in a blur as I thought about what we might face in the next hours. I might finally have all my mother's vessels in my possession, but if resurrecting one soul meant taking another, then how could I raise my mother and live with myself afterwards?

I'd suspected already that I'd have to sacrifice some part of myself to bring her back. But I'd also hoped the amulet Lucifer and I made together might negate that necessity.

What had happened with Parrish suggested Death needed payment. I wasn't ready to kill another human being, even if it was to restore my mother to her godhood. And I wasn't sure if I could let her take my life to do it. But where did that leave the cult? And what would that do to my bargain with Lucifer?

I might save my own life only to see people I loved suffer later.

"What do you think we'll find with Honey?" I asked finally.

"Well," he said with a thoughtful sigh. "I had to leave her with Emmett when Parrish sent me the text telling me I had to get my ass to Zach's. So I'm guessing we'll find a witch tied six ways to Sunday into some sort of prized hog arrangement."

I figured he meant it to sound light-hearted, but I didn't laugh. "I'm serious," I said. "Is it a trap?"

He squeezed my hand on his thigh. "I didn't mean to dismiss your worry," he said. "But I'm not about to let anything or anyone hurt you, Brie. No matter what we face, we'll do it together."

I sank into the seat and laid my head back, hoping the ache would just go away.

"You're tired," he said as he turned down the street that would bring us to his manse. "We'll get you a hot shower and some warm pajamas. And then you will sleep until it's time."

As much as I hated to think I was going to end up going unprepared to a meeting with Honey, the sound of a shower and rest seemed the most reasonable. There was no way I could face Honey again in the state I was in.

"You're probably right," I murmured, already feeling sleepy at the thought of warm sheets and a warm Layne lying next to me. "I don't think I'll be able to sleep, but I think I need to rest."

My fingers went to my temple, rubbing at the ache that seemed far deeper than a mere headache. And that worried me.

# CHAPTER 21

THERE WERE HOURS TO go before I had to face a witch with more experience than me and force her to hand over the things she'd stolen from me. The thought of a shower moved me silently along from the car to the manse as surely as Layne's gentle hand guided me there.

Neither of us spoke. I guessed we were both lost in the thought of what was going to come in the next short while. In the late afternoon hours, the sun had lost some of its warmth and I pulled my sweater closer around me.

Leaves from the maple trees on the property littered the grass. The scent of dying hydrangea blooms drifted on the breeze as the clusters caught and danced on the air currents. We shuffled up the paving stones to the back entrance, kicking through yellowed leaves, occasionally crunching them flat beneath our shoes.

It was a struggle at times to walk. I didn't realize how exhausted I was, but even the natural movement of a stride seemed almost too much.

"You're limping," Layne said as he rested his arm around my waist. "Did you hurt yourself?"

The worry in his voice bade me lift my eyes to his. "Just tired," I said.

That was all it took. In the next moment, he scooped beneath my knees and hugged me close, cradling me as he carried me the rest of the way to the manse. I leaned into him, listening to the sound of his heart. It raced along at a speed that seemed almost excited.

"I've got you," he said, and I believed him.

He carried me to his suite, where the familiar smell of him was almost overwhelming. A squeeze of emotion moved through my chest. I felt safe.

"You said your head hurt," he whispered as he laid me on the bed.

I nodded. "For a while there, I thought something was splitting it in half. But at least I didn't die."

I tried to smile for him, but could only manage a half grin. My head did still hurt, but it had dulled to an annoying ache that reached long tentacles of pain into my shoulders.

He climbed onto the bed with me and arranged me between his legs, my back against his chest.

"It's good you didn't die this time. It means you're getting some control, but I don't like that you're in pain. Thankfully," he said, "I have good hands."

With his hands in my hair, he exerted a small amount of pressure strategically along my scalp. Following the lines of my skull, he kneaded each millimeter, bit by bit, slowly, finding tension and working the spot until soft moans of relief escaped from me. The right side seemed worse, tighter, drew more of his attention. The sharp pain surrendered to his fingers as he found and worked each bit of tightness and knots till he made it to the base of my skull.

Seconds later, the tangle of ropes in my neck rooted his touch to the column of my throat. "Fuck," he said. "This goes all the way down."

A long moan of pleasure slipped through my lips. As the pain eased, he ignited a different sort of ache.

"You do have good hands," I quipped and relocated his hands to both of my breasts. "I've heard there are better things for headaches than massage."

He made a thoughtful sound that rumbled through his chest, vibrating into my back. My eyes closed, savoring the new massage more than the first. If I concentrated, I could almost ignore the headache that still nagged deep inside my skull.

"I promised you a shower," he said in a quiet voice thick with desire so languid I wanted to melt into him.

Before I could protest, his hands leaving my body, he had pushed off the bed and leaned over me instead.

Warm honey eyes roamed my face, fetching up on my mouth. I licked my lips. He was going to kiss me. My thighs squeezed reflexively.

"Is it cruel of me to want to fuck you right now?" he rasped. "When you're aching and tired, with God knows what awaiting you in a few hours?"

I shook my head and laid it on his chest. "It would be cruel if you didn't."

My hands slid down his waist to his hips. Before they could go further, he grappled my wrists in his hands.

"Are you sure?" he asked. "Is this really what you want right now?"

I nodded, holding his gaze. "It's not about want," I said. "It's about need." I tugged at my hands, trying to free them from his grasp, but he held them all the tighter, refusing to let go.

"You will not touch me," he growled. "This isn't about me right now. It's about you. And I plan to take my time showing you just how beautiful you are."

He held my hands up over my head as he unbuttoned my blouse with deliberate slowness. When my arms tired, and he was done, he let go, trusting I wouldn't interfere. He spread my blouse apart, then reached behind to unhook my bra.

He pulled lingerie and shirt off all at once and ran the backs of his knuckles along my breasts.

"You're so goddamned beautiful if I don't see the whole of you, raw and ready for me right now, I might not be able to control my wolf later long enough to drink you in."

I let him undress me, carefully, reverently, taking off every piece of clothing that remained. Each inch of skin he exposed drew his tongue or his fingers or his gaze in ways that brought shivers of delight and exquisite ache.

I was begging for him long before he hoisted me from the bed to straddle his waist. He stood, gravity and weight forcing me to slip from his waist lower, to his hips, making my legs coil around him tight.

His mouth took possession of mine the moment I dug my heels into his buttocks so I could piston myself along the thick hardness of him. He growled into my mouth and shoveled his hands into the curve of my backside, caging me against him and spreading me.

"You wear too many clothes," I said against his lips.

"You like my clothes," he said with a chuckle. "I'm incredibly well-dressed."

I snaked my arms tighter around his neck. The right one moved choppily, but I hooked my forearm with my left hand and held tight. "I like you better without them."

"Let's see how well you like me when you're spread over my bathroom vanity."

He strode with me to the bathroom, where he stuck the panel of switches with a flat palm. Every light came to life at the same moment, from the sconces lining the old-fashioned plaster walls to the vanity bulbs glowing softly with daylight hues to the overhead fixture with six white light bulbs.

I knew he could easily hold me without tiring, but he set me down on the wall length double sink vanity. The sharp cold of the tiles between the porcelain bowls made me gasp when my flesh touched down.

He peered down at me with eyes shuttered by lust.

"This isn't going to be quick," he said. "It's going to be long and lazy and by the time I'm finished with you, sleep will be the only thing your body can do. You'll rest like a baby. And if you don't, I'm going to do this again and again until you are a warm, squishy mess of exhausted clay."

My throat ached almost too much to nod at him, but when he spread me open and fell to his knees, it didn't hurt too much to let go a groan of pleasure.

He was right. It wasn't quick. The climax built beneath his mouth so slowly it was nearly painful to chase. As it rose, he backed off expertly, teasing other areas of my body and then returning. And only when I finally finished, did he peel down his trousers and scoop me onto his hips, letting me ride him until we both were satisfied.

Afterwards, feeling very much like warm putty, I let him lead me into a steaming shower and lather my hair. My limbs felt like lengths of silken scarves that had been beaten against a stone to come clean. As he held me close in the shower, and leaned me backwards to rinse the suds from my hair, I let everything go because I trusted him to hold me.

And he was right. When he put me to bed and pulled the sheets up around my chin, I had the best sleep of my life.

At least until he roused me hours later. It was dark in the room and I woke in confusion until he murmured to me that everything was fine.

"It's just time, is all," he said. "Emmett is waiting outside with the witch."

The witch. Honey. He wouldn't say her name, I noted. She'd been responsible for my near death and a dozen other atrocities. She didn't deserve to be called by anything other than the label that sounded like a slur on his tongue.

I sat up, naked but warm. I cast about for something to pull on over my skin and found his chest in the dark. My fingers trailed across the material of his T-shirt and a low rumble moved through him.

"Sweet Jesus, I thought I might be done with you for at least a dozen hours, but you're like a drug. You best get dressed before I change my mind about letting you go anywhere."

I stretched, lifting my arms high above my head, testing the way my muscles felt. They responded as they should, a bit slow and leaden, but that was no doubt the after effects of exertion. My headache had eased.

Whatever had caused the strange sensations in me after the spell seemed to have eased. There was some sluggishness on the right side, but nothing I couldn't manage.

I felt him move beside me, and realized he was standing beside the bed, not sitting on it. I flipped back the sheets and sought the floor for my clothes.

He passed me a bundle of fabric that turned out to be underwear, bra and thick yoga pants with a heavy plaid shirt once he turned on the bedside lamp and I could see what it was.

I dressed with him watching, my skin flushing as his eye traveled my skin.

"You move like a wolf," he said.

"I take it that's a compliment?"

"The best," he said and waited until I'd buttoned the plaid shirt before he gathered me into his arms. "Emmett says the witch is bringing us somewhere cold and damp." He kissed the top of my head. "Are you ready to do battle?"

"Let's hope it's not a fight and more a simple exchange of possessions." I angled my head back so I could see his face. "This isn't supposed to be a battle royale. She's just supposed to show me where she hid my mother's things."

He stepped back, dropping his hands to his sides, where they curled into fists.

"You know I will not let her leave there, right?"

I paused with my fingers on the waistband of the yoga pants as I tried to adjust them comfortably around my midsection. That he'd want vengeance was something I'd not truly considered. In truth, I'd not gone much farther than the possibility that she wouldn't bring us to the stash of things she'd stolen from me.

I scrubbed my hands through my hair. "You're a cop, Layne."

"I'm a werewolf first, a werewolf whose mate was hurt by this witch. As far as the world knows, she doesn't exist. She was supposed to have died half a century ago. I'll be more than happy to help her catch up with the devil. No one will miss her."

I crept toward him. "You don't want that," I said. "You don't want to be responsible for her death."

He canted his head at me as he slid his fingers behind my neck, rubbing the tension there that had returned with his words.

"I'm a predator, Brie," he said. "Not too long ago, I wasn't so civilized. You have no idea what I'm capable of, what I'm willing to do for you."

"Arrest her," I said.

He snorted. "Under what charges? She doesn't exist, remember?"

"Murder. Charge her with the deeds she's done."

He stepped into my space, pulling me against his chest. When he spoke, the words brushed over my hair. "You are too kind, and I love that about you. Because it's you, I will promise to try. But I won't make any promises to the end results," he said. "If she pulls anything, any little thing, she's dead. You understand this?"

I nodded.

He grunted in satisfaction. "Good," he said as he pulled away. "Emmett is waiting for us. You're ready?"

I nodded and he passed me a canvas bag. "To carry it all in. Emmett has orders to follow us back here when it's over."

I accepted the satchel and took a bracing breath. I didn't like going to the meeting with Emmett instead of Parrish. I didn't know him well. I knew Layne trusted him, but he didn't have a track record with me. I expected Layne felt much the same, but neither of us spoke of the woman who made as much impact by her absence as she did with her presence.

Trooping out to the vehicle, I expected to be stuffing ourselves in Layne's car, but it was a van that waited in the parking area of the rear of the manse. I took a moment to steel myself, breathing in the backwoods that Owen had left open behind his pack lands so the wolves could run.

I remembered standing outside with Parrish beside me as we released a resurrected owl. I had freaked her out over the animals raising from the dead from my touch. It had taken a bonding spell to remind her that she could trust me. I'd promised to never hurt her. I promised her she was my family. She had promised the same and then some. She'd protect me at all costs.

My heart squeezed at the thought of all we'd been through and now she was suffering some sort of near death that we didn't understand. What I was about to do, I did as much for her as my mother. I needed to reclaim my mother's power so the goddess Hecate could return to her form, but before I could do that, I had to learn how to guide a soul safely through the currents of death energy.

Only then would I dare attempt to call to the goddess. Only then could I hold my side of the bargain I'd made with the devil.

Because deals with the devil had a way of going wrong.

# CHAPTER 22

I LEFT THE MANSE as Brie, not Desiree. It made no sense to use the costume when Honey already knew it was me. Honey was already in the back seat with Emmett when we exited the manse and approached Layne's car. She wasn't tied up or gagged as I'd almost expected her to be. Rather, she sat casually with her hands primly resting in her lap.

Emmett kept giving her the side eye as if he thought she might turn into a cobra and strike him when he wasn't looking.

"We're trusting her now?" I said to Layne over the roof of the car.

"I trust Emmett," he said. "I told him who you are. He's onboard."

I said nothing to that. Pack bonds were still a mystery to me, but if Layne said Emmett could be trusted, then trust him, I would.

I slid into the passenger side, looking back at her and forcing her to meet my gaze. I wanted her to know this was me she was dealing with. I wanted her to know I was going to go to the mat to fight her and her coven and I'd do what I had to in order to break them.

If she saw all that in my gaze, she did nothing but smirk. When she yawned and dragged her eyes away from mine to look out the window, I hated her more in that instant than I thought I could hate anyone.

I slid into my seat and buckled up. Layne dropped his elbow on the backrest of his seat and angled his head toward her.

"So, where are we going?"

He was abrupt, no hint of emotion in his voice. I admired that. I didn't think I could keep the loathing from mine.

She swiveled her gaze to his and the glow from the backyard lights cut half of her face in two with shadow. "The old part of the city," she said. "There's a burnt out church right in the heart of it."

"The old Gothic cathedral and rectory," he murmured. "I know it. Burned three decades ago."

She played with the hem of her shirt. "It has a lovely underground crypt. Rumor has it the priest set the place on fire."

She looked up at him through her eyelashes. "I wonder what would have made a priest do such a thing." She lifted one shoulder in a shrug. "Lucky for me, I guess."

He made a noncommital sound as he turned back to the steering wheel. His hand found mine where it sat on my lap, and he squeezed my fingers reassuringly. "A few hours more," he said and glanced at the clock on his dash. "Ninety minutes till the witching hour."

From the back seat, Honey hummed a snippet of tune that sounded more like a chant than any song. I chose to ignore her.

"Emmett," Layne said. "If she so much as picks her nose, you will subdue her, you understand?"

Emmett's answer was a grunt that sounded very much like he wanted to do more than subdue the witch. I felt much better after that.

We drove in tense silence, with Honey only speaking up when she thought we could take a shortcut. Without comment, Layne followed them, and when we pulled into the long drive that lead to the cathedral, the very air in the cabin changed. I felt the electricity moving over my skin.

"There's magic here," I breathed.

"No shit, Sherlock," Honey said from the back seat.

We piled out to stand on the curved pavement of the driveway. I imagined Honey was drinking in the magic I sensed in the air. It was thick as fog and if I looked just so at the massive building that hunkered into the lot like a sleeping, black shrouded giant, I thought I could see the air wavering around it like heat on hot pave.

I remembered the church from my childhood, but then it had been a thriving community of believers. I didn't remember it burning, and guessed I'd run away by then. The church I remembered had been built of gray stone with turrets that made precarious squatting places for dead-eyed stone gargoyles. It wasn't so magnificent as Notre Dame, but it had the same feel.

"The items are in the crypt," Honey said, shattering the crystalline silence.

She gestured for us to follow her to the left of the building, where an overhang of scorched and splintered wood perched atop stone pillars.

"There are eight steps," she told us. "All granite and about two feet high, so mind your feet."

Layne waved Honey and Emmett forward first, and then he took position next, leaving me to bring up the rear. One after the other, we picked our way through the arched entry with its burnt out and collapsing roof and into a stairwell with granite treads so old grooves dug out the centers of the rock.

Spiders had nested in the gaps of stone and mortar and spun their nets out across the entrance. Those cobwebs reached for me as Layne brushed aside the webbings broken by Emmett and the witch. Their threads of gossamer clung to my hair, and I tried not to get creeped out by the sticky way they refused to brush away.

The door to the actual crypt was several paces from the stairwell nestled between two cast iron sconces that had rusted and burned and now hung crookedly on their rusty nails. The frame had warped and twisted what remained of the door. Several rotten slats littered the floor, leaving a gap of space in the door that we could see through.

Light came from inside. Impossible, but light just the same.

"Fucking creepy," Emmett muttered and Honey looked back at him.

"Scared, little wolf?" she asked.

He squared his shoulders. "A man who is not afraid of the unknown is stupid. A wolf who isn't careful is dead."

She grunted and stepped aside. "After you, then. Let's see what you've got."

Emmett shot a glance over his shoulder at Layne, who nodded.

"I'd rather have her out here with us," Layne said, and Emmett sketched a quick bow in response, then barged through what remained of the door. It splintered again as it flew open and banged against something on the inside.

The wood came to a creaking rest somewhere between open and closed. Honey strolled through as though an old world gentleman had just escorted her to a fancy ball. I clutched at the hem of Layne's jacket, afraid to get caught alone outside if something were to happen and leave me alone.

Inside, the crypt looked pristine. Whatever fire had taken its toll on the cathedral above had not touched the brickwork that rose from a herringbone brick floor to several arches that supported the ceiling above.

Thick hewn rafters, though shrouded in spiderwebs, remained intact. I guessed the rafters of the crypt acted as foundational joists for a tiled floor above, where the church's real face was.

From my spot just inside the door, I noted several arches lining the space and leading to a single stone altar at the other end. Beside me, to the left, it looked as though there was a multitude of nooks and crannies. Some of them wooden crates and wicker baskets that appeared as old as the stones that surrounded them.

My mother's canine familiar moved out from the shadows behind the altar, her head low, eyes blazing. I doubted anyone else saw it but me, but seeing Abbi there gave me no comfort. Too often, she acted as a harbinger of terrible things.

"This cathedral has been here for at least two hundred years," Honey said. "The crypt for longer." She strolled toward the altar, Emmett trailing along closely behind her. With a flick of her wrist, a hundred candles or more, scattered throughout the space, came to life.

From sconces, and bowls, and resting places within crannies and stones, they threw off an even eerier glow than whatever magic illumination she had left behind when she'd been there last. The scorching fragrance of burned wicks and wax permeated the air quickly.

"I don't give a flying fuck about the history of the place," Layne growled. "We didn't come for a sightseeing historical tour. Get Brie's things and let's be done with this."

She pivoted to face him, still walking backward. "So impatient," she said. "I told you we came here at the witching hour for a reason. You don't just grab for sacred objects and run. There are protocols to follow."

I came up beside Layne. "Meaning she spelled them," I said bitterly. "My mother's things. She spelled them and has to undo the casting in order for us to take them from this place."

Honey smiled and tapped her nose with her finger. "Smart for a new witch."

"I'm not a witch," I said, with venom in my tone. "I'm a demi-god and you'd do well to remember it."

At that, she laughed. "Consider me corrected. But whatever you are, none but the witch who hid them here can take them from this place." She cocked her head thoughtfully. "Well, the owner can, but I doubt Hecate will be able to claim them. At least not in her present state." She gave me a meaningful look.

I would have charged her, but Layne held me back with a controlled and calm grip. "Let her," he said. "More reason for me to tear her heart from her chest and eat it in front of her dying eyes."

Any other man might have made those words sound like a bluster, but the deadly seriousness of it made Honey's hand climb to her throat. She knew it was not an idle threat.

"I might need some help," she said, letting her gaze trail over her shoulder to the altar. "There's a sarcophagus behind the altar, but it's pretty snug in its little crevice."

I moved forward automatically, but again, Layne hooked me by the elbow. "I'll go," he said. "You stay back with Emmett."

With a nod, I let him go. Honey stepped neatly to the side, and the way she moved, the look on her face as she did so, set off alarm bells in my head. Abbi's front paws stomped, her lips peeled back. It was only then, as the sconces flared, no doubt from some infusion of her magic, that I saw what had been hidden by shadows before.

I turned to Emmett. "A Hecate's wheel," I said. "She's cast a circle."

I was already speeding toward Layne when my mate lifted his gaze to mine. "Don't," he said, racing back the way he'd come. "It's a trap."

The symbol had been cast in blood, the same as the one in the flophouse where Honey and her coven had sacrificed members of the coven to grant them power. It was the same as the one I'd found in the basement where Farrell had taken me to await the waning moon. The same as the ones I'd seen my mother draw out in salt and in blood depending on her spell.

I knew without having to be told why Honey had really brought us here. We were sacrifices.

I expected Layne to break through long before I reached him, but he hit the line of the circle and halted dead in his tracks.

I was still a few paces away, and confused that he couldn't come closer, I paused, instinct bidding me to stay where I was. I knew Honey's work well by now. Layne couldn't leave the circle. And that meant he was the one she was going to sacrifice. Him. Not me.

I spun to face her, ready to throw whatever magic I could at her. She stood out of my reach. With a flick of her wrist, the sconces flared brighter, casting a pinkish glow over the circle. I noted all the items I'd come to rescue lining points along the wheel. My amulet to the north, the grimoire to the south.

"You bitch," I said and drew my hand back as I flew at her. I might not understand how to wield my power as effortlessly as she did, but I could fight.

She stood motionless, waiting. Only when I was within striking distance did she flick her hand in my direction.

I fell to my knees as if someone had knocked the backs of my legs with a bat. I felt the blow physically, and I groaned when I went down.

"Emmett," I breathed out. "Layne. Get Layne out of there."

Honey's owl-eyed and innocent gaze flew to Emmett. "Emmett," she said. "What did your alpha say to you when we left?"

I looked at Emmett, whose face had screwed up into a mask of remorse and guilt. "He said I was to follow your orders."

Layne howled when he heard that.

"Traitorous bastard," I said to him, but he held my eye as though I was nothing. Certainly not his alpha's mate. He belonged to Owen, not Layne. "I'm going to kill you," I said icily. "When all this is done, I'm going to burn you from the inside out."

If he felt the remorse any more keenly, he said nothing. Instead, he shuffled toward Honey as though he was a marionette being gathered in by its makers' hands.

I felt Layne's energy as he prowled around the circle. I didn't dare look at him. His every movement was animalistic, and I had my doubts he was wholly a man anymore.

I pushed myself onto my palms and feet, looking up at Honey as she gathered Emmett in the way a mother hen might. She ran her hand over his hair as she watched me with an interested expression.

"I'm impressed, Brie," she said. "Usually, when I cast a rigor mortis spell, the poor subject can't move."

She crossed one arm over her chest and propped her elbow on it, her finger trailing her chin thoughtfully. "Maybe I need a bit more blood."

I knew what she was going to do, but I wasn't ready for it, even if I had made it to a sort of runner's lunge. She lifted her face to the vaulted ceiling and uttered a few words of incantation. As though he was an extension of her arm, Emmett lifted his wrist to his mouth. He bit down. Hard.

Blood dribbled from his wrist. I cried out too late, but he wouldn't have listened to me, anyway. From behind me, Layne let go a piercing and enraged howl. Fully wolf then. He'd shifted at some point and was no longer a man to reason with or speak to.

As though I didn't want to believe the evidence of my ears, I cast a look over my shoulder. No man met my gaze. Instead, a huge black wolf stared back at me. He leapt toward Honey, only to rebound against an invisible force.

As he hit the stone floor, he twisted, his front paws clutching at the grout even as his hind end struck the floor.

A heartbeat went by and he charged again. And again. And each time he came up against the same force. Each time he stuck it, a slash ripped over his hide. Blood splattered every which way.

"Stop," I said to him. "Please, Layne. Stop. You're going to hurt yourself."

Going to? He was already a bloody mess and still he went for Honey and still the magic took its toll.

I swung my gaze back to the witch. "I'm going to kill you too," I said. "You can't save yourself now. Not even if you give me all my mother's things back."

She cocked her hip, shoving Emmett aside. He fell like a rag to the stone floor and stayed there on his hands and knees.

"You really think I was going to give you those sacred objects?" She laughed. "You're a fool. But I'm not. You think I don't know you would kill me anyway once you have what you want? I haven't stayed alive all these years by trusting anyone other than myself."

"You're wrong," I said. "We would have spared you. Had you shown some remorse. Some humanity." I collapsed back onto my haunches, the effort of trying to push through the magic too much to keep up.

She stooped to dip her fingers into the pool of blood around Emmett. "What has humanity done for me?" she said, drawing symbols on the stone floor, moving from one side to the other, turning to draw more behind her and then again to the front. "My only hope was the coven. But they decided all I was good for was as a sacrifice. I'll kill them all before I let that happen."

"Is that what this is all about?" I asked her. "To gain you power to take over the coven?"

"Take over?" she barked out a harsh laugh. "I'm going to *become* the coven. And to do that, I believe you all need to die."

# CHAPTER 23

IN THE NEXT INSTANT, the nooks and crannies that held the bones of ancient nuns and priests came alive with the sounds of bones scraping against each other as they untangled themselves from ages of rest.

One by one, thigh bones, skulls, and skeletal hands sailed through the air at me.

I was able to shield myself at first. Tossing my arms up to hide my face and the top of my head, I could brunt the blows. But the crypt was ages old. There were a lot of skeletons. And each bit of debris and bone that freed itself from confining places became renewed projectiles as they struck me and fell with a clatter to the stone floor.

Layne's fierce growl was all but lost in the din of rubble striking stone and flesh, and my own grunts of discomfort and pain. By the time a third whirlwind of yellowed bone came swirling upon me, I abandoned hope of protecting myself.

The witching hour had come, and Honey had used the energy of the moment to enhance her magic. But if she was a witch able to use the power of that dark hour, then surely I, as the daughter of the witch queen, could bring that power to bear as well.

I was aware of Emmett's sagging form on the stone floor as he hunched over himself, bleeding from the wound he'd inflicted on his wrist. Honey had abandoned him after she'd used his blood to trigger her magic. Now, he was limp and unable to shift, no doubt because of one more piece of nefarious magic.

Behind me, Layne's prowling created a tension all its own as he slammed repeatedly into the barrier Honey had cast with the circle. Each thrust reverberated as keenly as if it were a physical wall he shouldered into time and again. It was a soundless force except for the corresponding snarls of fury, but those were enough to make the hairs rise on the back of my neck.

I took another blow, this time from a skull that cracked as it hit my shoulder. My eyes followed its path to the floor and beyond when it rolled a foot away, the thick fracture threatening to break the dead's skull in half.

I ached everywhere. The burning around my eyes suggested my skin was swelling near my cheekbones. Several gashes from rib bones had torn into my hands as I'd blocked them from my face.

Still, the bones came. Fast and swift, I knew it would take only one, pointed the right way, to pierce through vulnerable areas of my body, but I couldn't keep myself fully covered.

Time moved like strobe lights. Blackness flickered through the space and I wasn't entirely sure if it was the mass of missiles coming at me and blocking my view, or if Honey was doing something to the light.

I had to fight back. I couldn't count on Layne or Emmett or even Abbi, who was straining at the barrier, tearing at empty space with her teeth as she tried to free Layne. In a flash, it occurred to me that we hadn't been feeding her lately. She no doubt was using up whatever magic she had just to stay here, let alone try to break through the barrier.

She was losing that battle; I knew. She moved slower. The denseness of her body fading from view. It wouldn't be long before she'd be a mere ghost of herself, bound in this crypt by Honey's spell.

A pause in the projectiles gave me the opportunity to hunch downward, my shoulders set to take the brunt of the next blow. Honey's voice raised above the din as her lilting tenor released words of power to the air.

My initial panic and reaction to the unexpected assault had dulled. It was time to find the calm I needed to shut her out. To shut it all out: the blows, the fear, the sudden realization that I was powerless.

My fingers scrabbled for the nearest bone that hadn't yet risen again to attack me. Several times, I reached for one only to have it shoot away from me, gaining momentum to strike again.

Blood trickled down my cheek from a cut beneath my eye. The warmth of it burned a trail to my nostril and pooled there as I searched for yet one more shard of bone. My fingers were cut and abraded. Blood seeped from my fingers and hands. I was pretty sure a cut had opened up behind my temple because my hair felt wet.

Blood. So much of it. Blood pooled around Emmett. Dripping from me in tiny rivers.

Blood.

It was that moment of realization, that instant when I understood just how bad this was going that I realized I had exactly what I needed to fight back. I just had to find the courage to do so. The exact moment I knew I could change the tide, a wave of laughter boiled up through my throat.

"Not so smart after all, are you, bitch?" I ground out as I took a deep, bracing breath.

She must have heard me, because she paused in her incantation to swivel her gaze in my direction. I saw the look that crossed her face when I pushed myself onto my knees, when I heaved myself to a doddering stand.

I recognized the flash of fear that crossed her expression, and maybe it wasn't just because I had found my feet and legs. Maybe it was because whatever she saw on *my* face told her she couldn't win. Not now.

I blew out the bracing breath in a long stream and outstretched my arms, reaching with my fingers for the air, leaving my core vulnerable.

The clatter of bones racing each other toward me, vying to be the first to pierce my skin, echoed around the chamber like bats echo-locating.

I thought I heard Layne howl, but it was such a pained thing, so out of character, I wasn't sure if it was his voice or mine.

All I knew was that the moment a rib bone went into my belly, I saw the expression of triumph on Honey's face fade.

No doubt she understood what I did the moment my hand went to my chest. I staggered, but stood. I winced and shrank inward as my instincts bade me protect my softest flesh, but I held my ground. A smile moved my lips around the blood that burbled up through my throat.

"I win, bitch," I said, but I doubt she could make it out around the crack of magic that flew from my fingers when I touched down on my runes. My mother's runes. The runes that tied me to her and her magic and made my blood—blood Honey had spilled—transform into that of a demi-god.

My head dropped back. I didn't control it anymore. I moved out of pain and exhaustion, all my efforts going to my legs.

The magic building around me lifted me from my feet. The relief of not having to exert myself to remain standing was so acute, a sigh escaped me.

My head rolled to the side. I caught sight of Layne, fully transformed, panting as he watched me, frozen by worry or hope. His eyes were beams of yellow light in a swath of darkness, only relieved by splotches of red.

Sacrifice. That's what this moment needed. Honey had known it, which was why she'd forced Emmett to mortally wound himself. But he'd not cut the artery, as it seemed, because the blood was seeping out, not pulsing with each heartbeat.

Smart lady. Keep the blood flowing long enough to trigger her magic and hold on to it as she worked the spell. I had the feeling once she was done with the casting, she'd finish Emmett with a slice across his throat.

Layne was sacrificing what he could for me.

My offering was just the one to tip the scale.

I tried to smile for him but found I couldn't move my lips. If words of power were to be uttered, they would have to be from the language of pain and certain death. I traced one rune, imagining it in my head as I'd seen it dozens of times in the mirror these weeks. My fingers slid sideways, finding the next and knowing it by the heat it sent out, a sort of braille for the gods.

Honey saw me. I know she did, because she shouted at me and the sound of bones and projectiles whirling around me stopped. The clatter of them falling was like teeth chattering in the cold. Did she not realize my magic was the magic of death? Bones and blood made up the energies my power danced upon.

I could have looked at them. I could have looked at her.

I had eyes only for Layne, though. I held his gaze like it was my anchor, and he held mine.

He roared one more time and charged the barrier. I thought he might break through, but he needn't bother. A moment more and the magic would be an unstoppable swell. Once it was pregnant enough, it would blast into Honey and her magic would scatter.

The moment was coming. I felt it. My eyes squeezed closed of their own accord, spent of the visions of death and wanting no more. Honey made a small sound just as I felt the charge of magic. I remembered the way John Smith had laid his palm down on my blooded skin back in the hotel. I'd not realized what he'd done then, tracing the runes, speaking in the language of blood.

It was going to be over. Moments more. And yet I heard one more roar rip through the chamber. Layne. He sounded terrified. My eyes flew open.

Just in time to see Honey charging me.

In one motion she yanked the rib bone from my stomach. It sucked out of me and pulled with it a shriek of pain even as she simultaneously shoved me backward.

My hands fell away to my sides. The magic hiccupped as I careened along the air currents and landed on the stone floor far, far behind where I'd been.

The impact took my breath. It took several gasps to catch it and when I did, I curled into myself, cowering on my side as I cupped my wound. I couldn't feel any blood. When I peered at my fingers, they were clean.

No blood. What I'd bled, she'd taken. I saw it swirling above me, out of reach, swimming around the vaulted ceiling like a hologram.

Honey laughed. Maniacal. Relieved. She'd taken not just my blood, but any means to access my magic. No knife. No sharp and pointed bone shard. I was as good as any blunt object with no one to wield it.

I pushed myself onto my elbows, my head swimming, vision nothing but a swirl of colors. Half a second later, the hot breath of a canine—or wolf?—swam over my face. Layne. I was inside the circle. He whined and laid down on me, protecting me.

Honey's voice rose an octave. "I won't let you take what I've worked all these decades for," she shrieked.

Mad. She was completely mad.

She thrust a hand, palm forward, in the circle's direction, sending a blast of magic in our direction.

I tried and failed to shove Layne from my midsection, where he'd dropped his massive paws to protect me. My hands fell onto the ruff of his neck and I buried my fingers in his fur. He felt so warm. Everything felt so warm. Like a roaring campfire blazing through a cold night.

Layne whined again and nudged me with his nose. I blinked up at him. Yellow eyes stared back at me.

His whimper came from deep in his wolf's throat. A moment later, he shoved his muzzle under my back, rolling me to my side.

That was when I realized what she'd done. Flames circled us, drawing out the casting circle with white fire. I gaped at the flames licking upward, gaining height as the magic grew.

"I'm sorry you won't be able to raise your mother," Honey said from somewhere beyond the flames. "But since you were just going to die bringing her back anyway, at least I can use what's leaking out of you right now."

At her words, Layne swiveled his massive head back to me. He snuffed at my neck. The eyes grew hard and angry. The secret I'd kept from him, the thing he would never have let me do, swimming in the reflection of his eyes.

I swallowed down the panic that this massive werewolf might have lost the man's mind within at the thought that I was about to die.

A moment later, beyond the ever-growing flames around the circle, I heard a familiar voice. Male. Commanding. Through a break in the flames, I saw Emmett twitch at the voice despite how close to death he had to be.

That voice made one command. Short. Succinct. Yet it made Honey pause. She turned away from the fire and toward the voice.

Shift, that voice said. And damned if Emmett didn't try. I felt the power of the alpha waver through the air like the radiant heat of the fire.

Layne growled and bolted for the barrier even though the flames were still burning high, turning the blood to ash. His front paws pranced and danced on the floor with impatience.

I knew the voice just as Emmett and Layne did. But while they responded to the sound of their alpha's voice with hope, I knew the truth. It didn't matter if I was about to die.

Owen was here to help Honey kill us all.

# CHAPTER 24

IF I WAS GOING to die, I decided I was going to die on my feet. It took all I had to push myself onto my feet. I gripped my belly tight, the pain of the wound razoring through me with each movement.

From behind Layne, I faced the alpha of the Garder pack as he strolled toward his fallen pack member. Honey watched him moving with that insanely lithe grace more like a great cat than a wolf.

"Shift," he said again.

Emmett could barely lift his head, but when he did, just an inch off the stone floor, his eyes had become yellow lamp lights in the crypt's gloom. Honey took note with a casual, almost unfeeling glance.

"He's going to need more than an order to heal, I'm afraid," she said.

"What have you done to him?" Owen demanded.

She shrugged. "I needed a sacrifice." She jerked her chin toward Layne who was still prowling the circle and throwing himself against the barrier. "Would you rather I used your son?"

Owen's jaw tightened as she all but dismissed him, strolling toward the circle to watch Layne. "He's quite something," she said, eying the wolf that snarled at her from inside the circle. "I might keep him when this is over."

A low, thunderous growl moved throughout the chamber and I couldn't be sure if it came from Layne or his father or from them both at once. Honey seemed to think it was Owen because she faced him with her arms crossed over her chest.

"Careful," she said. "This isn't the time to regret decisions you made a century ago. But at least you're here. Just in time, too."

She flicked a gesture toward the relics that somehow lay untouched on the points of the circle. "I need you to retrieve those for me."

Owen's gaze swiveled stoically toward the casting circle, and if he took in the sight of his own son, snarling and gnashing his teeth as he fought against the force of the magic keeping us both trapped within it, he gave no sign.

"I will tend to my pack mate first," he said and those long legs of his ate up the distance between him and Emmett before Honey could protest. Which, of course, she did.

Owen ignored her and laid his hand on Emmett's shoulder. "Shift," he said.

The entire space filled with a shuddering power that had nothing to do with the magic of the circle or the witch who glared at the alpha of the Garder pack. This magic was all for Emmett, and it was enough that I saw him tremble beneath Owen's hand.

He wanted to change. He needed to change. He just couldn't.

Honey was unmoved. "He stays," she said. "I still have need of him."

Owen was still on one knee, his free hand slung over his thigh as he tried to impress Emmett with his will, but he spared a glare for the witch. "You've taken enough," he said. "This wasn't part of the deal."

"The *deal*," she said, emphasizing the word. "Was not with me. It was with the coven. I don't answer to their bargains."

Owen's fingers moved to Emmett's throat and when they came away again, he tested the stickiness of the blood by running his thumb over it thoughtfully.

"You. The coven. Does it matter?" he asked. "It's the same end."

I saw his throat move as he swallowed. Nervous. I'd seen enough anxiety in my field to know it when I saw it. I inched toward Layne almost intuitively, limping as my legs protested movement.

Honey groaned with impatience. "I suppose I should be grateful the deal works the same for you."

She edged along the circle, close enough for the firelight to wash her face with orange illumination but not near enough to Layne or I to touch. Her eye kept trailing to the relics.

"Perhaps it doesn't matter to you which is your master: me or the coven. But it matters to me."

"She is betraying the coven," I said, projecting my voice over the flames.

"I am not betraying them," she lamented loudly. "They betrayed me. They want to sacrifice me. They want to use my blood to consecrate their spell. Me. The witch who has brought them closer to their goal than they've been in a hundred years."

"So you stole the relics they've been searching for and are using them for your own ends." Owen's hand made a small soothing motion between Emmett's shoulders. "What would they think of that? Will they let you live?"

Her voice rose shrilly, bouncing off the rock and brick and grout all around us.

"They already tried to kill me," she said. "I'm not about to let them succeed. You came here for a reason, Owen," she said with contempt dripping from the syllables of his name in a way that made Layne's body vibrate beneath my hand. "You came here because I told you to come. You came because you knew the witch who will end your son's life is here in this very crypt and you want to end her before she can take your son's life."

Owen's voice went soft. "I know who she is," he said, and for a second, his gaze flitted to me. "She couldn't hide her true self from me beneath a bit of bad costume makeup."

His expression urged my arms around my midriff, my chin to lift defiantly. Honey watched it all with little emotion. Instead, she pivoted in her bare feet, and I wondered when she'd taken her shoes off, why she was suddenly naked when I hadn't noticed her taking off a stitch of clothing.

"You know the truth, Owen. The only way you can save your son now is to do as I say."

"You tricked us all," Owen ground out. "You betrayed your coven. You betrayed me."

She barked out a harsh laugh. "A witch does not betray a tool," she said. "You are mine to use. Like a candle or an herb. The bargain you made with the coven all those generations ago is extended to me as long as I am in the coven. So I'm using it. Your deal with them is a deal with me."

"What I did," he said. "I did for my pack, to separate them from this madness." His hand went to Emmett again, and the younger wolf leaned against him. "You may use me for whatever nefarious deeds you wish, but you have no right to use my pack mate for your dark magic. That was not the bargain. You have the use of *my* body. *My* blood. That was the deal."

Honey stomped toward him, completely unafraid, and I knew the truth of her belief. She owned him because the coven owned him. She wore that entitlement the way she wore her infuriated expression, and it was plain she wanted him to understand exactly how much she commanded him as she stormed the yards to his side.

She was a few feet away still when Owen dropped his gaze again to Emmett and whispered something to him. This time I saw a flare of color move through the younger man's eyes.

"You will shift, Emmett," Owen said. "If you die, you die a wolf. If you don't die, then you run. Go to Zach. Do you hear me?"

Emmett lifted his gaze past Owen, over his shoulder, toward me. I flinched at the look of pain on his face until I realized he wasn't looking at me at all. He sought the wolf who stood inside the circle with me.

Layne. The wolf halted his pacing as Emmett's eyes fell on him. His eyes had narrowed to slits. A shiver of power moved over my skin and I realized it wasn't just Owen's pack magic rushing to Emmett for help. It came from both the alpha and his second.

Layne was giving his pack mate what he could. I dropped my hand to his ruff and felt the vibration in his spine as he offered what he had.

"More," I whispered to him. "Give him what he needs. We'll face the bitch together once he's safe."

On her side of the circle, Honey had taken her place beside Owen. She held one hand behind her back.

"Enough already," she said.  "The hour is dying. We need to finish. I want you to fetch the relics." She planted a bare foot against Emmett's ribs and pushed, using what looked like all her weight.

Layne and Owen both snarled in unison as her foot met Emmett's body. The sound that came from Layne was a horror, but it was perfectly natural considering he wasn't human. But in Owen, still in his mortal guise the sound was so unnatural it made my spine want to creep out from beneath my skin.

As if that moment was what Emmett needed to shift, the awful noise of his bones cracking as they reshaped themselves echoed through the air.

Owen moved subtly, but it was fast and it was efficient, and in that one moment, he blocked Honey's arm as it came down with a blade toward Emmett's throat.

The man buckled as he transformed, and then he staggered as he almost stood but fell on all fours.

Fabric fell in tatters to the stone floor as his clothes ripped into scraps. A flash of skin caught the candlelight, then disappeared in the thicket of fur that sprang forth from every inch.

He cried out, the pain of the change and its force carrying on his voice.

Beneath my hand, Layne shuddered. I saw Owen shudder. Honey screamed in fury as the wolf darted back down the hallway and tore through the door that hung crookedly on its hinges.

"I needed him, you bastard," she shrieked. She stabbed downward with the blade, catching Owen in the shoulder.

She stepped back, chest heaving, as a spray of blood bloomed upward. His hand flew to cover the wound, his lips peeled back.

"That's all on you, you stupid bastard," she said. "Don't take that tone of face with me."

She flicked the tip of the blade toward the circle, pointing to the spot where Layne and I both had begun to pace in different directions.

"Get me the goddess's things," she demanded. "The fire has consecrated them by now and cleared any protective magic."

She took several deliberate paces to the altar and turned a brass knob. A door popped open, showing a copper chest.

"All that remains is this," she said, holding the knife in her hand like she was about to stab something with it. "Lay it onto the altar for me."

Owen sent her a sullen, hateful look, but he rose to his feet without a single look toward the door to see if Emmett had made it.

I prayed for Emmett's sake he'd healed enough to make it to Zach, but even then, I didn't know what he'd find. I sank to my haunches, spent and trembling. Every inch of my body ached. Dizziness swam in and out of my vision, warping everything I tried to blink into focus.

Beside me, Layne bristled and padded back and forth from one foot to the other.

Owen watched Honey closely as he crossed the chamber to her side. He stooped to pull on the circular handle that stuck out of the side of the chest. Without any seeming effort, and with Honey standing over him, he yanked the chest free of its cranny.

He two-handed it into his arms and rounded the altar to lay it atop. The scraping sound as copper met stone made me wince. Layne let go a low-throated growl.

Honey sighed a beleaguered, tolerant sigh. She hoisted the blade high.

"You wanted your pack member free? Well, now I suppose you'll have to pay his price."

She slashed sideways, with the blade's edge facing Owen. His head jerked and for a second, I thought she'd cut his throat. I cried out in shock and fear and Layne leaned into me, adding warmth to my cold body. His entire side quivered.

Then Owen fell back onto his palms, his chest straining in an arch toward the ceiling. Blood pooled around him.

Honey began chanting, ignoring the pool of red staining the floor as it ran from Owen's fingers and dripped to the stone until she bent to smear both hands into the fluid.

Rising again, she traced her cheekbones with her fingers, leaving streaks of blood that dribbled down toward her chin.

Her chant began then. I caught sight of Abbi behind her, nothing but a faded bit of white eyes like a deer in headlights. Beside me, Layne all but vibrated.

I thought of the last time they had trapped me in the coven's dark circle. Back in the hotel room where I'd nearly died, but for Abbi's interference. She'd used the magic stored in Farrell's body. She shared it with John Smith, whom I'd called to and whom Abbi had forced into the circle. He'd been able to use the magic of my blood to shield us from the coven's spell and throw it back at them.

There was no John Smith this time. The binding of my mother's vessels also bound the dog and the man, the same as it did me.

"It's over," I said as Honey's voice warbled on the air currents with each syllable. Not that I thought her magic was greater than mine. Not that her power could be called to easier.

It was just that this time, I had no John Smith to cut me deeply enough to bring my blood and connect with it like an electric charge. No blade with which to access my magic.

There was only me and a werewolf in the circle.

I stared at the massive face looking down into mine, the love and anger and hope in that gaze.

And I knew he was going to make all the difference.

# CHAPTER 25

THE WITCHING HOUR WAS dying. I felt it deep in my marrow. One glance toward Honey, where she stood at the altar, and I knew she was in the final throes of her spell. The candles guttered. Owen sagged against the other side of the altar, facing her, his palms supporting him.

At first, I thought he was watching Honey, but there was no response from him when her gaze darted down at him or when she so obviously indicated him with her spell. Whatever had his attention, it wasn't the witch who had stabbed him and was planning to use the rest of his blood to trigger the worst of her spell.

He was looking at something beyond the two of them, something I recognized. Two beams of whitish light that stared out from the shadows where Abbi crouched, watching the entire tableau as impotently as I did.

A muscle moved beneath his blood-stained dress shirt, jutting his shoulders into a tense knot. He wasn't sagging onto the altar any longer. He was bracing.

With a word of power from Honey, the lid of the chest swung open with a creak and a plume of dust. The witch dropped her head back at the same instant, a sign that it had been her magic that had cracked it open.

The unmistakable sound of bones clacking together with an awful echo reached me and I knew without having to see inside what the chest contained.

If I was unsure before, in the next moment, a blur of murky black smoke rose from the chest. I knew the shape of it like I knew my reflection in the mirror. I knew it like I knew the familiar Owen stared at so fixedly. I knew it like I'd known the shade that had visited me in my shop in the early weeks of this whole ordeal.

That chest held my mother's bones. It was her shade lifting from the copper casket these black witches had stuffed her into.

Honey had all my mother's vessels. What she'd not possessed before, she'd gained access to while she'd been at the manse. Either she had stolen them or Emmett had. However she'd got them, she now had access to all Hecate's powers.

My hand found Layne's chest, and I buried my fingers into his fur, clutching at whatever I could. "Bite me," I rasped out. "Break my skin. Make me bleed."

Layne's eyes darkened. He wouldn't do it. He wouldn't do what we needed to stop this because he wouldn't hurt me.

"Fuck you, Layne. Do it." I shrieked this, my voice raising in a pitch that hurt my ears. "Make me bleed, you bastard."

At that, Owen's head swiveled in my direction. I caught sight of his face then. He knew what I did. That Layne would not do me harm.

"Do it," he yelled at his son. "Kill her. She's not worth all this."

Layne growled in Owen's direction. Honey lifted her arms over her head as the shape above the chest grew darker. I knew it wouldn't take my mother's true form. She wasn't raising Hecate; she was using her spirit to pull the magic together.

"He's right," I said to Layne. "We can't let her have this power."

Layne growled. A wind lifted from some unseen chasm and whipped Honey's hair around her face. She didn't drop her arms to move the locks aside. She just kept chanting. The relics quivered and shook on the stones. I felt something tugging at me from deep inside.

A cry rose from deep within and gargled its way through my voice box. Layne dropped his huge paw on to my chest.

"Do it, Layne." Owen's voice, more frantic than I'd ever heard before. I wouldn't have thought he could be so anxious.

Layne's low rumble grew. I clutched at him, pulling him closer.

"You need to do this," I said. "If you don't, she will kill us all to take the power she is raising."

He whined. Stepped back.

From his place at the altar, Owen cursed.

The earth trembled beneath us. The wolf beside me stumbled. Every inch of my skin ached as though it had swollen to its limit as the magic inside tried to meet its maker. My veins burned like acid. Tears, hot and wet, streamed down my cheeks, the only response my body had the energy to make.

We were running out of time.

"Now, Layne," I said, grabbing for his face and bringing it to my chest. "Just fucking do it."

There was a lick of a long tongue in the cleft between my breasts, warning me, alerting me of his intent. It didn't matter. I was ready. I had to be.

With all I had, I sucked in a breath. I was still hauling in air when he bit down. It hurt. God, it hurt. His teeth buried into the swell of my skin, and I couldn't stop the cry of agony as my skin parted with a tear. My flesh was ready to let go. It was a swollen bladder waiting for the gentlest of touches to burst the skin.

I heard his whine and whimper as he let go and backed away. There was no way I was going to look into his eyes and see the pain I knew would be there for me. It didn't matter. Nothing else mattered except stopping Honey.

I didn't waste a single second. Before he settled onto his haunches, my hand flashed to the runes. Fresh blood met the pads of my fingers and I wept now with relief. I rolled away from Layne and used my free hand to grab for the amulet.

I had one second to pray that Lucifer would answer. His blood, my blood, combined there in the stone had cracked open a rift for Zach and brought him home. Perhaps it would take Honey.

With my mother's power surging all around me, swirling like a vortex toward her shade so that Honey could collect it up with a single sacrifice of blood, I had nothing left to me.

Lightning struck through empty air. Thunder rolled across the stone floor and rattled the bones that lay there.

Honey's head swiveled toward us, an ugly snarl curling her lip. She looked as much a beast as the wolf inside the circle, but I held onto the amulet. I held on even though it burned my skin and sent shocks radiating up my arm to my collarbone.

I held on even when she flicked her fingers in our direction, blocking a blast from the amulet. It zigzagged across the space. She grinned triumphantly.

As it ricocheted against the brick wall, it split in two. One awful stream of light shot toward the circle, striking Layne in the temple.

He fell. I screamed. Owen howled.

I didn't dare let go of the amulet. Not yet. With one hand clutched around the stone, I fell to my knees and landed awkwardly on my elbow. I splayed out onto my stomach, amulet held to the side, and tried to army crawl to Layne.

He wasn't breathing. There was no steady rise and fall of his chest. The haunches of the wolf were completely still. From behind him, I couldn't tell if his eyes were open or closed. I just knew I had to get to him.

I was still paces away when several things happened all at once. I wouldn't even know later, thinking it over what occurred first or if they all were simultaneous events.

As I army crawled to my mate, the amulet shot out branches of lightning all around. They lit the chamber brighter than the guttering candles, and for one clear second, I saw Abbi rise to all fours instead of the hunching shadow in the corner.

Owen saw her too. I knew that by the way he jerked as she leveled her gaze on him.

At the same moment, Honey raised the blade above her head. Owen swung his gaze toward Layne and I, not above himself or at Honey.

"Save him," he mouthed at me. And a second later, he lunged for the black shape of Abbi.

He collided with her at the same moment Honey brought the blade down. It struck the side of the altar instead of Owen. The blade deflected off the stone with a spark and caught her in the leg.

She screamed.

By then, I had reached Layne, and I knew he wasn't breathing.

"Layne," I said. "Please, Layne. Don't be dead. Don't be dead."

I laid my palm on his ribcage, hoping to feel the most subtle of movement to show he was breathing, even if it was shallow. Nothing. Not even a heartbeat.

I did my best to shield him from the bursts of magic still emanating from the amulet, bouncing off the walls, sizzling and cracking in the surrounding air.

The flames of the casting circle had died down sufficiently to see past into the chamber where Owen had embraced the huge dog as though she were a grizzly rearing on hind legs. Indeed, she was up on her hind feet, a massive black form that grew more solid the longer I watched.

The explosions of magic released from the amulet came down in sprays all around Honey.

She no longer stood solidly planted behind the altar, confident and cocky in her magic. Instead, she had her arms over her head, shielding her hair from the sparks of magic raining down and ricocheting from the walls. Like a coward.

Whatever shrouded form had begun gathering over the chest of bones was now wavering in and out of phase as the magics in the room collided with each other. Beneath my palm, Layne's chest was still. When my fingers trailed for his snout, seeking breath, it found a cold, dry tongue.

My breathing hitched. Everything around me went cold as I struggled with the knowledge that my mate was dead. That I'd been that instrument of his death just as Owen had said I would be.

My mouth, dry as a piece of stale cotton, fought to let the scream out that clotted between my cheeks.

I was vaguely aware that I still clutched the amulet. I looked down to where my fingers were wrapped so tightly around it that the knuckles were white. My head swam. Numb and dumb, I noted the blood trickling into my bra.

My head dropped onto Layne's hide, just behind his last rib, where his belly should have been warm but was growing ever colder.

A scream from the altar tried to wrest my attention away from Layne. I refused to give it credence. I was too deep in my own sorrow to care what happened now.

I tried and failed to pull my fingers from the death grip they had on the amulet. Instead, I yanked on the leather thong, once, twice, three times before it came free of my neck.

Thus freed, I draped my arm over Layne's still form, my cheek pressed against his ruff. I stared, almost blindly out past the casting circle to where the fire had all but died down. The lightning had fizzled out.

I had yanked the amulet free, but there was still enough illumination from the residual magic and the hundreds of candles to show me plenty of what was going on without me. Without Layne.

The struggle between Owen and Abbi had ended. The alpha lay on the stone floor, bleeding and inert. My mother's familiar had her snout eyeball deep in his belly.

Honey had backed up to the wall behind the altar. She palmed the bricks beside her as she inched her way sideways, obviously intending to slip past Abbi without notice.

My mother's ghost still hovered over the chest, and while it had taken a shape that looked like her, it was without true form. It almost looked like it was trying very hard to join with its physical parts that lay in a heap inside the casket.

I knew then that Honey didn't have the power to take her magic. The spell had failed. Whether it had failed because I'd stopped it or she'd never had the power, I couldn't be sure. I just knew she understood the full force of what was happening.

She wanted to escape.

"She's afraid," I heard myself mumble.

I looked from her to Hecate's familiar, now bigger and growing ever larger, the more she feasted on Owen's body.

"Don't waste it," I said, realizing exactly what Owen had meant when he'd mouthed the words, save him. He gave Abbi his magic so we could triumph over the witch, the coven, the bastards that had him enslaved, those who would steal my mate, his son, my damn life.

I would not let the Garder alpha's sacrifice go to waste.

Even if it meant my life was forfeit in order to stop her, I would win.

# CHAPTER 26

I STOOD ON SHAKY and aching legs, but I stood. Layne lay at my feet. The amulet lay discarded beside him. It glowed red in the dimming light.

With a bracing inhale, I stooped to pluck it from the floor.

I caught Honey's eye as she edged around the altar.

"You won't leave this crypt," I said to her. My voice was so low, I barely heard my own, trembling voice, but I know she did. The look on her face was evidence of that.

"You can't best me," she said. "I have your mother's vessels."

She gestured wildly toward the chest and the assembled relics. I saw the edge of the photo curling up toward the chest. The grimoire, with its bloodstained edges, lay open beside the photo. Honey still held the blade.

"You have some of the vessels," I said, as I strode purposefully toward the edge of the circle.

Abbi watched me, those glowing red eyes lifting momentarily from Owen's body. Honey swept her hair back over her shoulder, a nervous gesture that made me smile.

"Did you count the vessels, Honey?" I asked as I met the edge of the sulfur line. The blood had long been consumed. The sulfur was nothing but a faint hint of powder on the floor. I could only barely discern the Hecate wheel around me that held me captive.

"Did you think to mark the vessels the goddess placed here for safety?"

Her manic gaze held mine. She doubted herself at that moment. Everything in her features suggested she doubted her own careful planning. Had she accounted for them all? Was one missing?

"Hecate's grimoire," I said, lifting a finger and inclining my head in the altar's direction. I lifted a second finger and a third. "Her photo, her amulet, her bones." I grinned. "Hecate's familiar sits, enjoying a meal of magic right here in the crypt."

"And I have you," she said. "That's seven."

"Is it?" I asked her. "It seems to me there is one yet that isn't present here with us. You've met him, haven't you? You know him. Your cult sacrificed him, along with several others who were loyal to Hecate. But you didn't count on him being a vessel until you met him in the hotel."

Her hand flew to her throat, and I knew I had her. "John Smith," she rasped, and then cast a frantic look about the crypt, as though she expected him to step out from behind a column at her beckoning.

Something in the shape above the casket wavered. Honey saw it and she stumbled forward to grip the edge of the altar. She dropped the blade as she did so. It struck the stones of the floor with a loud crack. I didn't doubt for a second that the blade had chipped.

"Call him," I said calmly. "Call to him. Bring him here. You have the power. You hold the sixth of Hecate's power right here in this sacred place."

She ran a hateful gaze over me, noting my hands as I held them, shaking at my sides.

"Call him," I said. "You've come this far, too far, to back out now. You need him. You know you do. Neither of us will be free of this chamber until he enters it."

Her chest heaved, those heavy breasts moving up and down, the nipples swollen from heat and adrenaline. She knew I was right. She had come too far, killed too many, betrayed her cult all for the magic she was dying to possess. If she didn't call to Smith, all of that would be for nothing.

"Don't be afraid," I whispered.

Her shoulders jerked back. "I am not afraid."

At that, she ran her palms over the air above the relics, began her chant, quiet at first, slow and methodical. Power began to build at the tips of her fingers. The static of the magic started to swell enough to raise the hair on my arms.

I gave her the time she needed to intone her incantations, drawing Smith forth from the power of the vessels she held and the magic she'd created.

As she did, I looped the amulet around my neck. The stone needed blood. I planned to give it what it needed.

She had dropped her head back, taken by the spell and the magic it conjured when Abbi backed away from Owen's body finally.

The great dog ran her gaze over me, that sentience evident in the glow of her eyes. I nodded at her.

"Take her," I said.

I didn't need to raise my voice. I knew the dog would charge the witch because I felt the familiar's desire as strongly as if it were my own. Maybe it was my own. The seething need for vengeance burned like acid in my throat.

The moment she charged Honey, bloated with pack magic, I wrapped my fingers around the stone, fully expecting the magic pregnant in the chamber to take my life as purchase.

A surge of energy shot through me. The taste of copper, acute and astringent flooded my mouth. I almost choked on the viscous feel of fluid running down my throat.

Behind my eyelids, I saw bursts of color. I smelled the mold of old paper and ink. I laughed in memory of a camera flashing light in my eyes. A tightness coiled around me, threatening to force me into a ball. The sensation of flesh ripping through my teeth, razoring away to mulch and yielding flesh, billowed against my cheeks.

The witching hour had come on padded feet, and it wanted its sacrifice.

I felt as though something clutched at my waist, trying to throw me off my feet. I fought back, renewing my force, the weight of my body, the sheer will of my mind. I had to win. I had to take the witch down, no matter how she fought.

I staggered for a moment, and the grip fell away. Resistance came and went. Instead of fighting against power, I felt it fill me.

I was all the vessels at once and I was none of them. The magic in me tried to join to the magic stored. It tried to shake and rattle the bones in the chest. The billowing shape wavering above it lengthened and split in two. I heard it whispering and for a second, I thought I was back in my childhood basement, stealing looks at my mother's grave deeds.

It was now or never. With my feet planted and braced, I lifted my free hand to my chest to trace the runes still covered in dried blood.

Immediately, a blast of icy energy rocked me backward. Fine particles peppered my face, thrown up and around the chamber like sand. Each grain that struck me felt like a hot cinder of fiery ash.

This time, there was no Smith to shield me with magic. No purple burst of protective power blasted through the chamber to create a cocoon of safety. This was Honey's place. Her sacred sanctum and none of it was going to go down easily.

I held my ground against the whirlwind, the grains of salt from the circle, the bones that chattered as they were flung haphazardly through the space, the very ache of magic as it pressed upon me and threatened to lift me from the floor and toss me like a rag doll against the stones.

I caught sight of Owen as the magic lifted him and threw him toward the entrance. His heavy body slammed into the wood of the door and knocked it even further off kilter.

Honey wasn't dead yet. She fought. I knew she fought. I felt her rage knocking against the inside of my skull hard enough my fingers wanted to dig in and extract her through my ears.

It didn't occur to me at first that her rage had carried on the strings of her voice, that it was her screams that burrowed into my ears, making them hurt. I presumed it was Honey's voice, warbling on the high notes of terror once I realized it wasn't me screaming.

Except the sound was almost inhuman. Like the point of a sharp bone squealing down the face of an old-fashioned chalkboard, reverberating and redoubling a hundred times over.

As the cries died down, a blast of wind suffused the crypt. It blew me, stumbling, backward. An explosion of energy lifted my hair straight up.

The stone in my grip stung with the intensity of a hive of hornets, and that pain shot up my elbow and onward to my collarbone. It traveled along my bones to meet my other hand and that too went white hot with an agony so acute my stomach twisted.

I sagged onto my knees but held on. The heat from the flames burned my cheeks. I thought I heard laughter somewhere in the back of my mind. Dizziness swam in from the sides of my vision, warping the flames. I caught sight of Layne's body just there in my peripheral vision. Images of blood and death and artifice flashed through my mind's eye until I gasped and let go the stone out in panic.

My hands dropped to the stone floor. The warmth of the stones from the radiant heat only made my palms hurt more, and I rolled onto my shoulder.

I called out to Abbi. Silence echoed back at me so loudly I groaned from the vacuous stillness of it.

It took several moments for the surrounding fire to die down, an equal amount of time for me to gather myself enough to crawl onto my hands and knees. Every inch of my body ached. For a while, all I could do was lay my forehead against the stones and force myself to breathe while I took stock of my body and the state it was in.

Nothing broken, I didn't think.

"Hello?" I said, testing the chamber again. I could swear I heard the hard, heavy panting of my mother's familiar just beyond me. Stretching, I tried to look back over my shoulder toward the altar. A sharp pain razored down my neck.

So. Nope. No moving yet. The roots of my hair felt plucked upon as strings tightened too much against a fretboard.

At least, the splitting headache I'd been suffering and gritting my way through had gone. In its place, my head felt as though someone had planted a vast meadow filled with wildflowers. Birds chirped in the shrubbery. Fawns danced around their mothers. That was the extent of the relief, and I didn't discount it for a second.

Just when I thought the whole ordeal was over, that banshee scream began again. The bones lifted from the places they'd fallen. They swirled around me faster and faster, circling out and up, and rearranging themselves in midair.

My arms went over my head protectively, instinctively, and I fell back down onto my face with my arms over my head. The flames of the circle roared to life again, and I whimpered.

It was over. All over. I'd lost Layne. Owen had sacrificed himself for nothing. The stone was cracked and abandoned on the floor beside me, and now it seemed even Abbi had abandoned me.

"Stop," I begged. "Just stop. I give up. I'm no match for you. You win."

The clacking of the skeletons intensified. The heat of the circle radiated inward, and it forced me to back up, to find the center so the heat wouldn't singe my hair. I shoved off as I scuttled to the middle, and as I did so, I caught sight of those bones forming complete skeletons, neatly assembled in midair. Many of them sailed toward crannies and nooks within the wall of the crypt.

I fell back on my haunches, watching, rapt, as each form found its home again. The candles in the chamber surged with flame again. I waited, expecting Honey to step from behind the altar, perhaps bloody and wounded, but alive.

I lost my concern for what the witch might have done to Abbi the moment someone stepped from behind the altar.

Someone. A man. A man I knew well even though I hadn't seen him in twenty years.

My father.

# CHAPTER 27

I DIDN'T REALIZE I'D fainted until I woke on my side, with my hand flung over the stone floor. I blinked, taking in the bright lights of the crypt. A shadow crossed my vision. I groaned, rolled over onto my back.

Abbi peered down at me. She was gargantuan now. Those eyes glowed red. Her breath smelled of sulfur. I brushed her away, struggling to bring the last moments to mind.

I'd been engaged in a magic duel with Honey. Abbi had jumped her after chowing down on Layne's father. I squeezed my eyes closed at the memory. Layne was gone. That was the thought that came to me the moment all the memories came back.

Layne was gone, and I'd lost.

No. That wasn't it. Something else had happened.

The thought snapped my eyes back open. I jack-knifed to a sitting position and Abbi shifted to the side.

My father had died when I was a kid, and yet there he stood. He'd taken what was left of Owen's bloody shirt and pulled it over his shoulders. He was spare, much leaner and less muscled than Owen, so the tails came down to cover his hips.

I gawked at him, not sure I was seeing what I thought I was seeing.

"You're not real," I rasped out, and it sounded like fingers on sandpaper. "You're dead. I saw you... there. With Lucifer."

His smile was a wan one, barely creasing the pale face that looked back at me. Funny. I'd never thought of my father as pale, but he was. Even seeing him in Lucifer's lair, I'd not truly registered his appearance. I just knew it was him. My memory fed me mostly emotions and feelings and the odd detail like the scar on the side of his temple.

But there he was. In the flesh. He sported a head of hair so blond it looked like it came from a bottle. His eyes, though, they were black as pitch. Even from halfway across the chamber, they looked like endless pits.

My feet and knees and hands took me to Layne in seconds. I crouched there beside my lover, not sure whether I was protecting his body or seeking protection from it.

"You're not him," I said again to the man standing before me. "You can't be my father. Who are you?"

The familiar look of him was more than just the memory. He was more than that, and he was less. I just couldn't quite place it.

Searching my memories did no good. The adrenaline still pumping through my tissues created too much static in my mind to focus in on one specific flash of image. They throttled through at high speeds, showing me shades of dark bedrooms and laughter one moment, the next dank cellars with a tall shadow handing me a blade and urging me to run.

Then the specter in the crypt flashed a grin at me, and there was that characteristic detail that fired off the right memory, the side quirk of his mouth in a half smile, the flash of indulgence in his eye. My heart squeezed at the sight of it. My eyes might not want to believe, but my heart knew.

Tears burned the backs of my eyelids.

"Come, daughter," he said, gesturing me toward him. "You're safe. You may leave the circle. The witch's spell is broken."

Broken. Honey was dead. As impossible as it seemed, the witch who conspired to betray her coven and use me to take my mother's power for her own was gone. Her spell had broken. I could walk free.

I shook my head. There was more to this reluctance than fear. I couldn't leave the circle because I didn't want to. Abandoning it meant abandoning more than just a bit of stone floor.

My hands found Layne's ribcage, burrowed around until I found where the heart should be.

"He's gone," my father said.

"No."

He nodded slowly. "Yes. As are the rest of the mortals in this chamber."

"He's not mortal."

That grin again, this time sad and resigned. "None of us here are."

"I killed him, didn't I?" I said. "I killed him with my magic. I was ready to let it have my life, but I didn't want it to take his."

My father stepped closer. He smoothed down the shirt over his hips discretely. "Hecate wouldn't want that from you," he said. "She gave all she had to keep that from happening."

I shook my head. "She wanted you," I said.

He reached out his hand, and I stared at the blunt-tipped fingers. They were glossy. As though they had no fingerprints. My gaze flicked back up to his face. He was close enough now that I thought I recognized the features.

"Smith," I said. "You took Smith's body."

He lifted one shoulder, canted his head to the side thoughtfully. "I didn't take it. He gave it willingly. We are one now," he said. "I needed to come and he let me have his shape to do so. We share it."

"That's why John Smith wasn't here," I said, trying to work through the complicated magics to find the tethers that a witch might use to enhance her power. "Honey wasn't able to gather him to her. He wasn't just a mere object. He had a soul."

My father nodded. "A soul he let your mother bind to this realm with her magic. Mine gave him the ability to keep his form from fully fading if he died by magic or for magic."

He fiddled with the shirt, a modest gesture. "Once the coven used him as sacrifice to increase their power, he was neither specter nor mortal. That kept him here. For you. Because of us. He was a loyal man. We both loved him very much."

He sent a brief glance over his shoulder to where Abbi had lain down next to the altar. Her eyes burned like coals from the darkness of her face.

"Your mother's familiar was pure magic. Smith was not. He was real. It was the one thing next to you that could thwart the cult if push came to shove. Which it did."

My fingers trailed through Layne's fur, finding his ears. They were cold. As cold as the stone floor I sat upon. My head dropped back, the grief all but overwhelming me. Maybe we'd beaten Honey, but the coven was still out there. Layne had died for nothing.

I did not know how long my father let me sit there like that, lost in my sense of remorse and grief, but eventually, I felt his hand on my shoulder. I looked up, startled, because I hadn't heard him come any closer.

"There is no greater love than to lie down your life for another," he mused aloud. "It's honorable that you thought to use your life to save countless mortals from the evil that coven would have brought upon the world."

"But I haven't," I said. "It did nothing. I'm still alive and the coven is still out there."

I pushed his hand away and used the leverage of Layne's stiff body to help get to my feet.

I stood there, shaking, knowing I looked nearly dead as I swayed on my feet. My knees threatened to buckle. Blinking was painful.

I refused to look down at my lover's slack face, still wolf for whatever reason, while Owen lay curled on his side at the entrance as a human man.

"You need to kill me," I said.

The surprise that stole over his face did nothing to dissuade me.

"I mean it. You need to kill me. Honey's spell might be broken, but the coven is still a threat. We have Hecate's things. We have my blood saturated with her magic. It's not mine anymore, anyway." I thought of Zach telling me after testing it that my blood was changing. Becoming more canid instead of human. My mother's power making it into something she could use.

"Take me and use the magic to break the cult once and for all."

My fists were clenched by my sides, so when he took them and held them against his heart, they were still balled into a knot. Tears ran down my cheeks. My nose clogged up. I could barely see him anymore.

"Your death is useless," he said grimly. "Your mother would not have it so. That's what you don't understand. She wants you to live. I want you to live."

The tears moved faster at the words, but I shook my head. I didn't want to hear that.

"She needs to stop the cult. If I have to die to make that happen, I will. I've made my peace with it. I have nothing to live for, anyway. Not now."

"Daughter," he said in a voice so kind it nearly crumbled the shards of my broken heart. "Your grief consumes you, but even if it were true, you should live. That's what mortals were made to do. Not to be the toys of immortals."

I swallowed down the stubborn tears. Could I face tomorrow without Layne, knowing I'd killed him? Knowing I'd have to live day after day without him.

I snuffed up a long train of fluid. "No. I don't deserve it. I've conned and cheated and lied and I killed the man who loved me. I put my best friend in a coma. How can I live knowing all that? How can I forgive myself enough to make it thorough one more moment?"

A soft chuckled escaped him and he forced my fingers open to splay across his chest. His heart thrummed beneath the fabric of Owen's shirt.

"Don't you wonder at all how I'm here? Don't you want to know why?"

I felt myself swaying on my feet and had to open my eyes to keep from falling. When I did, his eyes, his face, were so close to mine I could see the flecks of gold within the irises. My head swam with memories. My heart swelled with hope.

"You called me here when you used the Blood Stone's magic to raise your friend," he said. "You opened the channels Lucifer gave you. I came hitched along on his energy and I hid inside you. I'm the one responsible for your friend's sleep. Lucifer doesn't give things without taking, and when I hitched a ride, I'm afraid he made a grab for the nearest breathing alternative."

"You?" I asked. "You are why Parrish is in a coma? Lucifer took her."

His head dropped, but I caught the briefest expression of embarrassment. "I had to. I needed to be here to do what you can't."

My eyebrows scuttled down. "I don't understand."

He sighed and dropped my hands to cross his arms.

"You are my daughter, but you're no full necromancer. You can dance across the realms when the magic is swelled, and you can pull a life back to a full body, but you can't bring back flesh to bone."

I blinked stupidly.

"It's my power that's needed to bring Hecate back to herself. Once she reclaims her a godhead, her magic can't be stolen. Not by the cult. Not by you. Not by anyone. That's why your death will be useless. Once I raise her, she will take back her magic and abandon the mortal coil. She alone can take from you what she put there."

I stared at him. "You mean..."

"I mean, I will raise Hecate, the goddess, and you will raise your lover. We'll use the same magic to power both spells." He dropped his hand on my shoulder and it was warm and comforting. "Plenty of blood has been spilled here tonight. We have no more need for your pain."

"And Parrish?" I asked. "What will happen to her?"

He quirked an eyebrow. "I felt her pain when I came," he said. "She suffers a centuries' old ache that hasn't healed in all this time of living. Do you really think she wants to return?"

"I know she does."

I didn't know, but the Parrish who had fought for Zach would want to see him alive. She would want to believe good things could happen. I wanted that for her. I wanted so much for her.

I hugged my waist as I scanned the area that Honey had turned into a war zone. Something good had to come from all this. Not just thwarting a black coven, but something better. Something lasting.

I looked up at him. "She would want to live," I insisted. "She has people who love her. People who can help her love again, too."

He nodded. "Then we shall do what we can." He laid his hand along the small of my back. "But we must hurry. The witching hour is waning."

He motioned for me to follow him to the altar. I kept my gaze averted from Honey's still form, but he stepped directly over her then crouched to smear both hands in the blood slowly congealing at her throat.

Abbi sidled sideways, out of the way. Her silent yip made him smile. When he dropped his head back, I followed his gaze.

And I wasn't the least surprised at what I saw.

# CHAPTER 28

MY MOTHER'S SHADE SWIRLED above us. In some ways, it reminded me of a caricature; it was a breeze of ragged and wispy shadow, the like of something penned by a graphic novel artist. I had to lean against the altar to support myself as I gazed over my head. It occurred to me she wasn't whole, that she hurt from the separation.

My father murmured to the shade as though he could hear it speaking, the chamber was silent to me other than the sound of our breath.

"Yes," he said. "She was too hasty. Too hungry for you, my love. She has paid for that. Now, it's time to make the rest of them pay."

At that, he smeared Honey's blood over his face and down his neck. Then he hunted for my hand. His fingers slid over my palm, finding the webbing of my fingers and clutching me in a greasy grip.

"I deal in death magic," he whispered. "The pain of the witch's passing, the blood she spilled as she moved from one realm to the next, those things are all we need to cast our own magic."

He gripped my hand that much tighter and Abbi padded closer, her snout raised, smelling the air. My own nostrils flared, sensing a shift in the chamber.

I felt as though I was on holy ground. The hairs on the back of my neck rose. A hush of reverence moved over me. The electricity of my father's touch created a static all over my skin that made my clothes nearly unbearable to wear. I wanted to pull myself free of them, bare myself to the air and the magics, let them dance on my skin.

But I couldn't move. We stood there, the two of us, until I thought he'd changed his mind about raising the dead. But then, one by one, the candles guttered. The bones in their crannies and nooks shook. Abbi edged ever closer.

"Do you feel the air, pregnant with magic?" he whispered. "Tell me, daughter. Tell me you feel it."

"Yes," I said, and the word seemed to draw out longer than I intended. The syllable felt like a snake coiling around my tonsils.

"Good," he said. "Then now it is time. Call to him," he said. "Call to your lover."

Call to him. Could it be so simple? A few words to erase the horror he'd endured for me? Such a thing seemed impossible and yet, I wanted to believe. I considered and discarded a dozen things before I groaned softly in despair.

"Do I use his name?" I asked. "Do I order him to come to me? What are the incantations? I don't know them."

"Words have power," my father said. "If you doubt it, think of hateful things said that you hold in anger years later. Think of those words that filled your heart with joy. Remember the things you couldn't say because they hurt your throat."

He squeezed my hand. "Say what your heart tells you is right. It's your spell, Brie. The words belong to you. But don't dally. We have much work to do still, and much of it is dangerous indeed."

The urgency in his voice suggested I was running out of time. Careful consideration was not possible. I squared my shoulders, preparing to trace the symbols on my chest, to lift the blade from the altar and bring the power in me to the surface.

He jerked me away when I reached for the knife. "No, child. The price has been paid already," he said. "You have only to say the words." He lifted his head to the ceiling again. The shade had grown fainter in the moments I hesitated.

"Say them," he said, this time stern.

I swallowed. There was only one thing I wanted to say to Layne. The one thing that mattered to me when all was said and done. If I never had one more moment with him except for the one where he could hear my voice one last time, then I'd want him to hear what mattered.

"I love you, Layne Garder," I said. "You are mine. I would give my life for yours. I would take a thousand lives to save you. Come back to me. Come back to us."

"Good," my father murmured. "Keep going. I will lend you my power, what I can spare, and you will keep talking until he is standing by your side. Trust me in this. You have what you need to bring him home."

So I kept talking. I repeated more times than I thought I could that I loved him, and quietly, on padded feet that were human and not wolf, he came to me. He had that same Smokey scent he always did, that hint of peppermint.

I didn't stop declaring my love even when his hand slipped into mine and tears burned a hole in my vision that was nothing but a blur of shadow and color. I kept telling him I loved him until my father let go my hand and I didn't stop even when Layne pulled me into his embrace and I felt his heart beating solidly against my cheek. I inhaled the warmth of him, the smell of his body that was only his, and I squeezed my eyes closed in sheer joy and peace.

We stood there for long moments, silent, then. I reveled in the feel of his warmth as it crept around me. Even when I felt my father moving behind me, guiding us away from the altar, I moved as one with Layne and he with me. I couldn't speak any more. My throat was too tight with emotion.

It was my father who broke the silence when something drew his attention to the door of the crypt.

"They come," he said and pivoted to face the door.

Indeed, a commotion sounded outside the crypt. I looked up at Layne, and those honeyed eyes regarded me the same as they always had. Full of trust and love, and I knew it was him. I knew it. I didn't care what price might have to be paid later to have him or what price had been paid already. I just knew it would be worth it.

"Parrish and Zach," he said in a harsh voice dusty with strain. "And Emmett."

Our pack. All safe. I sagged in his arms. His arms tightened around me.

I felt a hand on my arm, inviting attention. My father held out Owen's trousers to Layne, who took them with a sober hand. Pulling them on, his gaze trailed to where his father's body lay in a curled position. The material fetched up on his thighs, sticking from the blood soaked into the fabric. Layne yanked hard at the waistband till they slid over his hips. He swallowed convulsively and sighed. Whatever was going on behind his eyes, he kept it from me. Only letting his attention hold the necromancer in front of him.

When he stood there, half-dressed, my father waved toward the exit.

"They have to go now," my father said. "All of them. What needs to be done here will not be pleasant."

I nodded to show I understood, but Layne laid his arm over my chest. "She's not staying," he said, and I looked up at him in surprise.

"I made a deal with the devil," I said. "I can face whatever waits here."

Layne tried to tug me closer, to keep me from staying, but I resisted. "I need to do this," I said, looking up into his face. "I need to help."

I couldn't say that I wanted one moment of reunion. I wanted to look into my mother's face, hold my father's hand. I wanted that, and I wanted more. But I couldn't put any of the pack in harm's way to do it.

Layne lifted his chin as he peered down at me, those eyes hooded and thoughtful. "If you need this, then I'll stay with you."

"No," my father said, gesturing at us wildly now. "Brie needs to be here, but I can't have a mated werewolf standing by. You'll threaten the success with your need to protect her."

"So, you're going to hurt her?" His hands balled into fists. "I can't let you do that."

"Then you'll die."

Layne looked at him without fear. "I already died," he said quietly. "I'm not afraid of death. What I fear is hers." He jerked his chin toward me. "I vowed to protect her. I will do that until my last breath."

My father sighed. "You think her own father will do less?" he said. "You cannot be here. If you act to protect her, you will die and any pain she suffers will be for nothing. All you will accomplish is her pain when you are gone."

I took Layne's hand and held it against my chest so he could feel my heart.

"Please," I said. "Don't make me go through that again. Understand, I need to do this alone. I can't be worried about you. I can't worry about them."

I inclined my head to the door that was already opening. I caught sight of Parrish's signature red hair and suffered a moment of relief and panic. "Protect them," I said. "Take them away. I'll come to you afterwards."

Layne shot a glance toward my father, and he nodded. "I'll keep her safe."

"You better, old man," Layne growled. "Or I will kill you all over again."

My father smiled, slow and humorless. "I doubt that will be necessary."

With a long look in my direction, Layne backed off. His strides devoured the paces between me and the door, and he was shoving Parrish and Zach back through the opening long before they made it all the way into the room.

With a bracing breath, I turned to my father.

"Let's do this thing."

# CHAPTER 29

My father gave me a grim look.

"This isn't going to be easy," he said. "Not like bringing your lover back. He was freshly dead. Raising a goddess to herself using bones long dried and abandoned will be much harder."

I nodded. I could understand that. People got resuscitated all the time in emergency rooms, at accident scenes. I was willing to accept that whatever power I possessed simply tapped into the energy Layne had left to linger in the chamber.

"And Parrish?" I asked. "How is she whole again? Did I do that too?"

His foot tapped the floor four times, an echo of the werewolf's compulsion and grinned.

"You," I said, as comprehension swam over me. "It was you."

He seesawed his hand back and forth. "Not truly. I merely called to the she-wolf when Honey provided the channel as she died. Lucifer has had an equal swap to content him. So all your loved ones are returned with no balance owing."

His attention then went to the relics on the altar. He arranged them in a triangle: the grimoire at the top, the blood-spattered photo and amulet at the bottom. It took him several tries as a gust of wind from above kept moving the photo out of place. He finally decided to drop part of the necklace's chain down on the edge, holding it secure.

Only when he was satisfied did he pivot to face me.

"Your deal with Lucifer," he said. "Before we go further, if you're going to be here with me, I need to know what it was."

I cast a glance at the stone, cracked as it lay on the floor. "I told him I would take my mother's place. That I would ferry Persephone back and forth to his realm."

The news made his face go whiter still. He clutched at the altar. Abbi shuffled forward to twitch her nose against his bare leg.

"You don't know what you've promised," he said. "You can be forgiven that."

My hands wrung together. "I do know. It won't be pleasant, I realize, but it was what I had to pay to take down the cult. To get you and Hecate out of his realm."

His hand trembled as he reached for my face. "You think you know, Brie, but you don't. You couldn't." He looked up to where my mother's shade was fast fading but swirling still, an angry torrent demanding attention. "As the goddess, she could enter and leave again."

"As can I?" I protested, and he lifted an eyebrow.

"Indeed," he said. "I saw you. But that's not all." He turned his hand over in the air in front of me. "I was given use of this body by John," he murmured. "Your mother kept it from decaying by storing a part of her magic in him, but had she not, it would have been useless. I couldn't have taken it if it had been bones. There needs to be flesh too, Brie."

"I understand that."

"Do you? Do you really?" His fingers trailed over my chin, and then he pulled his hand back to his side.

"Where do you think Persephone is, Brie? Your mother was mortal for a hundred years. If Persephone is this side of the realm, then she'd be over a century old."

I hadn't thought of that. My arms moved to hug my waist. I leaned against the altar for support.

"I don't blame you," he said. "You couldn't know what you were promising. Your mother was able to ferry her back and forth not just because she has the magics to move on the energy of death magic, but because she is a goddess, she isn't destroyed by the things she must do to accomplish it."

My voice was nothing but a whisper. "What things?"

He dropped his gaze to his feet. "She grew tired of taking lives for Lucifer's lover to fill. Generations of killing beautiful women—or men, as his whims allowed—it took its toll even on Hecate. Sacrificing a fresh life so Persephone's spirit could live and breathe and inhabit the world you live in only to discard it as she returned to hell once again. Do you really want that for yourself, Brie? Do you think you can hold up under that sort of emotional strain?"

He had looked back up at me at that last, holding my eyes with a sort of determination that forced me to stand my ground in the face of his stare. Even though my stomach trembled at the thought of my promise. Even though the sick had started to boil in my belly.

"I didn't know," I said. "I was cocky. I thought—"

His hand came down on my shoulder in a gentle touch, cutting me off. "It doesn't matter."

He stepped back, his hand dropping to his sides as he craned his face toward the ceiling. "She knows," he murmured.

I looked up as well. The frantic movement of my mother's shade grew darker, a storm of black energy in its center.

"She isn't pleased."

He looked at me. "She is afraid," he said. "She wouldn't want that for you."

My mouth felt dry. It was too late. I'd made the deal. If the cult was to break, and it had to, I had to keep the bargain I'd made.

My father laid his hands on the altar, bracketing in the objects my mother had turned into vessels to store her magic, her spirit. All empty now and transferred to the three breathing vessels standing around the altar. When whispers moved through him, I realized he was talking to someone. Not me. Not Abbi. Someone not there in the flesh.

The air went cold. I shivered and pulled my collar tighter to my throat. It took several blinks to realize the room was getting darker. I squinted so I could see through the gloom and realized the darkness wasn't just a lack of light. The darkness had sentience. It had a presence.

The shade of Hecate had swelled to encompass the room. It was touching down on my skin. Where it brushed me, goose flesh rose to meet it.

"She says there is another way," my father said, and the tone of his voice dragged my gaze to his face. "She will reclaim the mantle of ferryman," he told me. "She will take the bargain from you and add it to her burdens."

A discordant sound echoed all around us, and he spun in place as it writhed throughout the chamber, following the noise with his body.

"Are you ready?" he asked me.

When I nodded, his smile came slowly. "I will need to drain whatever magic remains in you," he said. "It will hurt, but I will try to be swift." His gaze skirted the relics. "They are empty shells now, but they will serve to anchor the spell."

With that, he clutched the knife and ran the sharp edge over his palm. His sharp intake of breath came and went so quickly I barely registered it. He took deliberate care in holding his hand over each object until exactly seven drops fell onto each. Only then did he retract his hand back to swipe his palm over his shirt.

"I'll do the dog first," he murmured. "And then you."

"Alright," I said, nodding because I didn't truly know what else to do.

He let go a soft breath through his nose, then stepped closer to me. His arms had pulled me into a rough embrace.

"I am proud of you, daughter," he said in a soft voice. "No man alive or dead could be more so."

I was still struggling to find my voice when he pushed me away, and there wasn't time to find the words to explain how I felt for him, how much I'd missed him, how many times I'd wished he was there for me, because his attention had already drifted away, focused on his spell.

His chanting grew as he lifted his arms above his head. The free stones, those that had been dislodged from the walls or brought in as small pebbles over the centuries, rattled and rolled on the floor. They lifted to the air. Dozens of bones in their nooks chattered as they responded, like a string being plucked. His voice strummed the notes, and the dead hummed.

A yip of pain came from the corner and while he ignored it, my eye went to my mother's familiar.

Abbi leaped to her feet and began to spin in place, chasing her tail or some pain that badgered her unseen. Her eyes glazed over. All at once, the surprised yelps turned to howls.

I heard in the depths of her voice, a thousand or more canines lifting their own pained howls in unison. She shook. Her teeth bared at some invisible force as her tail dropped behind her.

For one terrifying instant, she met my eye, and I knew her pain. It suffused her altogether, and she begged me with her gaze to help. The animal in her that wasn't sentient wanted release.

I clutched my throat. I would have gone to her, but my feet were rooted to the floor. My father's voice intensified, even as it lowered in pitch. A brown sound, filled with darkness and gravel, rumbled through the timbre of it, twisting my bowels, my bladder. Even my stomach spasmed along with it.

A roar, very unlike that of a dog, and completely unrecognizable from anything I'd ever heard before, erupted from the familiar.

Someone began pounding on what was left of the the door as it hung from its hinges. Magic sealed the chamber shut, barring them from entry no matter how hard they fought to get in. Shouts and calls came from behind the splinters of wood, as those on the other side watched through the slats the things within that they were powerless to stop.

This was the moment. I knew it. The zenith of the spell, the climax of the moment. My father threw open his arms as though to catch a child flung along on its excitement to a long-lost parent returning home.

Abbi rose on her hind legs, her muzzle bristling, her hackles raised. She opened her mouth and the blackness of her coat just... peeled away from her, starting at the hindquarters and rolling forward. Her coat rippled over her, revealing a complete emptiness behind it as she plodded toward the man beckoning her.

She disappeared into his embrace with a rumble of thunder loud enough to shake the entire crypt.

I fell backward, landing on my palms.

My father spun in place to face me. I didn't recognize him in that second. His eyes blazed bright red. Teeth, long and canid, flashed as he shook his head, assimilating the muzzle into his own jaw. I scrabbled away from him instinctively.

Behind him, as the crypt settled, someone—probably Layne—began ramming their side of the door. The thuds were rhythmic and solid. A few more thrusts and the door would shudder beneath the weight. I had no idea how it was holding together; it had been such a rotten and unhinged thing when we came.

But I did know, really. Magic. Whether it was my father's or mother's, magic was keeping them from breaking in.

Adrenaline shook my core, and it trembled hard enough that it did not surprise me to hear my teeth clacking. The blackness of the crypt seemed just a bit more faded. I didn't dare look up. I wasn't sure I wanted to see the result of Abbi's assimilation.

My father shook out his hands at his sides and leveled me with a long, hard glance.

"Your turn," he said and his voice was so unlike his that it left my head shaking. Refusing him. What I'd seen in Abbi had been terrifying. I wasn't ready for that sort of hurt.

"No," I said. "I can't."

"You can, Brie. You have to. It's too late to stop now." He held his arms out. "Come to me, child. I'll take your pain if I can."

I didn't have time to respond. Pain razored straight through my stomach and up into my palette. I tasted blood. It bubbled up from the depths of my throat, choking me. I coughed and gagged, and even as I struggled to breathe, splinters like ice picks prickled beneath my nails. Hot firebrands seared my chest where the runes were. Each of them came alive as though separate fires had ignited beneath my skin.

My hands flew to my chest, seeking to pat out the flames, but it was hopeless. The fire wasn't real. The ice picks weren't real. The only true thing was the agony that shattered every molecule of my being.

I tried to scream. Instead, I swallowed down on the viscous fluid that threatened to choke me. I gagged. Spluttered.

By the time I'd fallen to my side, my father was there beside me. His hands ran down the length of my hair to my cheek.

"Let me take the pain," he said and in his voice, I recognized my mother's. I lifted my gaze to his face.

"Give it to me, child," he said and his voice was tight with worry. "Relinquish it to me."

I tried. I really did. The weight of the pain made my head so heavy I could barely blink without wincing. The pounding on the door intensified. Layne's voice had become a roar through the wood.

My whole body felt as though it was the bottom of an empty cup and someone was pulling on me with a straw, seeking the last molecule of liquid.

All I had the strength for was a whisper. "Yes," I said. "Take it."

"Then come to me," he said and opened his arms. "Come now. You won't live through another moment."

It was too much, and he knew it. Like my mortal body was too much for a god's magic, holding it when she wanted it back was too much for that body to bear.

I sucked in whatever air I could beyond the dizzying swim of my vision and found the strength to lurch into his arms.

I barely touched him when the white heat of agony climaxed. And it was too much. Blackness took me, and if it was the specter of my mother coming to claim what was hers, I didn't care. I just wanted it over. I sank into the oblivion of pain.

I woke seconds later, lying on my side. The first thing that came to mind was that I was cold. The second was that I lay on something lumpy and strangely soft, yet unyielding.

I blinked my eyes into focus and realized my father lay beneath me. His arms had fallen away, but I still lay across his chest.

I took stock and felt no pain. With tentative fingers, I prodded my chest, expecting to feel sticky with blood and to touch down on raw wounds. Hale and whole tissue met my palms. Gone was the blood. Sealed were the wounds. I didn't even wince when I blinked.

The sounds of frustrated rage beyond the door of the crypt sounded as though it was coming through leagues of icy water. One fearful look at my father's face told me he was dead.

My chest squeezed with emotion. I pushed away, not wanting to burden him a moment longer, even in death.

"The pain was too much," said a voice that might be amplified by several speakers, echoing through the chamber even though it was just loud enough to be heard. "Even for him."

I froze. Fear wrapped icy fingers around my heart. I knew when I lifted my gaze that I'd see my mother, and I didn't think I was ready for that.

"He took my pain," I said numbly. "And it killed him."

"He was ready to die," she said. "He was only here temporarily, and he knew it." A rustle of material drew my gaze upward.

There, stood a woman at least seven feet tall. Even as I registered the figure, with glossy black hair and a long raiment so deep black, it swallowed up any spark of light that touched it, the woman split into three.

Long black tresses, resembling the wig I'd worn for weeks as a disguise, caught an invisible breeze and whipped around three equally magnificent faces. Then, as swiftly as the goddess revealed the three facets, they joined to gather again, and then split, and then merged. It was a dizzying vision, only relieved now and then as Hecate transformed into a lean, muscled canine.

I had the feeling she was struggling to hold one form. I struggled to maintain my composure under the weight of her presence.

She was both beatific and terrifying. I felt the electricity of her like a pressure vacuum. My insides felt like they were crawling to get out. I fought to remain still, to keep from turning tail and bolting from the chamber. This wasn't my mother. I remembered my mother as a mournful shade of herself. Beautiful yes, but vulnerable and approachable.

Hecate was none of those things.

"You have been brave, child," she said. "A daughter worthy of a goddess. I am sorry you had to bear the burden of my faults, but that's over now. All over."

"My father?" I asked.

She crouched low, a movement that seemed as fluid as water, and she looked at me. "He is with me." She laid her hand on her chest. "And he is with you." She laid her other hand on mine. "There is nothing left for Lucifer to torture. And He and I have renewed our bargain, freeing you from yours."

She smiled a somewhat bitter smile. "I even have ten fresh lives to use for Persephone's needs. And I'll make sure each witch lives in limbo a very long time until I can use each one of them to ferry her back and forth. After all, what good is being a goddess if you can't take those who sacrifice themselves for you?"

I swallowed down a sudden flood of water at her touch. It was a grim thing, even if it was loving. She retracted her hand and stood. Several phases of her moved out of sync and back in again as she sent a look over her shoulder. The pounding and slamming of the door was almost too much. It vibrated through me like a bass note shaking my core.

"They will want in now," she said. "I can't hold them back much longer, so fierce is their rage."

Their rage: Layne's and Parrish's. Ready and willing to confront a goddess for me. I didn't deserve such love.

"You do," she said. "You deserve it all."

She waved her hand toward the door, and it crashed open. One glance my way, and a whisper of words floated to my ear, tinkling on her voice like discordant notes.

She disappeared as the storm of wolves exploded into the crypt.

I didn't have time to get to my feet before Layne had me scooped into his arms. Parrish was laughing out of relief and touching me everywhere Layne's kisses didn't land, saying over and over again that I was a stupid damn bitch and she was so glad I was alive.

Layne shoved her away, finally, and told her to back off before he had to kill her and she blew him a kiss that suggested she'd welcome the challenge.

As much as I loved the reunion, as much as I wanted to sink into Layne's arms and be done with it all, I also knew I needed to stand on my own. I needed to walk out of there as me. Brie. A mortal again, despite all that I'd endured.

"Put me down," I said, laying my palm on Layne's chest. "I can stand on my own."

"I believe you can," he said into my hair, "But promise me you will surrender to my arms tonight. I need to hold you. My wolf needs to feel your breath on its face. I don't think I'll be able to calm him unless you do."

"Agreed," I said, and let him steady me as I found my feet. I looked them over for a long moment, my chest heaving with the effort of standing, my eyes burning from unshed tears.

"It's over," I said.

Zach threw himself at me, embracing me so hard, my breath exploded from me in one blast. "You rocked it, girl," he said. "Totally worthy of our new alpha's mate."

I looked at Layne, whose gaze had drifted to his father's form. He nodded slowly, reverently, confirming the truth.

Parrish shot me a thumbs up, a quiet, simple gesture that made my heart swell. Well done, it said.

"And you too," I told her. "I imagine you'll be Layne's second?" I looked at Layne for confirmation.

"Zach is third," he said with a nod. "But they all come after you. You're my mate. You may not be wolf, but you have the heart of one." He touched my fingers to his chest. "And you have mine. Till the day I breathe my last. Every beat of my heart belongs to you."

"Is it too late to ask you to raise my Vi?" Parrish said, slinging her arm over my shoulder. "I happen to know where her bones are, and I—"

I peeled her arm off me. "Not a chance," I said. "What's dead should remain dead. Didn't a wise wolf once tell me that?"

She snorted. "So I'm wise now instead of rash and brash?" She shouldered me, guiding me along to the door behind Zach and Emmett, who looked back at me with something akin to awe on his face.

Then I noted that he wasn't looking at me, but at the altar and the relics we'd left behind. He'd seen some incredible magic in that room. I imagined he was reliving it all in the time he looked back. I didn't doubt he'd have nightmares for weeks.

But what he hadn't seen, what none of them had but me, was the actual face of the goddess who had made it all right again. The woman I'd called mother despite the trauma of my childhood.

I looked back at the room with him and bid it all goodbye. The pain of my childhood would rest like the dead. I thought of Sherry facing off against her father, of Scarlet falling to her abusive lover, of the old woman claiming the spirit from her mother's death mask, and I understood the value of facing your demons.

Because in those last words my mother had for me, I gained the understanding I'd needed all along.

She loved me. All along, she loved me. Losing herself had been worth it to know the joy of being a mother.

And that one truth was going to set me free.

# CHAPTER 30

IT TOOK FOUR DAYS for the runes to fade, and I was in my shop when the last of them went away with a pop that made my ears feel as though I'd just descended a great distance in a few seconds.

I'd gone to the store that morning despite Layne's protests. He thought I should rest longer. In my mind, twenty-four hours of near comatose sleep was enough. It took the proof of my body, letting him claim me and I him over a lengthy and exhausting bout of intimacy before he surrendered and agreed that I might be ready to leave the manse and start living.

He only told me that morning that he quit the force when I questioned why he wasn't going to work.

"I suppose you're rich now," I'd said. "No need to earn the man's money."

He brushed the backs of his knuckles against my cheeks. "*I'm* not rich," he said. "*We* are rich. Neither of us needs the man's money."

"But you're still going somewhere." I'd peered at him through shuttered lids as he buttoned up one of those Brioni suit jackets he was so fond of. "I know the look of a man dressing to impress."

He slid the tail of the tie smooth against his shirt. "I'm going to the office."

I lifted an eyebrow in query.

"My father left me everything of course, including the pack responsibilities."

I regarded him warily. I wasn't sure if I should broach the subject that haunted his expression and had ever since he'd pulled on his father's bloody trousers back in the crypt. I just knew I understood the emotion behind it because I'd been there, and I knew what it could do to his psyche if he let it fester.

"You're going to need to deal with it, you know," I said.

"Didn't I just say I was going to the office?"

"Not your father's business," I said and crossed my arms. "Your father's betrayal. His sacrifice."

He huffed. "What is there to do? He's dead. I would have wanted it to be me who tore his throat out, but so long as he's gone, I suppose I have to content myself."

I ran a hand down his arm and squeezed his elbow. "Would you really?" I asked. "Would you really have wanted to kill the man who did what he thought he had to in order to protect his pack? To protect you?"

He ran both hands through his hair. "I don't know, Brie." He dropped his head back. "It's all so fucking complicated; it's going to take a century to come to terms with it. All I know is that he threatened you to save me. I'm not sure I can ever forgive that." His gaze fell to mine and the intensity of it made me squirm.

"It would be nice if dealing with family was easy," I said. "But he's gone and you're alive. You're going to have to live a long time with the anger and guilt for loving him despite all he did."

His fingers brushed over my hair. "I know. And it's not like he's a god who can come back to life and help me deal."

I caught his hand and brought it to my mouth to kiss his palm. "Too bad the magic is gone," I said. "Maybe I could call to him and give you a chance to talk it out. I'm sure he'd be happy knowing you've stepped in to take his place."

His eyebrow raised a half-inch. "You do know that technically, it shouldn't be me who is alpha." He paused to adjust his tie as he gave me a meaningful look. "Packs have come a long way in the last few centuries, but none of them have allowed a human to take over."

My hand went to my throat. "You mean?"

He nodded. "You beat him, Brie. Were you wolf, you'd be alpha of the pack right now."

The thought of having all that burden after what I'd just endured made me sigh in relief that I was indeed still very much human. I ran my hand down his tie, smoothing it out just so I could touch him.

His hands went over mine. "You might not want to do that," he said in a gruff voice. "I do have to get to the office. The Garder pack has been in security and protection for centuries. Except now, I'm adding a branch."

"And that is?"

He crossed my hands over my waist chastely. "Body-guard detail. It's perfect for those wolves who want it and it gives the business a bit of leverage with clients who might have higher visibility and status. Politicians. Law makers."

He retraced his steps to the bureau of our suite and pulled out a pair of socks. He was sitting on the bed when he spoke again.

"If we end up getting outed someday, we can use the power and influence of those we are protecting to keep our anonymity."

I had doubted that would be the way it worked, but I didn't say anything. I was happy he was still doing what he loved, so long as it didn't interfere with my doing what I loved.

And I loved my shop. Standing behind the counter as I cleared away the dust from the counter, I paused to look it over and felt the last pop of my runes leaving me.

So that was it. I didn't have a single scar left of the ordeal to remind me. The runes were gone. The only thing that remained were the emotional scars of the battle with Honey. I ran my bare palm over the gouge in the counter left by the reaper.

No. That wasn't all that remained. I knew the love of my parents. I knew the love of a good man. The friendship of a woman so loyal she couldn't love another woman even a dozen decades past the death of her first.

Most women didn't have more than the inner strength gained after a large struggle like that. I had so much more. I smiled to myself as I considered all I'd gained.

The smile hadn't left my mouth when Parrish strolled through the front of the shop, looking very much like she had the first time I'd met her. Time spun for a second as I fought for words.

"I hear some witch is giving readings," she said. "Not that I believe in that sort of hooey."

A chuckle slipped free and I spread my arms out to my side to indicate a sort of ignorant helplessness. "No witches here," I said. "Just good old fashioned chicanery."

She laughed and drew up next to the counter. She traced the gouge in the counter with her index finger. "Too bad," she said. "I was hoping to communicate with the dead."

"You've come to the wrong shop for that," I said.

A long, hissing belch escaped her and she put her hand to her mouth primly. "Excuse me," she said. I had a bit too much honey a few days ago, and have had terrible indigestion ever since."

"You didn't," I said, staring at her in disbelief, but then waved away her answer before she could give it. There were some things I didn't want to know and with Parrish, I couldn't be sure she wasn't joking.

She spiked one hand to her hip, thrusting it at me. "Please," she said. "Wolves aren't scavengers. Don't get me wrong, had I been in the crypt with you, I'd have torn her entrails out through her nose. But to go back at her when she's rotting and most unhoneylike? I'd rather eat my own tail."

I should have believed her, but there was something about the way she wouldn't look me in the eye.

"You've been back there, though?"

"Of course. Layne needed the place cleaned. We had to gather up Owen's body. I had to prep it for cremation, send the notice of death to Zach so he could record it. All on the up and up." She winked.

I hadn't given the state of the crypt or the bodies within it much thought till that very moment. Thank heavens for Layne and his calm reason.

"And the others?" I said, not able to bring myself to mention John Smith by name and not willing to speak Honey's.

Parrish hitched herself up onto the counter. "The others were nothing but bones when we went. Their flesh had turned to ash. I suppose after living so long on borrowed energy, their flesh wasn't really authentic anymore. The copper chest was empty, so we left it there in the cupboard we found in the altar."

I nodded, remembering the space Honey had hidden it.

"We collected the bones in burlap sacks," she went on. "Tossed the witch into a pit and covered it with cement. She is now the cornerstone of the new solid waste treatment plant. "

She studied the thumbnail that sported a violent shade of purple. "And the other, Layne says he wants interred in the family crypt with his father's remains."

I eyed her quizzically.

"He's family, right?" she asked. "That's what Layne said."

She drew out air quotes as she tried on her best imitation of him. "He's pack. He housed my mate's father and sacrificed everything to keep our pack safe. He goes in the family crypt."

"Fuck," I said, not realizing I could love him more than I already did.

"Yeah," she said. "He told me what you said went on in there. I had no idea, Brie." She laid her hand on my shoulder. "You are one brave bitch."

Wetness slid down my cheeks and I brushed it away. "Not brave," I said. "Desperate."

She shrugged. "Ask any hero, they'll tell you the same thing. Courage is part desperation, part hope and all a willingness to face down madness."

She must have seen how uncomfortable her words made me feel because she hopped down from the counter and straightened her plaid shirt.

"Well," she said, "if you can't help me raise Violet, then I must complete the task Layne says is the most important of the day."

"And that is?"

She hefted her messenger bag off the floor and dug through it.

"He wanted me to give you these."

She laid the photo and grimoire and amulet on the counter between us.

"I can't destroy them," I said through a tight throat. "They're all I have of her."

"He thought so," she said with a nod. "He said it's up to you if you want to keep them, but it might be a good idea to inter them and your mother's papers in the crypt with John Smith. That way they're not gone but they're also not laying around for an inquisitive toddler to pick up."

I flushed at the insinuation. Children. I'd not thought of that, but I did want to be a mother. I looked at Parrish through watery eyes. I didn't trust my voice, but she understood anyway.

She hooked the bag over her shoulder and palmed the objects one by one, slipping them back inside the bag. I was considering how much I trusted her to do that when the shop bell rang. A young woman meandered into the shop, taking her time to peruse the candles.

I grabbed Parrish's arm, hooking her elbow before she could leave.

"Zach," I said. "Are you two alright?"

She sighed heavily. "It's complicated between the two of us, but we're working on it." Her expression flared with determination. "That doesn't mean we're going to be a thing. I don't swing that way."

"I know," I said, just happy they were working on getting along because that meant she was trying to find some sort of peace. "He knows it too."

"Damn straight," she said, then laughed. "Straight. Get it."

She chortled, and the woman who had come in started pretending an interest in the herb shelf.

I shoved Parrish gently toward the door. "Flip the sign to closed when you leave," I told her. "I have a real business to run."

I followed her as far as the candle shelf before I stopped and waited for her to flip the sign and wave goodbye.

With a bracing breath, I approached the young woman. I was still working through my introduction when she spun on me, hope and pain written over her face.

One glance over her shoulder at the shade behind her, dogging her heels, a female figure with a drawn and pinched expression, and I knew the fullness of my vocation.

My mother's magic might be gone, but I was still a necromancer's daughter.

And I wasn't a fake.

-The End-

***

## Dearest Reader

I hope you enjoyed this series. If you're curious about Lucifer's Boudoir, you'll find more in the Isabella Hush series. The series is filled with wounded characters worth rooting for and mortals discovering a world of magic beneath their noses.

If you'd like to keep updated on this and other series, plus get a bonus free ebook, sign up to my newsletter at theaatkinson.com

# AUTHOR NOTE

I sometimes have very vivid dreams that stick with me. Once I lived an entire lifetime through my dreams in ancient Egypt as an young scribe who fell in love with a sorceress. The dream was so vivid, I recalled the entire thing for days—just long enough to tell the story in a novella called Formed of Clay. It seemed so real it haunted me for a long time.

The crime scene at the beginning of this series was like that. I kept it as light as I could when describing it in Stone Magic because it was pretty grisly...and very visceral. I felt haunted by that scene for days as well.

That scene jumpstarted this series and while it's grisly, I am grateful to that scene as it propelled me through the story and gave me five full books that I hope you, the reader, have enjoyed.

# Acknowledgments

Several loyal readers have special places in my writer's heart. Some of them, like Caroline Jenkins and Denise Sherman always take the time to find my little oopsies and sometimes my big ones. An author needs readers like that. I also couldn't have felt good about this MS without the help of Debra Martin (a fabulous author of fantasy and romance) and Evelyn Dotson. Thank you to you all.

Then there's readers like Crystal Crystal Amason, who isn't just a reader, she's a sponsor, and you don't get more loyal than that. She is the first reader to make me feel like my tales were worth reading. Thank you, Crystal. I hope I can continue to write stories you enjoy.

To my other patrons who prefer to remain anonymous, I thank you. You know who you are.

I really appreciate you all.

-thea-

# About Author

Thea is a NEW YORK TIMES and USA TODAY Best-selling Author. She used to have a black lab at her feet when she wrote, warming up the calves. It can be cold in rural Nova Scotia. Now it's just a cuppa tea keeping her warm.

Whether she's finding ways to lure Isabella Hush into the Shadow Bazaar or throwing the switch on a new monster, her urban fantasy pulses with dark themes and action-packed intrigue. Her characters are always deeply wounded creatures struggling for redemption. The romance is slow-burn but worth it, and the humor just might have a touch of Canadiana.

As a fan of Dannika Dark and Patricia Briggs, she hopes you enjoy slipping into the skin of her characters as much as she enjoy theirs.

Hang out with her on the socials:

# MORE BY THEA

**What are you missing?**

**By Series**

**THE IRON KING'S ASSASSIN**

**ISABELLA HUSH SERIES**

**COUNTERFEIT PSYCHIC**

**WITCHES OF ETLANTUM**

**VAMPIRE ADDICTIONS**

**REAPERS REDEMPTION**

**GRAVES FILES**

**ROGUE HUNTRESS**

**THETA WAVES**

**QUEEN OF SKY AND SHADOW**

Hale Saint

**Mainstream and Stand-alones**

One Insular Tahiti

Anomaly

Secret Language of Crows

Throwing Clay Shadows

www.ingramcontent.com/pod-product-compliance
Lightning Source LLC
Chambersburg PA
CBHW020650120726
47906CB00001B/205